THE DEVIL'S LINE

MARRISSE WHITTAKER

Lots of love,,

Marrisse Whittaker (signature)

BLOODHOUND
— BOOKS —

www.bloodhoundbooks.com

Print ISBN 978-1-914614-52-1

ALSO BY MARRISSE WHITTAKER

The Magpie

Daryn Robinson, one inspirational wheelchair warrior.

1

DEATH OF A PRINCESS

The date she was born, was also the date that she died. Friday the thirteenth. Considered unlucky for some. It most certainly was for Sophie Grey. But as the teenager began her final journey, destination unknown, she had no suspicion at all that the station clock was already counting down the minutes to her horrific end. The devil was also in another detail – that her ride on the death train fell poignantly on her thirteenth birthday.

Sophie checked the clock. Only ten minutes to wait, thank heavens. Not in her wildest dreams could she have imagined that on the day she finally became a teenager, she would find herself standing in a strange train station, far away from home. Nor that she would be downing a cheeseburger from a big chain takeaway, rather than a slice of especially made birthday cake. Luckily, she also had no idea that this lacklustre celebration tea was to be her last supper.

Still, these things happened, and it wasn't like she was a Teenie anymore. She was a fully-fledged Runner now. The amount of cocaine, crack and heroin strapped between layers of her clothing was evidence of that. The Beast had said that this trip was a birthday present. Going solo. Showed that she had respect from the other soldiers. She wiggled her toes in her brand-new trainers. They looked cool. Got them with her own paper notes and there was room to strap extra weed around her toes. Win-win situation.

Sophie checked the clock once again. The action was starting to turn into a nervous twitch, but her connecting train to some tiny postcode she'd never even heard of, had already been cancelled twice and the trains there were few and far between. She didn't fancy spending the night on a station bench, not with this amount of street candy on her. Chance of Feds picking her up. She could just imagine Mum and Dad's faces, but they hadn't exactly pushed the idea of a happy fam birthday party, so what else was she to do?

Eight minutes to go. Sophie tried not to look at a huge poster facing her on the other side of the train track. A teenager's face stared out from behind prison bars. The words printed in tall letters underneath the huge photo declared 'CRIME DOESN'T PAY'. It was referring to people thinking of not buying a train ticket, rather than those like Sophie who were carrying enough drugs to buy a house. She shivered, looking away. The Beast had said not to get all shook in these situations, and he was an Older, so he should know. She'd never actually met him, but he'd sounded nice when he'd called on the mobile, the one she'd just dumped. He'd made it clear that she was banned from having his number on her burner with stash on her. Anyway, she had her blade down her sock, so she was ready if any beef kicked off.

Sophie spotted a cold hard seat on the platform and sat down, keeping her little bag of horrors on her back. She pulled a tiny mirror out of her pocket, brushed her long fair hair aside, ignoring the spot erupting on her chin, and checked that her eyebrows were still on fleek. Mum said she'd started wearing too much make-up, but Razor said she looked like one proper scrum wifey, and he was thinking of making her his baby-mother any day now. Her old fam was washed out – history, he said.

Razor was a Drill musician as well as a main man in a gang. Got to give him respect. She loved to watch him on the video platforms. He'd let her choose which mask he would use when they'd last put feet on the street, all gassed up, then gone to the next neighbourhood. Told her she could be the one to spray their signature all over the walls. He even made sure to feature her hand in the recording, as proof she had done her initiation.

Sophie reflected that it helped that she had always been good at languages, so she'd taken to the street slang like a duck to water and she'd also been musically talented all of her life. She popped her earphones in now, finding the video footage on her mobile where Razor had cheffed up with his huge Rambo knife and began the beat, threatened to ching anyone who ventured onto their strip again.

The low battery sign flashed up. Sophie quickly switched off. She needed some juice left to make contact. She'd been briefed. An Elder would be waiting at the Trap House. No way would he give the address of the Cuckoo's nest until she set foot on local turf.

She glanced at the station clock yet again. Only five minutes to go. Her gaze fell onto another commuter, a man who looked a bit like her dad. He was taking a seat at the upright piano on the station concourse. Every train station seemed to have one these days. Sophie felt her soul sing as the first notes filled the space of the high Victorian arched roof.

He's playing my song, Sophie thought to herself with a smile. That's what her dad called this composition; Ravel's 'Pavane pour une infante défunte'. He'd taught her to play it. In fact, she could walk right up to that piano now and perform better than the guy sitting there. Get her blade out, tell him to shove over, impress the other travellers. That's if she wasn't keeping a low profile, like a real pro.

The beautiful piece of music acted like a calming balm. At one time Sophie had dreamed of becoming a professional musician, just like her dad. She'd passed all of her music grades way earlier than most kids her age and had always played solo at the school concerts. Her old school that was, before Mum and Dad's divorce. Nowadays in the flat she shared with Mum, there wasn't space to swing a dead cat, let alone squeeze a piano in.

Anyway, the kids at her new school had called her a geek when they'd found out she played old-time tunes. Slammed the lid down on her fingers when the music teacher's back was turned. She wouldn't make that mistake again. She couldn't even play at Dad's. He was always away doing concerts. Then again, Mum was constantly at her new boyfriend's. As the parents weren't speaking these days, both had just taken her word for it when she had said she was sleeping over at the other's place on her birthday. Win, win, yet again.

Sophie stood up and headed for the platform. The clock said only two minutes to go. She couldn't resist passing close to the piano, pausing for a split second. The man looked up and smiled.

'It's my birthday,' Sophie suddenly blurted out, for some mad reason wanting the man who looked like her dad to know the fact.

'Happy birthday,' the man answered softly, smiling again, 'I'm dedicating this piece to you.' He continued playing the haunting melody. A loud tannoy announcement broke the moment, advising people to step away from the platform, as a fast train was approaching. Sophie put her head down, suddenly embarrassed, moving quickly away.

It was at that moment that she felt a hard jolt. Someone was trying to grab the bag on her back. Her heart leaped as she tore away. A kick sent her lurching forward and then a blow that felt like a punch, landed in her side. Sophie started to run, whilst reaching down to her sock to pull out her blade. She'd never actually had to use it before, just practised in the mirror, but it was more than her life was worth to get robbed with this amount of gear on her.

Whether it was the final kick in her back or the fact that she was still struggling to reach for her craft-knife that caused Sophie to overbalance, no one knew for sure. But what was certain was that the birthday girl hurtled through the air onto the track and straight into the path of the rapidly approaching train.

It was to be hoped that at least her favourite piece of music was the last thing that she was aware of in her short life, rather than the smell of big chain burgers and coffee, or the sound of shrieking brakes, as the driver, who would be forever traumatised by the scene, attempted to avoid the inevitable.

Without a doubt, it was this same tune, Ravel's 'Pavane for a Dead Princess', that Sophie's heartbroken dad performed on the church piano at her harrowing funeral. His last belated birthday gift to his very own precious princess, recently so brimful of dreams, possibilities, and potential, now completely lost to the world. As indeed was Sophie's mother; too heavily sedated to make this very final family gathering, too devastated to ever recover from the shock.

A HEADY COCKTAIL OF DEATH

S trip-club owner Christy Callaghan also had a look of surprise in his bulging eyes. He clearly hadn't seen his own death coming, nor the fact that it would have links to a teenage girl whom he had never met in life. They were certainly on the same journey now.

Until today, he had been an old-time gangland boss, not a clairvoyant, after all. But then even Nostradamus couldn't have foretold that the man who held the criminal purse strings in this area would be parted from his wallet in quite such an unexpected manner. Proving, Billie considered, that crime *really* didn't pay. Right now, his severed head was staring at Billie from the centre of a large serving platter.

'Welcome back.' Senior crime scene investigator Charlie Holden gave a cheery grin, his eternally rosy, round cheeks giving him the air of a children's storybook character. 'Like the party we've laid on for you?' he asked, nodding to the garish nightclub decorations and giant glitter ball above the dance floor, where the serving platter lay.

'Sorry I'm not dressed for the occasion,' Billie counter-joked, dropping into the well-trodden team banter used to cope with facing scenarios that would give the average person nightmares for life. 'Still no sign of his body yet?' Billie asked, as she pulled on her white forensic overalls. 'I've just bumped into Jesus O'Brian's lads, heading off for his last supper. First thoughts are that it's likely to be a tit for tat job.' Charlie shook his head.

'No way of being certain yet. Jesus, of course, ruled next door's patch, but word has it from their CSI team that his was a blade job and Josta's thinking an axe was used here.'

As Charlie got on with his work, Billie glanced across to where forensic pathologist Josta King was staring into the eyes of Christy Callaghan. She looked up, giving Billie a wave. Billie responded as she pulled on her gloves. It felt good to be back. After recent devastating events, she reflected, work colleagues were the only family she had left.

'Dearest heart. So good to see you back. Don't forget you promised to come around for supper this weekend.'

It never failed to amaze Billie how Josta could talk about eating in any situation, including when she was leaning over a freshly killed corpse.

'Not if you are doing seafood.' Billie wrinkled her nose as the heady cocktail of death and shellfish filled the area around the serving platter. Christy's head was surrounded by a ring of sweating shrimp. Two dozen tiny black beady eyes stared up at her. They were laid out on floppy lettuce leaves and dressed with a Marie Rose sauce, of Christy's own making.

'An axe job, you think? Could our friendly neighbourhood gangsters be getting all handbags at dawn after being on cordial terms for such a long time?'

Billie gave Christy's head the once-over. It wasn't a pretty sight. To be fair, Christy Callaghan had never been a particularly attractive-looking individual in life, bulbous-nosed and balding, having just made it to his three score years and ten. Had his head not been separated from his shoulders, Billie knew that

7

she would have seen a snowy sprinkling of dandruff there, but still, she couldn't help feeling a little stab of sorrow for his demise.

No doubt he could be a formidable piece of work if any of his fellow crooks got on the wrong side of him, but though he was a familiar character, she'd had little to do with Christy Callaghan professionally since she had taken her role as head of the murder investigation team. If slayings had taken place in his murky world, the corpses never showed up on her turf. These old-fashioned gentlemen criminals took pride in a code of conduct, albeit a slightly warped one. They kept their misdemeanours amongst themselves and cleared up their own dirty work. Jesus O'Brian had been made of similar material. The two rarely strayed onto one another's patch, nor involved average members of the public in their shenanigans.

Indeed, many residents thought of Christy Callaghan as a latter-day Robin Hood, turning a blind eye to his criminal escapades and odd stretches in prison, which now and then hit the press. It was hard not to do so. He was a local lad, and the regional newspapers were more regularly full of feel-good stories of Christy having donated money for a new children's ward at the local hospital, arranged for a dying child to go to Disneyland or having sent a lorryload of essential supplies to the food bank. No doubt there would be a crowd of tearful Joe Public lining the route of his funeral procession. That would have to wait however, until his head was reunited with the rest of his body.

Billie glanced around, expecting the next of Christy's family in line for promotion to come over and introduce themselves. She was aware that the local crime gangs generally ran on hereditary lines, much like the Royal Family.

'Who's the acting head honcho now?' Billie called across to a woman in her mid-thirties, with swollen eyes, tear-stained face and a hanky tightly held in her fist. She wanted to try and get any info on the crime sooner rather than later, when the shock factor might make someone spill. Christy's crew would clam up once one of his kin stepped forward to take over. Like all crooks they worked on the principle that the less said to the police, the better. The woman shook her head, blowing her nose hard as Billie approached. There didn't seem to be anyone else, besides the crime-scene investigation team, around.

'Nobody could replace Christy,' she started to sob. 'He was a good man. Paid for my Tommy to go to RADA. He said that he could see the same talent for entertainment in him as I've got... I'm a dancer, you see...'

'Here?' Billie asked, looking away from the general dance floor to the half a dozen raised podiums, which wove their way through the seated areas; poles inserted from floor to ceiling at the centre of each. The woman nodded, her pretty but worn face showed a lifetime's struggle reaching for the stars.

'My Tommy's made it big time now, all thanks to Christy. He's on the cruise ships, well, the ferry from the Port of Tyne to Amsterdam. He's a singer. Not that it's all beer and skittles, mind. He has to strap himself to the seat when he plays his guitar because of the size of the waves in winter.'

The woman's words conjured up a sobering vision. Billie added both mother and son's jobs to the list of those she would rather be shot dead than be forced to do, but then it took all sorts and you had to wonder at the sort of person who wanted, as she did, to deal with violent death for a living. Horses for courses and all that.

'I don't know what I'm going to do now. Christy was an amazing boss. He was like a father to me.' Billie momentarily thought of her own father, well aware that he had a dark side, too, and had also made deadly enemies.

'Did he have kids, relatives?' Billie probed deeper. Someone must be waiting in the wings to take on Christy Callaghan's criminal crown. The woman shook her head.

'He was brought up in a children's home. Pulled himself up by his bootstraps did Christy. He couldn't have any kids of his own, that's why he was like Father Xmas to other people's little mites. The other guys working for him, well they're all old-timers, they were all talking only the other day about retiring from the business, after what happened to Jesus O'Brian. There's no proper code of conduct these days.'

'Do you have any gossip on who committed that murder, em...?'

'Cilla Saunders,' the woman answered, wiping her eyes. 'Outsiders. Vicious criminals. They all want locking up!' she added fiercely, clearly not having registered the irony of her words.

'The whole area is being swamped. Stab you to death as soon as look at you and then disappear back to the Big Smoke, or wherever, only to be replaced by new ones, just as ruthless as the last lot. They carry guns as well, come at you from out of nowhere. One of the guys, old Sid, got stabbed only the other day, when he was picking up rent. He's got a bad heart and he's just had a hip replacement. They nearly did for him, good and proper. What do you call them, county lines gangs or something?' She shook her head in despair.

The collection of protection money from businesses, together with slot-machine crimes, running dodgy nightclubs and prostitution, with a modicum of low-level drug dealing thrown in to satisfy the local junkies, had been the modus operandi of Christy Callaghan for so many years that Cilla clearly thought of it as a legitimate business. True, he had given back to the community, but he had certainly taken from it too. It was beginning to look like a new operation had swept in and taken the lot from him, as well as Jesus O'Brian, on next door's patch.

Billie shivered. She hoped that Cilla was simply second-guessing the situation. County lines drug dealing had never, to date, reached this far north, even though she was well aware that the phenomenon had been spreading like Covid across the rest of the UK. Billie knew that if there was any truth in the pole dancer's words, then one of the deadliest of all criminal activities had put down its school bag bang on her patch. The worst part was that most of the perpetrators of the crimes, as well as those manipulated and murdered, would turn out to be children.

'Call for you, ma'am.' A uniformed officer approached, holding a police issue mobile in his hand. 'DS Green,' he added. Billie took the mobile, remembering that Jo Green had just achieved her new promotion thanks to her work on Billie's last investigation. Billie had recommended her, which was ironic in itself, as they had started off as sworn enemies.

'DS Green.' Billie emphasised the 'sergeant' part of the address, vowing to drop the nickname of 'The Grass' from now on. She'd paid her dues, big time.

'Yes, ma'am. Thank you,' Jo Green replied. Billie smiled to herself. Jo was always going to be an oddity – one of those eccentric characters that you rub shoulders with now and then in life. Billie had decided to welcome such people in, rather than keep them at arm's length. She'd learned a lot in the time that she had been away on leave.

'Ditto,' Billie replied. 'What's up?'

'I'm at an incident at the central train station, ma'am. Witness statements point to a homicide. Might you be free?'

Billie ran her fingers through her hair. First hour back at work and two dicey deaths already. She had missed the job. Looking around, she could see the crime-scene investigation team preparing to remove Christy Callaghan's head and one of her gang, notebook in hand, already leading Cilla to a seat. There was nothing more she could do here right now. Josta was clearing up. She would grab her and speed straight to the new location.

'On my way. You're not looking at a body without a head, by any chance, are you?'

'Em, yes, ma'am,' Jo replied.

'It isn't Christy Callaghan's, is it?'

'No, ma'am. Looks like a drugs mule. There are class A to C narcotics spread all across the track... a child by the looks of it.'

Billie was unable to answer for a moment. It was one thing to come face to face with the admittedly gruesome murder of a full-time criminal. Quite another to deal with the heartbreaking and horrific demise of a child.

She tried to tune into the exercises taught to her during counselling sessions after the last investigation. They all seemed to centre on strategies that accepted not being able to change events, but instead, to change the way one thought about them. Putting on a positive spin. Easier said than done when one was in the thick of a murder investigation.

'Witness says she told him it was her birthday,' Jo added, to fill the gap in conversation.

'Okay. On my way.' Billie ended the call, already imagining the harrowing anniversary surprise she was about to spring on the deceased's parents, knowing that it would be a visit that they were never likely to forget. She would pass on counselling them to try putting a positive spin on this particular piece of devastating news.

A THORN IN THE SIDE

Cinderella had her glass slipper, Sophie Grey her trainer. Black and white, big brand. Not cheap. The type coveted by most teenagers. At the moment that her body had either collided with her murderer, or the train, the new birthday shoe had flown off, landing on the platform. It was the only bit of Sophie Grey still intact.

'Looks new. Size three.' Jo crouched down next to Billie, staring through her round-rimmed magnifying specs at the still box-fresh, white insole holding printed details.

Billie sighed, glancing at the harrowing view on the track, which had been quickly shielded from any stray members of the public still desperate to get onto the station concourse, determined to travel. Not a chance. Yet despite the obvious no-go situation, a crowd of disgruntled travellers constantly inched forward against the scene-of-crime bunting as though they were at a cake sale scrum at the local fair, rather than the location of a devastating death. Billie mentally took a cattle prodder to them all. A far-flung platform was still open for the odd incoming train, allowing people to disembark only, otherwise she would have had the whole station closed down.

'Any comment to make for tonight's edition?'

Billie heard the voice cut through the melee and inwardly groaned. She looked up to see local newspaper reporter, Perry Gooch, pointing her camera straight at Billie. The woman was a regular thorn in Billie's side.

'Not at the moment. The incident is under investigation.' Billie gave her a hard stare. 'And please keep back behind the tape.'

'Anything to say on the earlier incident, Christy Callaghan's decapitation then?' The crowd reacted in fascinated horror.

Billie strode forward, her face close to Perry's, furious that someone had already spilled the beans on the earlier crime.

'Who, exactly, is your informant?'

Christy Callaghan's head wouldn't be the only thing rolling, if she discovered that someone in the force was spilling confidential details.

'Can't say. Anyway, I'm simply stating the facts.' Perry was a big woman with a strong personality of her own. Not the sort to be easily intimidated. She smirked at Billie.

'What's your problem, DSI Wilde? You've just got no body.' She smirked. 'Story of your life really.'

Bearing in mind recent events involving her former fiancée, Billie wanted to tear the crime-scene tape aside and hurl the reporter away to hell, but she knew that that was exactly the sort of reaction Perry Gooch wanted to capture on her ever-present camera. She wasn't going to go there, despite the fact that the journalist was snapping away in Billie's face once again. Instead, she turned and waved a uniformed officer in her direction.

'Move that lot back to the entrance. Extend the perimeter.' She couldn't help flashing a final disparaging look in the direction of Perry Gooch, who had been waiting for it. She clicked the camera, getting the shot in one. Billie silently damned her. She turned back to the job in hand.

'This may help with an identification,' Billie shouted over to the CSI photographer, pointing to the shoe which had so recently held the small foot. 'We need it recorded and bagged up.' He nodded, getting onto the job immediately.

'CCTV footage available yet?' Billie knew that cameras would be situated around the station.

'On to it, ma'am.' Jo Green almost leapt to attention, before setting off like a dog after a bone. Her manner had been an irritation to Billie in the past, but now she knew more of the young detective's life story, she was amazed that such eccentricities were all that she had been left with. It had taken a lot of work on Billie's part to have emerged relatively unscathed from her own crazy background and Jo's would beat her in any competition for the most totally warped family in the world award.

A uniformed officer approached Billie, as she watched the CSI team carefully climb down onto the train track now that the area had been made safe.

'Ma'am, the witness wants to know if he can go?' He indicated a man sitting at the station piano, clearly no longer in the mood to tinkle the ivories with a happy tune. In fact, he had his head in his hands, so didn't detect Billie's approach.

'DSI Billie Wilde,' she announced, 'are you feeling okay, sir?' He looked up, ashen-faced.

'Not really, but that policeman told me to wait here to give a statement when my legs wouldn't seem to hold me up. I'd like to go now.'

'Stay there,' Billie advised. He did look on the brink of keeling over and she didn't want to have to bring paramedics into the cordoned-off area, other than those who had been essential to pronounce life deceased.

'It all happened so quickly...' he started, shaking his head in horror. Billie's ears pricked up.

'She was just a child, maybe a teenager but she looked younger, long fair hair, pretty... I have a daughter of my own.' He shook his head again. 'I'd like to get back to her if...' He started to get off the seat. Billie gently touched his shoulder, keeping him in place.

'We just need a few more details, sir, to help identify her, in order to inform the parents.' He closed his eyes tightly, understanding, having seen the incident, that Billie had little other than his description to go on right now.

'It was her birthday,' he said, 'she came past as I was playing...' He couldn't bring himself to name the piece. '... Ravel.' He shook his head in horror. 'Then a gang of kids wearing hoodies, just set about her. It all happened so quickly,' he repeated. 'Then they scattered, like rats...'

Billie suddenly felt a grip on her arm. She spun around ready to threaten arrest, expecting Perry Gooch, who had never been one to take *bog off* for an answer. Instead, she found herself glaring into the eyes of the chief of police, dressed in a civvy suit. He wasn't looking happy.

'When I called around first thing this morning to let you know you could start work again, I didn't expect to come back to *this* mess,' he hissed.

Billie did hope he wasn't referring to the scene on the track. He might be her chief and also her godfather, but she felt her temper rise.

'Bit uncalled for, sir' – she always addressed him formally at work – 'that's a child lying on the track.' She folded her arms.

'Oh Christ, I didn't mean *that* mess, I meant all this!' He waved his arm around. 'I've been at a meeting in Durham and my damn train has been delayed by an hour. Get the team to crack on with the clear-up and stop pussyfooting around!'

He started to march off across the concourse. Billie strode after him, ducking under the scene-of-crime tape and through the crowds, hot on his heels as he made for the taxi rank outside.

'You've heard the news about Christy Callaghan?' Billie caught up with him.

'Yes, sounds like a simple revenge job for O'Brian's demise. Should tie that up in no time.' A taxi pulled forward. The chief opened the door.

'We haven't located his body yet,' Billie persisted.

'Don't expect you ever will. Probably fish food by now. Put it down to O'Brian and wrap the case up.'

'But, sir…' There wasn't a hope in hell that Billie would wind up a murder investigation with so little input, no matter who the deceased was.

'Look, Christy Callaghan and Jesus O'Brian both knew the score when they decided to get into their business. Crime doesn't pay. Their sad demise sets out a great message to the public. No one is going to care that the bad guys have been taken off the streets. Concentrate on clearing up this kiddie case. Pulls at people's heartstrings when a child has been killed.'

The chief put his hand out and hooked a stray curl, which hung over Billie's eye, around her ear. She shook it away, hating that he did that. He flashed his expensive grin.

'And don't forget that you have exactly an hour and a half before you are due at tonight's event,' he added.

'What?' Billie questioned.

'The Community Awards do. You're presenting a prize, remember?' Billie had totally forgotten.

'But, sir, I can't exactly leave the scene of crime,' she started. He cut over her defence.

'Delegate, Billie. Delegate. You claim that you've got a crack team. I don't want you taking on too much, like last time.' He hooked the curl back over her ear. 'Don't let me down now, I'm counting on you. By the way, David's mother will be there.'

'Christ, no!' Billie exclaimed. The chief laughed out loud. He was well aware that no love was lost between the two women.

'You've always been a stroppy kid.' He shook his head, then gave her a quick peck on the cheek. 'Cut her some slack and send her some positive vibes. She's hurt you haven't been in touch. She was looking forward to being the matriarch of the next generation of the Silver family. Now poor thing's reduced to flower arranging classes three times a week. You've got to get over all that negativity from the past. Dig out your rose-tinted specs.'

Billie held her tongue with some effort. The chief had no idea what a dangerous woman he was dealing with, but she reasoned that he was a big boy now and could take care of himself.

'Don't let me down, darling goddaughter.' He jumped into the back of the cab and slammed the door shut.

Billie cursed out loud and strode back into the station. The man who had been at the piano appeared to have scarpered. She swore again. She had absolutely no intention of leaving the scene until she was sure that she had overseen all of the steps necessary to get justice for the little mite on the tracks. But she also didn't want to let down the chief, not when he had just let her come back to work, especially as she recalled now that it was the Outstanding Young Citizen award that she was due to present.

Billie looked down at her hoodie and jeans which she had slung on that morning, not even having expected to be back on duty today, let alone attending a ball.

Forget her godfather's wishes, what she needed right now was a fairy godmother if she was going to make it to the ball on time, tonight.

4

THE KISS OF DEATH

As Billie finally left the station and raced across town, unable to shake murder from her mind, she had no idea that she was not alone in her thoughts of evil deeds. Her return on the scene had attracted attention and not all of it the welcome back to work kind.

A pen was dropped onto a table, followed by a sealed envelope addressed with Billie's name. A deep red rose fell on top.

Thoughts flew through the writer's mind. *The waiting is over. No one will hear her screams for mercy, nor her cries as I call with my deathly kiss.*

Footsteps could be heard across the floor. Male or female? It was hard to tell. A door slammed as the writer set out, mind focused on their journey. Finally taking the first steps towards the union that they had been dreaming of night and day. It was time to turn fantasies into deadly reality.

5

A ROSE IN A GARDEN OF WEEDS

B illie tripped on the delicate silver sandals she was wearing and almost cartwheeled down the last few stairs into Boo's sitting room, where her great friend and trusted colleague was sipping a large glass of wine.

'I do have a lift in the house if you'd wanted to use it,' Boo joked. 'Even I could do a better job of walking in high heels and that's saying something.' She spun her wheelchair around, surveying Billie who was now smoothing down her borrowed dress over her hips.

'Thanks for this. I owe you. I could never have gotten home and back in time.' Billie stopped to catch her breath, gratefully taking the glass of wine being offered. Inheriting her birth mother's beautiful house, overlooking the sea in the stunning location of Alnmouth was like a dream come true, but on nights like these Billie wondered if she had been too quick to sell the penthouse flat in the city that she had shared with David.

'Free room here anytime you want it.' Boo looked Billie up and down. 'Wow, you look a hell of a lot better in that get-up than I ever did,' she exclaimed. 'I hope you're ready for some full-on male attention.'

'I'm not interested in any of that.' Billie brushed away the sudden thought of Max Strong, the criminal psychologist who had called and accompanied her to put flowers on her mother's grave only that morning. It seemed like a lifetime ago now. She'd nearly made a fool of herself with him again, almost invited him back to her place. When his phone call had cut dead their outing, he clearly hadn't been able to rush off quick enough. She flushed with embarrassment at the memory.

'If you want to bring anyone back to look at your crime-scene etchings,' Boo teased, 'the spare bed is all made up. Want me to put on the satin sheets?'

'Stop it!' Billie giggled despite herself. Boo had been amazing in uplifting her spirits since, well, since the last inquiry she had headed up had resulted in so many personal deaths. Billie was sincerely grateful, whilst also feeling truly awkward. It seemed like a lifetime since she had worn a dress, especially a number like this black velvet one, which clung to her body and plunged to a deep V at the base of her spine.

'It was either this or one of your spangly numbers. That lot would put a contestant from *Strictly* to shame. I have no doubt that they look lovely on you with your stunning ebony skin and beaded braids, but look at me, I'm so pale I look like I've crawled out from under a stone.' She caught herself in a mirror, tried twisting up her long red curls, pulled a face and let them drop down her back again.

'Jeez. Forget the updo. I need the back coverage big time.' Billie took a sip of wine. Dealing with dead corpses was one thing but dressing up was way out of her comfort zone.

'Not from where I'm sitting. Funny, it's so long ago since I wore that dress, it's practically vintage.' Boo backed up her wheelchair to allow Billie to rest her already weary feet. She gladly sank into the big cushions on Boo's sofa, glancing at the clock like a prisoner on death row. She felt guilty.

'Still got the child on your mind?' Boo patted Billie's arm.

'I should be at work, trying to locate her parents and the people who did this to her, not to mention Christy Callaghan's killers, rather than hobnobbing at some event–'

'Hey,' Boo interrupted, 'you're giving out an award to a young person. It no doubt means the world to them. Encouragement, that's what kids need and an interest in their lives. Maybe your little drug mule never had that. What you are doing tonight *is* important, Billie.'

'Thanks.' Billie sighed heavily, wishing that her taxi wouldn't be arriving at any moment.

'I wish I still had that feeling that I'm making a difference,' Boo added quietly. A look of regret swept across her face. Billie was taken aback.

Boo's nickname was taken from Boudicca, the brave and fearless warrior princess. As the murder team's office manager, she had the major responsibility of running the incident room. It was an absolutely key post, the importance of which couldn't be overstated. It was Boo's job to control all of the information coming in, ensure that all tasks requested by Billie were completed and to spot anything that needed following up, ensuring it was done and done thoroughly. It was a post that would only be offered by Billie to an officer who was highly efficient and could be absolutely trusted.

'What's brought this on?' Billie was alarmed at Boo's comment.

'I guess I just miss front line policing.' Boo shrugged. A car horn peeped outside. 'Cinderella, your carriage is awaiting.' Boo suddenly grinned, blocking any further conversation on the subject.

'We'll talk about this tomorrow, right?' Billie stroked Boo's hand, concerned. It was rare to see a chink in Boo's emotional armour. Injured whilst working on an investigation, resulting in her losing the use of her legs, Boo had seemed to rally like the superstar she truly was, continuing to do vital policing work, even if it was from behind a desk, rather than on the streets.

'Keep those glass slippers. Let's face it, I won't be wearing them again,' she quipped as Billie pulled a face on standing up and making for the door, 'and if you see any handsome princes, send them my way.'

Billie smiled and waved but vowed to get to the bottom of Boo's sadness. She had been dealing with her own grief during the weeks of her enforced leave and could spot the signs that Boo still had issues to be addressed from her past.

As for Billie, she intended to do her duty then run away as soon as possible from the ball. She intended to be back at her desk at work tonight, long before midnight.

'Don't eat the shrimp.' Billie was thrilled to find that the empty seat next to her on the smart table in the hotel ballroom reserved for those giving out awards, was about to be filled by Josta King. The older woman flopped down, eyeing up the menu on the tabletop.

'What a day! Red please and make it a large one.' She caught the eye of a waitress who was about to pass with a drinks tray.

'I don't think I'll ever eat seafood again.' Billie pulled a face at the memory of the first crime scene that afternoon, whilst trying to wipe away the even more harrowing memory of the second. Autopsies on both would take place in the morning. Billie took a sip of her sparkling water. She intended to keep a clear head. There was much work to do on both investigations and her brain was already buzzing.

'I could eat a horse right now,' Josta added, unfolding her

napkin. Dissecting dead bodies all day never seemed to take the edge off her appetite.

'You've probably had one of those in your fridge at some point, complete with stab wounds,' Billie teased. Josta was notorious for serving up joints of meat at dinner parties complete with a variety of knife injuries inflicted upon them, due to the forensic psychologist having compared victims' stab wounds to those inflicted by her on the kitchen table. Billie reflected that she wasn't the only one who took her work home with her. Josta was legendary for her expertise in the business; her outstanding ability to help the dead bring the tale of their final moments to life.

'Well, I do remember those terrible horse attacks in the nineties,' Josta mused, leading Billie to realise that she probably had indeed housed a horse's head in her fridge at some time.

'Now, I can't remember what award I'm giving out tonight...' Josta opened an envelope situated at the side of her plate and took out the card inside, squinting through the spectacles perched on her nose. 'Ahh, Butcher of the Year.' Very apt, she quipped.

Billie giggled. Thinking herself lucky to have colleagues who were such good company. Pseudo family, on the other hand, offered only tension and stress. She was reminded of the fact when the chief swept in, always a man with an eye for the ladies, with the mother of her former fiancé clinging on to his arm. He had tried to persuade Billie otherwise at the station, but the truth was that there would never, ever, be any love lost between the older and younger woman. Indeed, it had taken a lot of in-depth conversations with herself, before Billie had decided to drop the idea of attempting criminal charges against her almost mother-in-law.

She inwardly groaned even further as the new couple took the seats immediately opposite. David's mother had been smiling inanely to all and sundry around the room as she had walked across to their table. The fake smile dropped now as she looked from Billie to Josta.

'Darling, I had no idea that we would be sitting in the cheap seats.' She let the chief remove her expensive shawl, as she sat down. To Billie's relief, the last two VIPs arrived at that moment, causing a welcome distraction.

Local newspaper tycoon, Lance Harris, owned the *Daily Herald, Evening Herald, Saturday Sports Herald, Sunday Herald* and Friday's *Woman's Herald*, presumably because he thought the local females would be more drawn to glossy fashion photos and adverts for beauty products than hard news. Together the publications claimed to be the voice of local people, though Lance Harris didn't actually reside in the area at all. In fact, he owned similar groups of rags all over the country and his own main home was a villa of mansion proportions in Spain.

Billie guessed that this would be a fleeting visit, as his company were sponsoring the awards. It was a clever publicity stunt, establishing him in local people's minds as the caring voice of the region. In reality, his papers were largely purveyors of PR messages, offering a view of the realities of local life slanted towards the purse of the highest bidder, instead of addressing the true concerns of the community.

Win a brand-new house. Entry forms in **The Herald** *all this week!* Billie remembered one recent competition in the *Daily Herald*. No doubt one lucky local had received the keys to a tiny, two-bed modern 'mews' house – a sardine-can style new build with paper-thin walls and no garden, on the edge of a vast estate. But the land it had been built on had once housed playing fields for the children and allotments, providing freshly grown food. The handful of so-called 'affordable housing' way beyond the purse strings of most locals, had instead all been snapped up by holiday home investors, leaving entire neighbourhoods broken. When the children finally grew up, they would no doubt have to move away, to find truly affordable accommodation.

Lance Harris introduced his strikingly pretty dinner date to the other guests around the table. She was tall, cappuccino-skinned, with black eyes and a tumble of glossy dark hair.

'May I introduce Dr Luciana Martinez. She will be presenting the Environmental Award tonight. Dr Martinez heads up Precioso Global, based in South America, which oversees sustainable business models worldwide. She is on a high-pressured business tour of the country, so we are very honoured to have her with us tonight.'

'He must have some ulterior motive, dear. Especially if he's paying her expenses,' Josta whispered to Billie, as greetings were exchanged with Lance Harris's stunning partner.

David's mother was all eyes and teeth, fawning over the important guest, admiring her dress, her shoes, her jewellery. Billie left her to it, knowing how important reflected glory was to the woman.

'What a beautiful corsage.' Dr Martinez finally relented, no doubt feeling that she had to return at least one compliment. She was looking at a red rose pinned onto David's mother's dress.

'Yes, it was a gift from my companion.' She looked beneath her eyelashes coquettishly at the chief, then shot a glance at Billie. 'Some of us like to try, as a mark of respect for the award winners. Others appear to be happy to simply dig an old black dress out from the charity bag.'

Billie refused to rise to the bait. Josta patted her protectively on the hand.

'You are indeed a rose in a garden of weeds, Mrs Silver,' Josta boomed theatrically and not without a little hint of dryness, causing Billie to hide a grin.

The awards ceremony swung into play. Josta handed out her award to an incredibly grateful butcher, afterwards doing a deal on regular deliveries of prime sausages throughout the coming year, Dr Martinez delivered a stirring speech on the environment and Billie presented her own Outstanding Young Citizen Award to a charming young lad, sixteen-year-old Josh Hallows, who had set up an online help site and counselling service for children who were being bullied.

During the interval, Billie made her way to the ladies' bathroom, waiting to swap places in the cubicle with Dr Martinez, who smiled as she emerged, showing a row of perfect white teeth as she checked her profile in the mirror over the washbasin.

'Great speech,' Billie offered, having been impressed by Dr Martinez's impassioned address to the audience on saving the planet.

'Thank you, DSI Wilde. Stunning dress by the way. Sorry we've not had a chance to talk. I've heard so much about your talent for catching serial killers. If you ever come to Columbia, I am sure our security team at Precioso Global could make great use of your talents. We have some extremely dangerous predators in our country.' A dark shadow fell over her perfect features.

'And drug lords too...' Josta announced as she bundled out of the adjoining cubicle, having overheard the conversation, '... interesting you talk about our joint responsibility for the environment. Do you know, I once did a scientific study on freshwater shrimp in rural rivers in Suffolk England and what do you think I found?'

Billie shook her head, bewildered at the turn in conversation, whilst Dr Martinez viewed the short and wide Josta, with her brogue shoes and cropped hair, with hardly veiled disdain.

'Columbian cocaine, that's what. Every single shoal was high on the stuff. Now when you talk of cause and effect and the whole world being responsible for the environment, I applaud you. Who would have thought that the effects of illegal farming in South America would come to haunt every catch of shrimp bathing in the waterways of a quaint English town?'

'But I have just eaten your local seafood cocktail.' Dr Martinez looked aghast. Billie tried to hide a chuckle. She and Josta had made more considered choices.

'Moral of the story is stick to alternative appetisers on your foreign travels, dear, then you won't overload and end up getting caught short on a random drugs test.'

Luciana Martinez shot a furious glance at Josta before storming out, leaving Billie staring at her colleague, gobsmacked.

'What?' Josta responded. 'I wasn't born yesterday, dear.' She swung the door wide open to the cubicle Dr Martinez had just vacated. Traces of white powder could be clearly seen scattered across the toilet seat, like talcum powder.

'I could hear her honking up the stuff. That's the trouble with those who preach to us lesser mortals. Her snorting cocaine is having a direct effect on the Amazon rainforest she claims to love so much. A toxic cocktail of cement powder, bleach, kerosene, and sulphuric acid are needed to extract cocaine alkaloid from cocoa leaves. It doesn't do much for the environment when it runs into the Amazon River and it doesn't do much for our own ecosystem either. Cause and effect. Every action in life has its consequences, dear. The doctor should know that.'

Billie loved the way that Josta wasn't afraid to call a spade a spade. It was no wonder that she had found herself falling for Max, Josta's son, no matter how much she tried to sweep that thought aside.

'I'm done,' Billie answered. 'Do you want me to drop you off home or is Max going to pick you up? I'm happy to wait a little while with you until he comes.' Billie crossed her fingers that she had successfully covered the hopeful note in her voice on the second option.

'I'd be thrilled to take you up on the offer of a lift, dear heart, let me just go and say a few goodbyes. Max isn't around. He jetted off this afternoon on one of his secret missions. Rush job. Goodness knows when he'll be back. I get more gossip out of my stiffs than my darling son.'

Billie felt her heart sink. When Max had taken a call on his mobile outside of the cemetery, where she had been with him earlier that day, then rushed off, she had secretly hoped that she would get another chance to see him sooner rather than later.

She had truly tried to put him out of her mind, during those weeks when she had healed alone from the horrors of her past investigation, but as soon as he had called at the door of her new home, flowers in hand, all of her resolve had immediately evaporated. Right now, she found her heart fluttering at the mere mention of his name, like a silly schoolgirl.

As they emerged from the ladies' bathroom, Josta set off towards the ballroom to press the flesh and say her goodbyes. Billie suddenly found herself looking into the wary eyes of Josh Hallows, the young lad to whom she had just presented her award. He was leaning against the opposite wall, one leg tapping nervously, as though he had been fretfully waiting for her to emerge.

'Hey, well done for taking on such a big responsibility. It takes some guts to stand up to bullies, but you've helped all those other kids. Every little action has its consequences.' Billie echoed Josta's sentiments from moments earlier. She smiled, giving Josh a little clap to show how impressed she was.

'Em, well that's what I wanted to talk about.' Josh looked

shiftily from side to side, as though worried that someone might overhear the conversation. Billie was immediately alert. 'Honestly, I felt like announcing it on stage, but I was too much of a coward...' He trailed off, as though he was having second thoughts about the conversation. His eyes filled with tears. Billy touched his arm in concern.

'What's worrying you, Josh? You can tell me anything, in confidence–'

'It's about the murder.' His breathing suddenly became shallow, panicked. Billie moved nearer.

'Christy Callaghan? It's okay.' She lowered her voice. 'I'll make sure that you're safe if that's scaring you. Tell me what you know–'

'I know it all–' Josh started. Perry Gooch suddenly clattered through the door from the hall, looking Billie and Josh up and down. She appeared slightly drunk.

'Sorry to break up your intimate little... party...' She looked at Billie's hand on the boy's arm and smirked. Billie dropped her arm to her side, suddenly feeling guilty for no reason. '...but I need to get in there.' Perry pushed between them and into the ladies' bathroom. A look of sheer panic crossed Josh's face.

'Forget it.' He started to move off. 'I've got to go.' Billie followed, catching his arm once more to slow the boy down. Her voice was low.

'What if we talk about this tomorrow? I can come to your school.'

'No!' Josh appeared petrified at the thought. He wiped his hand over his face. 'I've got a free period tomorrow. I could meet you, at the playing fields, by the railway track, after school starts.' He started to pull away, as Perry Gooch appeared behind them once again.

'Don't mind me, playing gooseberry,' she taunted, making a big show of tiptoeing past them, towards the ballroom. Billie wanted to grab hold of her and ram her against the wall for her snide remarks, bearing in mind Josh was sixteen years old and in full school uniform.

A door at the end of the corridor leading to the back exit opened and a man popped his head inside. He looked like a middle-aged version of the boy.

'Taxi's here, Josh!' He clocked Billie. 'I hope you've thanked DSI Wilde for your award. Sorry, he's got to go early. He's got a revision programme for his exams.' He pulled a face at Billie. 'The pressure on kids these days, eh?' He rolled his eyes but clearly, professional parent that he was, he wasn't going to let Josh ease up on his studies even for one special night. He stepped back out, waving to the taxi, whilst holding the door open.

'I've gotta go.' Josh was acting like a scalded cat.

'All right. I'll be there tomorrow,' Billie started.

'Alone!' Josh retorted. 'By the railway viaduct. Don't say a word to anyone. Promise, or I won't spill.'

'Spill what, Josh?' Billie pressed.

'I know who killed them!' Josh's voice cracked before he pulled away and rushed out of the exit door.

Billie stood frozen to the spot. Had she heard right? Josh had said 'them'. Who was he talking about? Could there be murders on her patch unknown to her, or was he referring to Christy Callaghan and the girl who had been slaughtered at the train station. Surely the two couldn't be connected, could they?

6

TOO MUCH TO DO, TOO LITTLE TIME

Billie used her security pass to enter the darkened murder inquiry room and felt for the light switch.

'Good God! You gave me a shock there.' Long-serving officer Derek Blythe's head flew up from the screen on which he had been concentrating, as Billie clattered in.

'Bedtime, Derek.' Billie kicked off the silver high-heeled sandals, with a sigh of utter relief.

'Is that an offer?' he joked in response. He had taken Billie under his wing from the very first day that she had become a detective, so she didn't take offence. Derek, being an old-timer, sometimes cracked jokes that weren't exactly politically correct in this day and age, but Billie was of the opinion that she couldn't have wished for a more loyal team member.

'If you were offering a bag of chips on the way to the sack,' Billie retorted as she headed across the room to her office. 'I've just been to one of those work dos where the food was as boring as the entertainment and I'm looking at a long night here.'

'I can always nip out and get a takeaway?' Derek offered, but Billie shook her head with a smile as she shrugged off her coat. 'Seeing as you've dressed up especially,' he added, nodding to her backless dress as he followed her. Billie chuckled.

'Believe me, I'm about to turn into a pumpkin in about five minutes.' She glanced at the clock whilst firing up her PC. 'When I dig out my sweaty old training kit from the sports bag I left it in when I went on my extended holiday. It will probably have a field of mushrooms growing on it,' she added.

'Great to have you back.' Derek chuckled. 'You are about the only one who's always had the same passion for the job as I do,' he added.

Billie wondered whether to confide in Derek about her conversation with Josh. She had so much to get her head around, having not even expected to be back at work when she had left home that morning. She decided instead to catch her breath and take stock of the events that had unfolded throughout the day.

'Get yourself home, Dexie.' She used her affectionate nickname for him. 'Because I'm going to need you tomorrow, all guns firing. You wouldn't consider putting off your retirement, would you?'

Billie was only half-joking. Derek Blythe was the most experienced officer in her team and currently she was without trusty wingman Ash Sanghera, who was still recovering from the life-changing injuries he had recently acquired.

'No way, Jose. I've gone as far as I'm going in this business. I'm looking to new adventures. Got too much to do, too little time...'

Billie wanted to quip 'looks like it', with Derek still labouring in the office at nearly 10pm. In truth she felt it was going to hit him hard, retirement. Derek, though prone to cynicism, was one smart cookie.

'You did all those drugs courses, didn't you? I could do with a narcotics king on my team for this one.' Billie didn't want to sound like she was pleading, but she hated wasting talent and Derek Blythe would no doubt be able to shine some light on why a young girl would end up on a train track with nearly half a million quid's worth of narcotics on her.

'You just want to get out of hosting my retirement party,' Derek quipped.

Now he came to mention it, Billie accepted that his words did have a ring of truth to them. It was one thing offering to arrange his leaving do when she was still off work recuperating from earlier events, quite another thing when she was in the middle of what could be a double murder investigation.

'You wouldn't do me a big favour and attend the autopsies tomorrow?' Billie asked. A senior officer needed to be present, and she could count on Derek to do the job properly.

'What's wrong with The Grass then? Thought she was teacher's pet these days?'

'That joke's over now. We'll be using her proper name in future.' Billie felt a pang of guilt for starting that nickname in the first place. It smacked of the sort of bullying that schoolboy Josh Hallows had just won an award for stamping out. By Billie herself. She flushed. 'You're the best man for the job, Dexie. I'm counting on you.' Billie smiled.

'In that case it will be an honour, ma'am.' Derek Blythe bent forward in a jokey bow. Billie had already decided that she needed Jo to chase up the piano-playing witness who had gone AWOL due to her having been distracted by the chief at the train station and she couldn't miss the meeting with Josh at the playground. In addition, she needed to get two investigations under way.

'Shut the door when you go.' Billie was already starting to peel off her borrowed dress, as she rifled through a cupboard, searching for her sports bag. Suddenly her mobile rang. Billie rushed back to her desk and emptied out the tiny black velvet bag that Boo had loaned her for the evening's event.

Josta was on the line, sounding uncharacteristically panic-stricken. Billie frowned. She had only dropped her off in high spirits fifteen minutes earlier, chilled out with red wine and a pound of sausages on her lap donated from her new fan, the award-winning butcher.

'Oh, my dear girl. I'm so sorry to bother you, but something absolutely terrible has happened.'

Billie's heart leaped in her chest. She hoped to God that whatever Josta was referring to didn't involve Max.

7

A SHADOW OF HERSELF

'Do you think she was raped?' Billie whispered to Josta, who shrugged, worry etched on her face.

'I have no idea. We haven't got that far. I still can't get much sense out of her. It appears she's been fleeced at the hotel she was staying at. I wanted to call the emergency number, but you were the only one she would allow me to contact.'

They were standing in the hallway of her Victorian villa in the smart suburbs of the city. Through the half-open door, Billie could see Josta's wife, Lola Strong, looking a shadow of her usually magnificent self. She was wrapped in a shawl, sitting hunched on the floor in front of the fire and visibly shaking, though the house was as warm and inviting as usual. Her striking long silver hair was dishevelled, her face drawn and ashen.

Billie followed Josta into the room, her concern for Lola wiping away the pang of relief she had experienced on learning that Max was not in any danger.

'Lola.' Billie softly touched her shoulder. She jumped. 'Whatever's happened?' Lola pulled her shawl more tightly round her.

'I don't know...' she answered in a whisper, rather than her usual confident and well projected actress voice. 'I can remember being on stage...' she started.

'She's been playing the nurse, in *Romeo and Juliet*,' Josta informed Billie, 'along the highways and byways of the kingdom. I can't keep up with which theatre she's at in any given week.'

'Cambridge.' Lola looked up, catching Josta's hand for comfort. 'The show finished there on Saturday...'

'But it's Monday today.' Billie exchanged glances with Josta.

'Is it?' Lola, who was normally full of sharp wit and charm, appeared to be totally spaced out. 'I can remember watching the Friar Lawrence scene from the wings, where he gives Juliet the drug...' Josta rolled her eyes and sighed.

'People talk about the MeToo business today, female abuse in films and the like, but there was Shakespeare writing tales in which a holy man has an ancient form of GHB on hand that would knock a girl out for two days.'

'Could be what's happened here.' Billie nodded towards Lola, who was drowsily staring into space. She had long since arrived at the conclusion that Josta and Lola had a fairly open marriage. It was an attraction of opposites, for sure. Billie guessed that it was unlikely that the hugely attractive bohemian actress, did not have the occasional liaison with other like-minded members of her ever-touring theatre group. Especially as performers came and left depending on the specific play being performed.

If she did so, then Josta happily turned a blind eye to the situation as it allowed her to be devoted to her own other great love, forensic pathology. Whilst Lola needed a live audience at all times, Josta had a craving for serious engagement with the dead. It was an unusual set-up, Billie reflected, but it seemed to have resulted in a long and happy relationship and the creation of Max, the enigmatic psychologist whom Billie simply couldn't get out of her mind. The situation did, however, make the business of investigating the truth of how Lola came to arrive home in such a state, slightly delicate.

'Can you remember leaving the theatre?' Billie asked, crouching down beside Lola, catching the heady scent of her perfume, immediately being reminded once again of her son, Max, and his intoxicating lemony cologne. Like mother, like son. His other mum, Josta, preferred plain soap and water, together with a dousing of antiseptic gel, to wash away the smell of her autopsy suite.

'I recall a woman waiting as I left the stage door.' Lola frowned. 'She had an autograph book in her hand, I think, or a programme. She handed me a pen...' She trailed off again, looking into the flames of the fire.

'Then what?' Josta asked. 'Did you take her back to your place?' Billie swallowed hard. She was glad it was Josta who had asked the question. Lola shook her head, appearing genuinely shocked at the idea. Then she suddenly seemed to have another recollection.

'I bent down to sign my photograph. It was dark and I remember now, I didn't want to put my specs on...' Josta rolled her eyes. Lola looked up at Billie. 'Then she blew something in my face, a white powder. That's the last thing I remember, before waking up in my rental lodgings this afternoon. The cleaner was banging on the door to get in, but my head was thumping, and I still feel so woozy.' Tears started to roll down her cheeks. Josta put her arms around her and with Billie's help sat Lola on a richly embroidered fireside chair.

'I'll take some samples.' Josta stroked Lola's hair. 'See if we can find any evidence of poisons. Possibly nothing in the blood now, but a hair-strand test might turn up something.'

'There you go, the joys of having a one-woman forensic testing unit at your disposal,' Billie gently joked.

'But first we need toast.' Billie clocked the term 'we' as Josta swept off to make food, comfort eating being her default action at times of distress.

'Do you remember having a drink at all?' Billie sat on the arm of the chair as in her mind she ran through a list of drugs, modern-day versions of Friar Lawrence's famous potion, such as ketamine, rohypnol and Josta's aforementioned GHB, which could have had the effect that she was witnessing, but after two days, it was unusual to see a victim still so affected.

'I don't remember anything, that's the problem.' Lola sighed. 'Not after the powder blew in my face.'

'And they took your wallet, jewellery? Any other valuables?' Billie questioned. Lola was lost in thought for a moment, before looking up. 'No, that's the strange thing. The room was absolutely ransacked, drawers pulled out and upturned on the floor, the wardrobe emptied.' She rubbed her wrist. 'This watch is worth a small fortune. Josta bought it for our wedding anniversary, but they didn't touch it, nor me, for that matter. I'm still wearing the same clothes I was when I left the theatre.'

Josta bustled back in, breathing a sigh of relief on witnessing that news.

'So, whatever did they take, dear heart?' Josta fussed around putting a tray of buttered toast and tea on Lola's knee.

'Photos of the family. The ones I always carry in my bag.' Lola reached out for Josta's hand. 'All of the photos of Max.' Billie's stomach lurched at the name once more. 'The ones of the two of us alone were left scattered on the floor.'

'Anything else you can think of?' Billie's mind was racing. Lola nodded, utterly exhausted by her harrowing experience.

'My address book.' A chill swept through Billie's body.

8

A WILDE ROSE

Billie was up, if not exactly bright, then certainly early. That had been easy. After leaving Lola and Josta, she had returned straight back to the office and continued working throughout the night.

Hard slog had been the only way to still the unsettling thoughts looming in her mind, such as why anyone would go to the trouble to drug up one of Max's mums, ransack her room yet only take personal photographs of her son and her address book, leaving all of the normal target valuables behind.

Billie shivered. If Josta had been as worried as her, she hadn't shared her fears, bar commenting gently, as she had kissed Lola on the top of her head and stroked her hair, that she would have all of their house locks changed today.

Billie hadn't wanted to spook the couple any further, but after meeting Josh Hallows that afternoon, she would call by Max Strong's house, just to check that everything was in order. She didn't want him to come home to find that his own place had been similarly trashed.

Being well aware that some of the people that a criminal psychologist came into contact with could bear grudges and be just as deranged as her own past acquaintances, made Billie shudder. She would need to have a word with Max about personal safety. Billie scorned herself. She just wanted to have a word with him full stop, try as she might to hide that truth, even from herself.

Billie stood back to look at her work. Enlarged pictures covered the right wall of the room. These featured Christy Callaghan in life, for those members of the team who may have been living on Mars and therefore had no idea what the man looked like when he was still breathing. Alongside them were various photos taken at the crime scene, showing a head, registering a shocked expression, surrounded by a frame of staring pink shrimp.

For those who found the wall on the right hard to stomach, Billie had created an alternative and equally gruesome view to the left. Here hung death-scene photos of the Jane Doe drugs mule. Not that there was much left of the poor child. The train had first smashed into her slight body, bouncing it off the engine like a rag doll and then onto the tracks ahead, before running her over. The pictures sadly showed the horrific results, which included decapitation and electrocution.

Billie pitied any of the team arriving with a breakfast butty in hand. The new wallpaper wasn't full of scenes for the faint-hearted. Billie herself was nibbling in an absent-minded fashion at an ancient trail bar, way past its sell-by date, which she had dug out of her musty sports training bag.

She was hopeful that the recovered CCTV footage and a description of the piano-playing witness, should Jo Green be able to track him down, would enable the team to match the female victim's description with current young mispers. The autopsies this morning would no doubt give more vital pieces of much needed information on both cases.

'Looks like you had a good night.' Boo crashed through the

door in her wheelchair, shaving a strip of paintwork off in the process. She grinned at Billie, handing her a carrier bag.

'Your day clothes, ma'am. When you popped back to my place, you must have been thinking about other things.' Boo winked. 'So forgot to take them. Top marks for me having spotted the sheets in the spare room were untouched, so spill. Whose bed did you end up sleeping in last night?' Billie took the bag, nodding her thanks.

'I just got a couple of hours on the sofa in my office.' Billie flicked her head in the direction of her tiny corner room, indicating a mountainous pile of folders under which there had once been a sofa. Clearly, no checks had been made to verify the fact that this was still the case, for months. Boo certainly looked unconvinced.

'I haven't always sat in this office like a lemon you know, I used to be a fully paid up, card carrying member of the CID.' Billie sensed that even though Boo was teasing, there was a hard edge to her comment. She reminded herself to get to the bottom of their conversation the night before on that very subject.

'I'm not with you.' Billie shrugged, waving her arm around. 'I lost sense of time, so I just stayed here. Look around. I've been decorating the room.'

Boo dug in her bag before pulling out a white envelope, with a single red rose taped to it.

'That's a wild rose, if you get my meaning, DSI Wilde, so somebody's sending you one hot message. It was on my kitchen table this morning. So how did it get on there when you're claiming to have been here all night?' Billie took the envelope from Boo's hands, frowning as she looked at the name. It was definitely addressed to her.

'Beats me,' she mused, tearing the envelope open and squinting at the writing scrawled across the single sheet of paper. Billie scanned the words speedily, aware that the team were gathering at their places. Then she stopped, frozen in shock for a split second before slowly reading it again. 'Shit,' she whispered, almost under her breath as the meaning of the words sank into her brain.

I feel her Wilde calling, songs from the soul she cries,
calling me to take her Wilde life,
her Wilde beauty calls for defacement,
her Wilde tresses call out to be scalped,
her Wilde body calls for disfigurement,
her Wilde soul calls out for the devil,
she hears my Wilde cries; she calls me not.
No one will hear her Wilde calls for mercy.
Nor her Wilde cries of pain as I finally call with the kiss of death.

'What?' Boo frowned, aware of Billie's change in demeanour.

'Looks like I've only gone and got myself a stalker.' Billie shrugged, chuckling as she dropped the notepaper in Boo's lap. 'Just some crazy having a joke,' she added.

'But how did they get in my kitchen?' Boo questioned.

'Maybe you put the dustbins out early and forgot to shut the door when you went up to shower?' Billie sounded totally unperturbed as she headed to the front of the room, ready to address the team.

'No,' she heard Boo reply. Clearly, she hadn't put her friend's mind at rest. Not that Billie believed her own hastily thought up explanation either. She couldn't help noticing, from the corner of her eye, as she launched into her briefing, Boo's reaction on having finished reading the note. The look on her face gave the game away. There wasn't a hope in hell that her friend and colleague agreed with her that the wild rose and warped love letter was any sort of laughing matter, at all.

Billie slammed her brakes on, slapping her hand hard on the car horn as a dark car with blacked out windows sped past her, pulled in sharply to avoid a collision with an oncoming lorry, then shot off again, overtaking the three vehicles in front in one jump.

On another occasion, Billie might have chased after the car and apprehended the crazy driver. There was no doubt the person behind the wheel would create carnage sooner or later. But right now, she was talking to Josta on her car phone, en route to her meeting with Josh Hallows. With the volume of outstanding tasks on her mind, she didn't have time for any distractions with dangerous driver fun and games. All her team were hard at work, no doubt having lunch on the hoof as they focused on their different, but equally vital tasks. As for the phantom stalker, Billie had arranged for someone to go around and change all of Boo's locks. Her friend had done her a good turn last night. She didn't want her to be terrified that a mad person had access to her home and might be planning to pop back again tonight.

'The girl also had a stab wound to her leg.' Josta was ending her summary on the train death. 'Unfortunately that came via a craft-knife that appears to have been her own, tucked into her sock. The blade must have been clean of the casing at the time of the incident.'

Billie sighed. 'Jeez, what's the world coming to, when a child is partially killed by her own weapon of destruction?' she asked.

'No different from how the world has always been,' Josta replied. 'It's just that in the past, we were all complacent that armies of child killers were getting on with their deadly deeds in some far-off uncivilised country. Now, my dear, I'm afraid they are right on our doorstep via county lines drug dealing. I don't want to second-guess your enquiry, but I'm postulating that is the case here. Fortunately, we found part of the torso that was still intact...'

Billie tried to keep the memory of the dead child in situ on the rail track at bay, whilst she concentrated on the road ahead. Her fellow road users were already at risk from the maniac driver, who had now disappeared from view.

'...it reveals evidence that a hernia operation was carried out, almost certainly when she was a baby. It's a common surgery, but the fact might help you narrow down an identification.'

'Thanks, Josta, we've located a witness who's coming in this afternoon to work on a facial composite.'

Jo had been like a dog with a bone as usual, not least because the irritating Perry Gooch had managed to get her damn claws into the man who had been playing the station piano when Billie had been distracted, chasing the chief across the concourse. As a result, the key witness's photo was on the front of today's *Daily Herald*. It ensured that the public had full details of evidence that Billie might have wanted to protect in order to get a conviction, much to her annoyance.

'She was alive when the train hit her...' Josta added, a detached professional air to her voice as was usual when discussing cases, no matter how gruesome. Billie reacted by squeezing her eyes shut in horror for a split second. She opened them, glanced into her back mirror, and blinked. Was that the same car with blacked out windows, the one that had just sped past, coming up behind her again?

'Are you still there?' Josta asked.

Billie didn't engage the car indicator as she spun the wheel to the left. Fortunately, she was planning to turn at that junction anyway. The dark car shot past. Was it the same one, or was she more spooked than she had let on to Boo, by the strange note that she had received that morning?

'Hello?' Josta enquired more forcefully.

'Yes, sorry,' Billie responded, deciding she was letting her imagination run wild.

'Did I mention earlier that Christy Callaghan was also alive when his beheading took place?'

Billie pulled into a parking space overlooking the park playground. It was a pretty spot, in the dip of a valley. A train thundered over the viaduct that straddled the leafy, tree-surrounded area. No sign of Josh Hallows yet. Billie reminded herself not to get autopsy updates whilst driving in future. Derek had already returned and dropped both files on her desk, but she hadn't had a chance to read them fully before leaving base, hence putting in the call.

'Yep.' Billie undid her seat belt and tried to take stock for a moment. 'Sorry I couldn't make the examinations. Was Derek Blythe, okay?'

'Well, no one could compensate for your attendance in the flesh, dear heart,' Josta joked, 'but all went well. Sergeant Blythe took an avid interest in both cases, though he seemed genuinely shaken by the child. Of course, as expected, he fell into his usual politically incorrect, prehistoric-era quips about Christy Callaghan having lost his head, etcetera.'

'I guess it's too late to teach an old dog new tricks.' Billy smiled.

Derek had started in the police force long before political correctness had kicked off its high-heeled shoes and tucked its gender-neutral feet under the table. Despite having once called Boo 'handicapped', a passing remark made in her hearing that he had barely survived, and constantly flinging out sexist wisecracks way past their sell-by, he had somehow managed to keep his place in the force until retirement. True, he hadn't reached any heady heights, due to his reluctance to take on new ways of policing, but he was certainly shit-hot at his job and one of Billie's greatest supporters. She would be sorry to lose him, everything considered.

'Is Lola all right today?' Billie needed a brief respite from talk of dead bodies.

'Rallying. The show must go on and all that. Thanks for helping last night at the end of such a long day. She does have a soft spot for you.'

'No problem,' Billie reassured.

'But she's still not at her best,' Josta continued. 'Up before dawn and out for a walk to clear her thoughts. When I woke up, I was worried sick. Of course, the news on this morning's TV didn't help things.'

'What news?' Billie had been totally focused on the murder enquiries. The rest of the world could have come to an end without her having noticed the fact.

'A major South American drug lord taken out. Six people killed in the armed tussle retrieving a hostage. Said to be a birdwatcher, but more likely an operative.'

'And?' Billie ran her fingers through her hair, sensing something troubling in Josta's voice, but quite unable to decipher the reason why. Josta was silent for a beat, as though weighing up whether to say anything.

'Max, as you know, was an officer in the British Army SAS.' Billie waited for more information. 'Since becoming a criminal psychologist, his vast talents are in even greater demand, the world over, especially in hostage situations.'

Billie felt a cold chill skitter through her body. 'He often shoots off to different locations at a moment's notice. We can rarely get him to spill the beans on where he's been, but he has long-standing connections with South America. He has certainly travelled there before. The last time, as recently as just a few weeks ago.'

Billie felt sick. Her last investigation had been so personally destructive that she had been ordered to take time off to recuperate and relaunch her life. She had often wondered why Max had not made any contact at all. True, he had made it clear during that previous investigation that it wasn't wise to engage in a relationship due to his own personal circumstances, not to mention Billie's harrowing situation. But there was still *something* between them and Billie had hoped that given time, it might even develop beyond friendship, especially when he had turned up at her door yesterday, out of the blue.

'Rumour has it that the British Army operate in vicinities such as Columbia. In an advisory capacity, allegedly, assisting in the war against illegal drug production. I have no idea whether that is true or not,' Josta continued.

'Have you heard from him yet?' Billie rifled her fingers through her hair again, a nervous tick she had fallen into at times of stress, since her childhood days.

'No, but then rather like the rest of the family, when he's concentrating on his work, he does tend to forget everybody else. Talking of South America, do you remember my conversation with the delectable Dr Martinez on the subject of krill? Did Sergeant Blythe convey to you the results of the seafood garnish around Christy Callaghan's head?' Josta queried, demonstrating her point about her family's laser focus on their jobs.

'How could I forget?' Billie replied. 'The stoned shrimp of Suffolk story. I'll be dining out on that tale for a while.'

'I'm afraid it turns out that junkie shrimps have swum further afield, arriving on our own fair shores in the far north of England. The seafood menu in Christy Callaghan's club, states that all of the shellfish is locally caught, and my tests produced positive results that every single shrimp on the platter was full to the gills on cocaine. Drug waste is very much alive and kicking on our home territory.'

'You're kidding me.' Billie was stunned at the news and horrified that Cilla the dancer's talk of drugs gangs from far afield suddenly swamping the local area, seemed to be turning out to be true.

'I never like to upset you, dear girl, but this looks like bad news for the home-grown wildlife as well as the resident population.'

Billie was scanning the park as she talked, keen to make herself known the moment that Josh Hallows appeared in view. Suddenly, across the furthest perimeter of the park she saw a dark flash cross behind the trees. Was it the same car that had appeared to be following her, *again*?

'Sorry. I've got to go.' Billie ended the call, jumping out of the car and rushing into the park. She stared at the thick clump of trees way beyond the viaduct area, where the old stone arches straddled the usual banana slide and roundabout formations of an English children's playground. There it was again, in a gap between the foliage. Billie started to stride quickly across the grass.

Suddenly she was aware of a figure moving speedily in the high grass beside one of the stone arches, or was it two people? She quickly changed direction and moved fast towards that area, reasoning that it could be a dog walker or maybe just Josh Hallows, trying to keep a low profile until her arrival. The shapes dropped from view again. Billie frowned as she arrived in the vicinity, looking all around and up at the inside of the arch as another train thundered on the track immediately overhead.

'Hello?' she shouted. Her voice carried away on the breeze that made the long grass wave like a golden head of hair. Somehow it made Billie recall the so far nameless girl's head lying on the rail track. She shivered as she stepped out from under the arch, checking her watch. Josh was due any minute.

The splash of blood on her wrist made her jump back in

shock, a split second before a body fell, ricocheting onto the ground at her feet. Josh Hallows, having landed at a frighteningly weird angle, neck clearly broken, stared up at her with an unseeing gaze. Blood trickled from his mouth.

Billie snapped into action. She could hear footsteps running overhead, stepped back for a second to see if she could spot the culprit, clocked the metal ladders that ran up the side of the arch and took a step to give chase, before making the decision to turn all of her attention to Josh. Blood poured from his chest, covering Billie, as she attempted to stem the flow and find a pulse, knowing in truth that her attempts would be futile. Cradling the young figure in her arms, she felt tears run down her cheeks as she reached for her mobile and called in her team, devastated that this young soul would never be caught telling tales out of class again.

'Ma'am, I think we've got an ident on the girl,' Jo Green announced, as Billie clicked on her mobile, noticing that the keys were sticky with blood. She put the phone on hands-free instead, as Jo ran through the address details.

All around her the crime scene investigation team were hard at work, Josta at the fore, bent over Josh Hallows' broken body. Billie suddenly had a memory of his proud dad from the night before. She totally dreaded the task of breaking the devastating news about his precious award-winning boy.

She pushed the thought away, marvelling instead on Josta's ability to have reached the crime scene in record time. It felt to Billie as though she had just been around the corner when the suspicious death was called in, rather than at the mortuary across the other side of town.

'On my way,' Billie replied. 'I've asked the chief to bring in a specialist drugs officer to assist with the briefing later this afternoon.' Billie had made the decision that the team urgently needed a crash course in county lines drug dealing.

'We may have time to inform the family before then, ma'am. The victim's parents only live in Durham. Divorced, but I understand currently together at the father's house, worried sick about the whereabouts of their daughter. Both were under the impression she was at the other's home last night, celebrating her birthday.'

Billie sighed. Breaking the news of two suspicious young-person deaths in one day was not a job for the faint-hearted, but it came with the job and though harrowing, offered a real opportunity to gather vital evidence.

She had to admit that she was quietly surprised at the location of the girl's home. For some reason, she had not expected that a child drugs mule could have been residing less than thirty miles away in the beautiful city of Durham, known for its magnificent cathedral, outstanding university, and breathtaking scenery. She reminded herself that her own background had been full of hidden family horrors, despite her also having grown up in a middle-class, perfect English country garden scenario.

'Can you take care of this for me?' Billie called over to Derek Blythe who was just arriving at the scene, truly relieved that he hadn't retired yet and wondering if she could have another stab at getting him to stick around awhile. With her trusty wingman Ash still off work on sick leave and three suspicious deaths in two days, her team was currently sorely stretched. 'Looks like we've found the girl's parents. I need to nip off and break the jolly news,' she said, her face grim.

'Rather you than me.' Derek Blythe shook his head. 'You might need to brush up a bit.' He got his hanky out of his pocket and rubbed Billie's face as though she were a child. 'Don't want you scaring the horses.' Billie rolled her eyes at Derek, before clocking that his hanky was smeared with blood. She rubbed her face.

'Thanks.' Billie suddenly looked down at her top, realising that she was a bit of a bloody mess, racking her brains for any other clothing options at all that she might have stashed in the back of her office.

'I've got a jacket I can loan you to cover that,' Derek offered, 'let me just nip back to my car.'

Billie called her goodbyes to Josta before heading off to her own vehicle. She was aware of her hand shaking as she clicked on the electronic key to open the door. Whatever show of bravado police liked to play for people not in the force, about being at murder scenes, the truth was one never got used to such scenarios. Billie often woke in the dead of night reliving incidents. She would be glad of the short journey back to base in order to centre herself again and remember all that stuff she'd been taught in counselling about not being able to change events, but instead alter her perception of them. Reframing, it was called. She was having trouble making that theory work for her now she was back grafting at the crime-scene coalface.

The electronic car key clicked but didn't seem to engage with the door. Billie grabbed the handle, immediately realising that the driver's door was already open. Chiding herself for having forgotten to engage the lock, she swung the door wide and then froze on the spot. A single wild red rose on a thorny stem lay on the seat. The joke was beginning to wear a bit thin.

'Got you.' Billie nearly leaped two feet in the air, as Derek Blythe slapped his hand on her shoulder. She whipped around as he handed her a zip-up police-issue fleece, almost vintage it was so ancient-looking.

'Got this out of the ark, did you?' Billie quipped to cover her jumpiness.

'I usually only wear it for gardening, but it won't frighten the relatives half as much as your current get-up.'

'Thanks, Dexie, you're a gem.' Billie took the jacket, whisking the rose off her seat. 'Ow!' she exclaimed, catching her hand on a sharp thorn in the process. She sucked her finger as a drop of blood appeared. Derek Blythe bent down and picked up the rose, which had spiralled onto the kerb spilling petals like confetti.

'Aye, aye, what's all this then? Got a secret admirer, have you?' he teased.

'Lunatic more like.' Billie rolled her eyes. 'Keep it as a mark of my appreciation,' she added, handing it to him as she swung into her seat behind the wheel. Derek Blythe chuckled.

'I might wear it behind my ear, cheer this whole scene up,' he joked.

'I wouldn't put anything past you,' Billie called after him, starting the engine.

She thanked God that Derek had lightened the moment. She had been seriously spooked for a second, wondering if maybe she should take this stalker thing more seriously. Perhaps she should have kept the rose, sent it to forensics?

She shook the thought away, deciding that she had enough on her plate with her current investigations without making herself into a victim over a couple of roses and a rambling page of words. Instead, she turned her mind to the serious business ahead, beginning with the trip to old Durham town and the soul-shattering police door knock of death.

9

WILDE MURDER

'A spot of blood, ma'am.' The Grass indicated a corkscrew curl, still carrying the remains of Josh Hallows, framing Billie's face.

Billie quickly tucked the hair behind her ear and zipped Derek Blythe's jacket fully up as she hit the brass door knocker of the smart Victorian villa within Durham's spectacular World Heritage site. The tall windows had panoramic views down to the medieval city huddled below and across the River Wear to the iconic edifice, Durham Cathedral.

The shrine of Saint Cuthbert lay here. Rumour had it that when King Henry VIII's henchmen had visited in 1539 to strip the ornate tomb of gold and jewels, they had found the bones of St Cuthbert still completely intact, covered with skin and tissue and sporting a fully grown beard, despite him having flipped his mortal coil in 687AD.

Billie was praying for some sort of similar miracle here, experience telling her that the grief-stricken parents of the victim now expected to be thirteen-year-old Sophie Grey, would demand to see the body of their fallen child as a matter of urgency. A request that if granted, could only riddle their souls with never-ending torment.

The police artist's facial composite had resulted in an almost identical photo to that on file at the UK Missing Persons Unit, including the scattering of freckles on Sophie's nose and the slight scar on her forehead where she had fallen out of her pram once as a baby, though DNA and dental records could further confirm, without causing excruciating distress. Billie reminded herself to ask if Sophie had ever undergone a hernia operation.

Jo had run all of the details so far gleaned, by Billie on the journey from base. It turned out that Sophie had already gone missing a couple of times before, for a day or two – even a week at one point, hence a photo being on file. All absences from home having occurred since her parents' divorce. She had each time resolutely refused to give particulars of her whereabouts after having returned from these sudden walkabouts.

A quick call by Jo to both schools Sophie had attended in the past few months, listed on the Missing Persons' files, revealed that Sophie and her parents had presented as the perfect happy family for many years. Then Dad had gotten overfamiliar with a rather talented first violinist within his orchestra, triggering the less than amicable break-up. Mum had moved out, nabbing a new flat, new haircut and new lover in the shape of her rather fit Zumba teacher.

Sophie had been lifted to a new school and had moved between both homes as decreed by a court order. In between Father making sweet music with his latest amour and Mum getting into the rhythm with her spanking new amigo, it appeared that Sophie felt that she had been relegated to the cheap seats as a result of her parents less than applause-worthy performance. Instead of accepting that the show must go on, despite the huge upheaval to her life, the girl had searched out entertainment elsewhere. With devastating consequences.

All of these details were running through Billie's mind as the door swung open. A tall man looked from Billie to Jo, his eyes puffed up and red.

'DSI Wilde. May we come in, sir? It's about your daughter, Sophie.' The man neither nodded in acquiescence or shut the door in their faces. He simply turned around as though in a daze and wandered back across the hallway. Billie glanced at Jo. It was clear that the terrible news had reached him already, the question was, how?

'It's more police...' The man trailed off as a woman with newly bleached hair, expensive manicure and colour co-ordinated dance practice kit, emerged from a room, looking equally spaced out. Thick mascara streaming down her face could have given rock star Alice Cooper a run for his money. She looked utterly deranged as she ran across the polished parquet floor in her dance shoes and caught Billie's arm.

'I want to see my baby,' she practically screamed. 'I told her that I wanted to see my baby girl no matter what she looks like!' She started sobbing, almost keeling over with the waves of grief racking her body.

Billie took both arms gently yet firmly and steered Sophie's mother back in the direction of the room she had just come from. No one less enjoyed breaking the news of a sudden death than she did, especially the fatality of a child, but normally at least she and her fellow officer were in a position to break the information gradually and control the reaction. Billie had known it range from utter shocked silence to crazed aggression, hence the need for two officers in such situations.

'Your colleague said it wouldn't be a pretty sight.' Sophie's dad flicked his head back in the direction of the room. Tears welled up in his eyes. 'She said that her body was... scattered all over the track.' His hand flew up over his mouth as if to prevent himself from throwing up.

Billie looked towards Jo again. She still gave the impression of not having long left childhood behind herself, with her short stature, cropped spiky hair and Harry Potter specs. She was blinking hard, as taken aback as Billie had been by the welcome. Clearly it wasn't her that Sophie's dad had been referring to. As far as Billie knew, the investigation team were the only people who were currently in possession of the information on the identity of the victim.

As Billie practically held Sophie Grey's mum up now in her arms, the woman being at the brink of collapse, they entered the grand living room of the house, a space with a stunningly scenic view to Durham Cathedral, featuring a grand piano in front of one of the tall windows. The ceiling was high and ornate, the fireplace surround cut from the palest marble, expensive antique furniture adding to the air of exclusivity.

Like a blot on the landscape, slap bang in the centre of one of the gold-hued, overstuffed silk sofas, sat reporter Perry Gooch, notebook balanced on her ample knees. She held a cup of tea in one hand, slice of cake in the other. Happy family photos of Mum, Dad and Sophie Grey were spread across sofa, coffee tables and floor. She had obviously been looking forward to a telltale tea party featuring stirring stories of the newly departed, hot from the mouths of her heartbroken parents. Billie felt an incandescent rage flood through her body.

'The impersonation of a police officer is a very serious offence.' Jo found her voice first, Billie having been stricken momentarily speechless at the sight.

'You're not a police officer?' Sophie Grey's father stammered, looking from Perry Gooch to Billie.

'I never said–' Perry Gooch started to announce with confidence, as Jo grabbed the cup of tea and cake swiftly from her, before Billie yanked her hefty frame upright, marching her forcefully towards the door. Sophie Grey's parents stood like rabbits trapped in headlights as Perry made a grab for a large portrait photo of their daughter, looking particularly angelic in school uniform, on a coffee table en route.

'Don't even think of it,' Billie warned, giving the journalist a push into the hallway.

'What the hell are you playing at? I should book you right now. You could get six months in the nick for that sicko trick.' Billie pinned Perry Gooch up against the hall wall. Another photo, large, framed and right above their heads, showed Sophie sitting at a piano, smiling proudly. Perry Gooch pulled away, smirking at Billie.

'Good luck with that, officer, I can't help it if they jump to conclusions, due to their grief–'

'Who's feeding you stories?' Billie cut in. Infuriating as the fact was, she knew that Perry Gooch was right about making the charge stick, whatever the truth of the scenario when Sophie's parents had opened the door and found the reporter skulking on the step. Perry Gooch smirked again, straightening her jacket.

'I'm just a crack investigative journo, DSI Wilde. Perhaps if you were a bit quicker off the mark, you would have got to break the sad news instead of me. Watch and learn, love, watch, and learn.' She threw the words back as she headed out of the door.

It took all of Billie's inner strength not to chase after her, but at that moment a delivery driver passed Perry Gooch, climbing the steep stone stairs to the door. He handed Billie a bouquet. In the fury of the moment, she didn't question the fact that no one should have had the knowledge necessary to even consider sending condolence gifts.

She walked back into the room, handing the flowers to Sophie's father. The wild red roses looked well past their sell-by to Billie. An alarm bell started ringing in her head even in the split second before he glanced at the card. From his face it was clear that his bewilderment had reached breaking point. His voice was totally flat as he handed the bouquet back to Billie.

'DSI Wilde you said? I think these are for you.'

A flush of mortification raced through Billie's body. She could already see the writing on the card positioned in the centre of the dismal arrangement.

Wilde murder, it read. This was getting past a joke.

10

TRAPPED

Billie took the stairs two at a time, determined to make the team briefing with the police drugs expert dead on time. She still felt stung by Perry Gooch's comments about having needed to be quicker off the mark.

The feeling had nothing at all to do with her having any respect for the journalist, but a lot to do with the same old feeling she had never been able to shake off, despite several weeks of counselling as a result of her last, albeit ultimately successful, investigation. Had nepotism played a big part in her having risen through the ranks so spectacularly? Her late dad had been a former chief of police, the current one her godfather. Billie could see how rumours could circulate on the subject.

Billie was also still furious about the delivery of the damn dead flowers, right in the middle of engaging with Sophie Grey's parents. Luckily, Jo had been alert to the faux pas and had swiftly taken the dismal bouquet from her, asking for directions to the dustbin outside of the back door. It had given Billie a chance to focus on the parents in an attempt to salvage the situation with Mum and Dad and glean any details about their daughter that might prove useful to the investigation.

Jo had been astute enough not to question Billie about the strange delivery on the drive back to base, perhaps assuming that the grim flowers were linked to a lover's tiff. Though her relationship with Jo was on a totally different footing nowadays from the time she had last assisted Billie, it was still very much on professional terms. Neither had any wish to fall out, as they had done so spectacularly in the past.

Billie had pocketed the card that had been clipped to the flowers, for later perusal. She mused that maybe she would recognise the scrawl of someone that she had recently antagonised. She mentally rolled her eyes at the thought. The list would be endless. Not many criminals she had come into contact with were likely to have her at the top of their Xmas card list, after all. In any case, from what little Billie knew about stalkers, if that was indeed what she had suddenly acquired like a bad dose of the clap, was that they were attention seekers. Her plan, in so much that it even crossed her mind, was to cut off the idea that she was even slightly affected by their game. Not when her brain was fully focused on murder.

Below the staircase, in the smart reception area, a TV was transmitting the news. It included further details of the South American hostage situation, including an interview with the relieved freed English hostage. He insisted yet again that he had simply been trying to get photos of a rare hummingbird, hidden deep in the Andean Mountain range. Unfortunate perhaps, that his search had taken him into territory known as the wild west of Columbia and the lair of more deadly creatures – a major drugs cartel. He'd got entangled, like a spider in a web, with the group who operated a very lucrative sideline in ransom income.

Thinking of the deaths involved in the man's rescue, Billie felt queasy. No further details had been given on the identity of those who had been killed. The truth was that the honest-looking birdwatcher could well have really been an undercover operative, despite appearances, upping the stakes for both sides. Billie couldn't help thoughts of Max smashing against the hard emotional shield that she attempted to wrap around herself during murder investigations. She desperately hoped that he would make contact soon.

'Ah, DSI Wilde.' The chief always used her formal title when she was accompanied by a fellow officer and no welcoming hugs today, thank God, Billie noted.

'I'm just having a quick word with the drugs specialist that you requested. He's on permanent attachment to the National Crime Agency. He's one of the best in the business and he's offered to be on hand until your investigation is over. Make sure you treat him nicely now,' he teased.

'Is that level of interference called for, sir?' Billie felt her heart sink. She wondered if the chief was taking a sledgehammer to crack a nut here. She made a note to be more careful in future with what she wished for.

'I might have been a bit laid-back about Christy Callaghan flipping his mortal coil, but the two kids are making the media think that all of their Xmases have come at once and we don't want to look like the jokes in the crackers,' he quipped. 'Just as you flagged up, we need some drugs education. I'll send him in when I've given him fair warning about you,' he added, grinning.

Billie rolled her eyes as she walked past him. True, she had wanted her team to be fully briefed on the latest intelligence in connection with county lines drug dealing, but she had not expected input from the NCA.

She had come up against some of their operatives before. Focused on the most high-risk offenders involved in serious organised crime across the world, they often made it clear that policing at a local level was way beneath their pay grade. Billie didn't know what strings the chief had pulled, but in truth the operative would probably be keen to hotfoot it away as soon as the opportunity arose. She guessed that she would be the one first in line to wave him goodbye.

Billie began to run her team through the evidence to date, full of regret that she hadn't got the vital information from Josh Hallows the night before. She desperately tried not to dwell on the fact that it might just have saved his life. Sophie's parents, for their part, had given little useful information, save for the fact that there was no love lost between the two of them.

Though they had got as far as agreeing that Sophie had been secretive and distant recently, the warring couple had put her behaviour down to her change of school or accused the other partner of having had their eye off the ball. As Billie and Jo had left, a simmering tit-for-tat spat was already coming near to boiling point, now that the initial mind-numbing smack of shock had worn off. Sophie, until yesterday their only remaining joint love, would lie bleeding forever between them, her sickening death a gaping wound too grave to ever heal. Poignantly, she had often lay in bed dreaming of her parents reuniting, never for a moment guessing that she would be the one to have dealt the last fatal blow to her already departed, yet once happy, family.

Apart from the vast haul of drugs on Sophie Grey's body, a pay-as-you-go phone had been found nearby on the train track. It appeared to have been brand new and used for the first time that afternoon, to visit the same social media video channel, several times, showing a group of young men engaging in a 'Drill' performance.

A small female hand, wearing a similar ring on her finger to the one worn by Sophie, could be seen in a freeze-frame, spray-painting the name of the gang onto the wall of a rival group.

Billie briefed that members of the team were already trying to locate the performers, in a bid to work out if the spray-painting, along with the antagonistic lyrics of the Drill rappers, may have helped hasten her death.

Calling for a quick refreshment break, Billie unzipped Derek Blythe's jacket and slid it off, feeling overheated in the overcrowded room. The assembled attendees were collectively silenced at the vision. Billie had unwittingly revealed an eye-catching abstract design in heavily splattered dried blood across her upper body. A poignant imprint of Josh Hallows' death mask was stamped onto the white fabric. It was clear to all that she had held the boy's head close to her heart, as his life blood and oh-so promising future, had ebbed away. Though there was no evidence on show of the salty tears she had cried, the picture told the story of the boy's sad demise more forcefully than any crime-scene diagrams ever could.

'Sorry,' she said, racing to her office to see if she could locate yesterday's clothes delivered in the carrier bag by Boo that morning. She hoped that Derek Blythe was having more success on his visit to the schoolboy's home, to impart the devastating news, than Billie had achieved earlier with Sophie Grey's parents. She gave silent thanks that he had stepped in and offered to make the doorstep death call, taking some of the load off her shoulders. He had volunteered to take a rookie cop along with him to show him the ropes. The young detective was his nephew, Andy, who had just joined the team. His enthusiasm gave Billie hope that he would turn out to be just as dedicated to his job as Dexie. As Billie dragged off her T-shirt, she vowed again to try to persuade the mature officer to stay until the cases were wound up. Experience like his was worth its weight in gold.

'DSI Wilde–' The door flew open. Billie was trapped, topless save for her bra, which was also soaked with bloodstains. 'This

Is Ellis Darque, from the Serious Crime Investigation Agenc–'
The chief stopped mid-sentence, realising that Billie, flushing
bright puce, was in no fit state to receive guests at that very
moment.

Billie flung her top over her head and pulled it down,
flicking her head up, ready to brazen the situation out. She held
out her hand.

'Hi.' She finally looked up. Then did a double take. She had
met the man in front of her only the day before. The last time
their paths had crossed, he'd had a cocky air and worn a grey
baggy tracksuit as he had trailed behind the funeral cortège of
the region's other newly dead gangster, Jesus O'Brian. Today, he
was freshly shaved and wearing a sharply tailored suit.

'Now I recognise you. With your clothes on,' he quipped,
clearly enjoying her embarrassment. The chief looked from one
to the other quizzically.

'Ellis Darque?' Billie counter-attacked. 'Is that the name
you're using on Tinder these days?'

Billie clocked that he was certainly more date worthy than
his undercover alter ego, criminal hard guy Glenn Baxter,
though both ghost person and the man in front of her shared a
similar cheeky charm. But then she was just a bit biased. Glenn
Baxter, whoever he may never have been, had probably saved
her life, thanks to a chance meeting during the last investigation.

'She's trouble this one, chief.' Ellis Darque winked at Billie.

'Tell me about it,' the chief agreed, relieved that the
introduction had gone better than he had guessed it would.

'I'll leave you two boys to chew the fat shall I, whilst the rest
of us get on with a triple murder enquiry? Some cups need
washing if you've got nothing better to do,' Billie added, showing
that she was more than up to their boyish banter.

Instead, the chief went back to his big office with the view over the city and Ellis Darque followed her into the briefing room. Billie introduced the crack officer to her team. Their eye-popping lesson on the realities of county lines drug crime was about to begin.

'Do any of you have kids?' he started. A handful of people in the room nodded.

'Kids like these?' He switched on the CCTV footage from the train station. A shaky view of the concourse appeared on a big white screen at the end of the room. Sophie Grey could be seen, getting up from her seat, passing a man playing the piano and pausing for a moment before moving towards the platform. Three hooded, tracksuit-bottomed figures rushed into shot. Two of them could be seen tussling with Sophie before her body ricocheted onto the track at the very same moment the fast train from Edinburgh to London hurtled through. He froze the frame.

'Anybody?' He looked around the room. Nobody responded. 'Nobody got a kid over eleven years old, or maybe as young as eight?' He pointed from one child to the other. The third figure hovered just on the edge of shot, perhaps acting as a lookout. 'Nobody got a boy, nobody got a girl?' Various people nodded again, not sure where he was going with the questions.

'Every one of the children on this piece of CCTV is likely to be a drug dealer. Maybe a mule, maybe a runner, maybe running a Trap House, maybe just about to go home where mum will be waiting to put their fish fingers and chips on the table. She probably thinks that her precious sprog has simply been at after-school club.' Ellis paused. 'Six-year-old drug runners aren't unheard of.'

Various members of the team reacted in astonishment.

'Everyone knows what their kids are doing at this minute?' People started nervously checking their phones, texting messages.

'I can tell you one thing for sure. Your kid knows a drug dealer.'

'Not my nephew, Jimmy, mate.' Derek Blythe had just entered, back from his deathly knock at Josh Hallows' parents' door. 'Andy's little brother. He comes from a good home.'

'So did Sophie Grey,' Billie replied, 'she had a precocious talent, top of the class in all of her subjects, not short of pocket money. But she was carrying drugs adding up to a street value of £485,000 on her body at the time of her death. Mostly cocaine and heroin with several wraps of hash plugged in both of her lower body orifices and in between her toes.' Billie suddenly felt sick at the thought.

'That's what everybody thinks. It couldn't be my little Jimmy.' Ellis nodded. Billie noted that he was totally focused, brimful of passion for the subject. It was clear just how much he cared. She had already had a glimpse of the danger and sacrifices he must have made to get to the top of the tree in his chosen area of policing. He looked like a man on a mission.

'People think, it only happens to poor kids with rough family backgrounds, relatives who are chavs or druggies or on the game,' Ellis continued. 'You're right, those vulnerable kids are sitting ducks for county lines criminals, but nowadays kids don't have to be living in a dive to be dragged into the drug game. County lines business comes to them via their social media apps.'

'I check my Lexi's Facebook account. I'm a friend,' one of the officers piped up, reassuring herself that it simply couldn't happen to her child. Ellis smiled sadly to himself.

'Your kids will have apps on their devices that you don't even know exist. Sophie's parents will be astonished to learn that their good little girl was involved in gang culture. She had a walk-on part in a Drill video, which is an ultra-violent form of music sweeping the country. Let me show you...'

Ellis clicked on his laptop and footage of a Drill video burst into life on the screen. The young male performers filled the screen looking seriously dangerous. They were dressed in designer street fashion, posturing with knives and guns and murderous mimes. The lyrics told stories of drug dealing, machete attacks, misogyny, and beefs.

'It might look scary to us lot, Mr and Mrs Middle-Aged, but it's a lifestyle many kids aspire to. No newspaper delivery jobs around nowadays and even if there were, no kid today wants to save up several hundred quid for a pair of the latest designer trainers, only to find that by the time they've managed that, they've already gone out of fashion. So, they become a county lines delivery boy or girl instead. Their ultimate dream being that they're in with a chance of becoming a social media star like the big boys here.' Ellis's face looked grim. 'But real life doesn't turn out to be anything like the stories portrayed by the flash boys, even if your little Jimmys and Lexis do end up carrying the weapons you are watching on screen here.'

'No different from punk rockers in my day,' Derek Blythe challenged, 'just a bit of smart-arse posturing. They all grow out of it. I did.'

Billie suddenly had a vision of Derek Blythe sporting a pink Mohican hairstyle and bin-bag trousers complete with safety pins and razor blades. It made her smile, lifting her spirits somewhat.

'I'm sorry to tell you times have changed, mate,' Ellis replied. 'Kids like Sophie Grey, they don't get a chance to grow out of it.' Derek looked suitably huffed by the nod to his superior age.

'Whether the kids are part of the gang culture, or at the mercy of a single Mr Big, which is more the case in the north of the UK, this is how it works.' Ellis settled down on the corner of a desk and clicked on his laptop. A large map of the UK appeared on the screen; major cities circled in red.

'In the past, the drugs business centred on urban areas – big towns and cities. Low-level dealing would take place via the local criminal kingpins such as Christy Callaghan and Jesus O'Brian. They largely kept dealing to their own turf, predominantly via their own nightclubs and to grown-ups who lived up the street. Everyone rubbed along nicely, give or take the odd OD and tussle.'

Ellis surveyed the room, to ensure everyone was keeping up with his explanation.

'Now county lines dealing, is a totally different kettle of fish. It predominantly relies, for one, on child exploitation. We're talking grooming, bonded labour and extreme violence. The drugs, mostly cocaine and heroin, arrive in the country by various means and are sold in bulk – just like any other imported goods – to the county lines' Mr Big Spuds.'

'Doesn't look like your lot are doing much to control it then. Thought you lot like to think of yourselves as the Mr Big Spuds?' Derek Blythe goaded.

'I've personally asked for specialist assistance with this.' Billie stepped forward, folding her arms as she stared at Derek. He flushed. She hated calling him out in front of a room full of people, but she sensed that Ellis was imparting information that was vital to this investigation and she was determined to get justice for Josh, Sophie and even Christy Callaghan. 'Can we all just concentrate?'

Everyone stopped texting their kids, finished their drinks and biscuits and finally settled down. Billie glanced back at Derek. He looked away. She kicked herself. He only had another day to go on the job and by the look on his face, any chance of persuading him otherwise appeared to be fading fast.

'The deals are done via encrypted phones. Almost impossible to crack. Upshot is the main man we're primarily after is protected all along the line. Once the drugs haul is in his sweaty hands, it will be split into smaller wraps ready for individual buyers. Crack cocaine can be made at base, from cocaine concentrate. Doesn't need to be a factory, it could simply be someone's kitchen. I'm happy to swap recipes. You've probably got the stuff in the back of your kitchen cupboard. But right now, the making of it is not important, the fact that it can be addictive after just one snort is.'

Ellis had briefly flicked the photo on the big screen to shots of heroin, cocaine and crack laid out on a kitchen table.

'The word "county", in county lines, explains what is going to happen to the drugs next. They are heading out to county towns across the country, ending up in respectable homes down sleepy lanes, eventually pissed out into the sort of streams beside which you take your families to picnic in summer. Soon as any local competition has been removed. Goodbye Jesus O'Brian and Christy Callaghan.'

Billie recalled Josta's recent preoccupation with the narcotic-imbued shrimps. This was turning into a horror story.

'Kids like yours, perhaps actually yours, will be taking the heroin and coke there. Usually by train, just like Sophie Grey. Sometimes by coach. Reason being that until recently no one thought to stop a kid in connection with drugs. But if they are caught, then the "Bics", as child drug runners are called, are disposable, just like a single-use shaving razor.'

Billie ran her fingers through her long red curls. She was glad she hadn't had to share that particular heartbreaking piece of information with Sophie Grey's parents.

'The main man stays safe, as the kid has been given a "burner phone",' Ellis continued. 'Bought for cash and equally disposable. The buyers make an order, ringing the unique number for the county line. Then the main man rings the child in the Trap House via the kid's burner phone, to arrange delivery.

'The county line is often branded with a name, just like any product. Business cards and flyers, with two-for-one offers and seasonal deals will be stuck on bus shelters and posted through doors of known local drug consumers. Which, believe me, are often teachers and lawyers and other professionals. Drug users are not just the down-and-out types looking like they might cut your throat, that you step over slumped in a sleeping bag right next to your bank's cash machine.'

'So how does a child arrive at a strange town and start selling drugs without being noticed? Where do they stay for starters? Any hotel would surely be suspicious if a lone child tried to book in,' Billie asked.

'That's where the Trap House comes into play.' Ellis clicked onto a photo. 'Here's one we came across earlier.' He revealed a bare-walled, filthy room, piled high with drugs paraphernalia on a table. In the background a kitchenette showed a bin overflowing with takeaway boxes and a mountain of dirty dishes.

'But before the kids arrive, all they see are photos like this one, on a big social media snap-sharing site, where kids are regularly groomed to be drugs mules.'

Ellis clicked again. A similar house, this time spanking clean, had a boy of around Sophie Grey's age standing at the centre. He was wearing new trainers, holding a shiny gun, and surrounded by piles of money.

'A vulnerable person living in the target town will have been befriended, via free drugs if they are a junkie, or friendship if they are feeling isolated for some reason and are therefore ripe for grooming. Before they know it, their home will have been taken over and become the hub for the drugs dealing. Threats and actual use of violence keep the "Cuckoo" quiet.'

'How long will they stay there?' Billie was hooked on the subject now.

'The child who is carrying the drugs will stay in the Trap House until all of the drugs are sold. That way they stay out of view. During this time, they are on twenty-four-hour alert. No sleeping, no washing, no leaving their burner phone or stash unattended, even for a second. If an order is made on the county line number they will be called on their burner phone to facilitate delivery. They have to answer their burner within two rings or there will be violent repercussions.

'Local children are often coerced to deliver. Check the rubber ends on your kids bicycles when you get home. Great place for concealing wraps. Runners are generally known as Youngers, young teenagers; Elders, older teens, may also be based in the Trap House. They often carry guns as well as blades, policing their patch and carrying out higher value handovers.'

'I can't believe that all this can be happening right under our noses.' Billie shook her head in frustration and shock.

'Street slang doesn't help.' Ellis looked at her with some sympathy. 'So don't beat yourself up about it. You could be standing next to your niece whilst she's talking about doing a drugs deal and you wouldn't have a clue if she was simply setting up a pizza party with her mates.'

'Never had this when there were bobbies on the beat,' Derek huffed under his breath. Billie had to admit there was a lot to be said for more full-on community policing.

'Anyway, once the drugs are sold,' Ellis continued, 'the child makes the return run by train or coach again, taking the money back to the main man. Another child runner will take their place, heading back to the county, carrying more drugs and a different burner phone. The Cuckoo house will be changed regularly too. That makes it difficult for police and local officials to pinpoint the centre of activity and criminals involved, or to follow the line back to the main perpetrator. The original child runner may now be heading for a completely different county to do the whole business again. Any questions?'

Jo held up her hand. 'So why don't the children just run away with the money and spend it on trainers, job done?' she asked.

'Good question,' Ellis replied. 'At the beginning, the kids don't even realise that they have been groomed. They think that they are movers and shakers, chosen people. Part of a cutting-edge alternative family, just like the Drill stars. The kind of people no one dares to mess with. Goodbye old family, who are now kept away at arm's length. Then violence and intimidation kick in. Once a child has become embroiled in the world, there is no way of opting out. Technology allows the youngster to be coerced, controlled, blackmailed, and tracked.'

'But what if they get robbed?' Billie asked, concerned. 'Surely word gets out in small towns about some little kid carrying drugs. Aren't they at risk of getting fleeced every five minutes?'

'They will get fleeced, that's for certain. What may come as a surprise is that a mugging will be arranged by their own Mr Big Spuds, whilst carrying his drugs.'

Ellis clicked onto another shot. It showed a close-up of a mortuary slab holding a bottom half of a torso, waist to upper thigh, facing down, with a large stab wound on either cheek. There was a collective intake of breath.

'That is what I believe happened here with Sophie Grey. Her lower torso remained intact on impact with the train, so we have the opportunity to see clearly that she carries a signature wound of a county lines gang.

'Of course, you will want to investigate, to confirm whether a rival drug gang was involved, and this was in fact a premeditated murder. But this is generally the sort of wound inflicted at the point where the child enters bonded labour.'

Derek Blythe shook his head, appearing to not buy the

explanation, but not willing to speak out loud again in Billie's hearing.

'Had Sophie Grey survived, but been parted from her drugs delivery, she would now be in hock to Mr Big Spuds to the tune of £485,000 quid, with interest. There is no way of ever paying it off, but she will be expected to be at Mr Big's beck and call night and day for evermore, running drugs, selling her body, encouraging her friends to get involved...' Billie felt rage rush through her soul.

'Please, God, I'm the first one to get my hands on the sick bastard who did this.'

Billie let her thoughts tumble out loud. From others' expressions of horror, it was clear to see that she wasn't the only one of her team to appear outraged at the fate of Sophie Grey.

'Robbery is only one of the devices used to control the children,' Ellis continued, obviously so used to the sordid world he was describing in such detail, that he hadn't fully realised the impact his revelations were having on Billie's team.

'Social media comes to the fore again. In order to keep the kids in line they may be filmed being sexually abused, gang raped for example, boys as well as girls, with threats carried out to upload the footage online. Often tracking devices are used to live stream their whereabouts twenty-four seven. Known as "remote mothering". If they should try to run away, they will be quickly tracked down. Children may also be sent photos of a family member's home, with threats to firebomb the house should they step out of line.

'It's impossible to exit the set-up. If they manage to wriggle away, and we have many safe houses set up for this very purpose, you can bet another family member will be made to suffer. It's not unusual to find siblings or even parents being forced to take on the debt, by continuing to deliver drugs.'

'If you ask me, it sounds like you are fighting a losing battle,' Derek Blythe grunted.

'I fear you're right,' Ellis agreed. 'But the time has come for us all to wise up. Get a grip on this. Yesterday it was Sophie Grey. Josh Hallows today. Unless we put a lid on county lines, you could find yourself standing at the graveside of your own child, tomorrow.'

11

OLD FRIENDS

The playground shark was swimming in a sea of blood, towards the dead boy. Billie ran her fingers through her hair as she perused the crime-scene photos of Josh Hallows' murder, in preparation for his autopsy at the hands of Josta first thing in the morning. The scenario merely emphasised the poignancy of the event. A youth who had just won an award for trying to make the world a better place didn't deserve to suffer such a monstrous death.

Josh had no doubt chosen the playground location as a way of making sure that his meeting with Billie would take place in a spot of supreme safety. She had another flush of guilt that she hadn't ensured that was the case. One thing was certain – Billie was hell-bent on finding the vicious predator responsible. Her biggest fear after Ellis Darque's briefing was that it would turn out to be a child of similar age.

With three totally different murder scenarios seemingly linked, Billie had stayed behind late to ensure that members of the team were clear on their individual investigative assignments. It was proving to be a complex job. She desperately wished that her wingman, Ash Sanghera, was alongside her.

Unfortunately, the last investigation that they had faced together had caused a total upheaval in Ash's personal life, equal to the trauma of Billie's own. Ash had, in addition, suffered physical injuries that were taking time to heal. Billie was grateful that at least their relationship had recovered. It had certainly been a true test of enduring friendship. Had they not had such a strong bond, Billie reflected, then the revelations unearthed during that period would have blown both their personal and professional closeness to smithereens.

She glanced at the clock. It was nearly ten pm, but then she didn't have anything special to run home for, except a clean change of clothes. The silence offered her an opportunity to concentrate on her countless tasks without the crazy buzz of noise and questions created by the all-hands-on-deck approach amongst her trusted team.

Spoke too soon, she chided, as the outer door to the office banged hard against the wall. She looked up. The inner door smashed open now. It could only mean one thing.

'Hi. Didn't you get the message to take the rest of the day off?' Billie called, her words disguising the fact that she felt utterly relieved to hear the clatter of wheelchair against furniture which signalled Boo had just entered the building.

On arrival back at the office after visiting Sophie's parents, Billie had been given the news that Boo had been called away on a family emergency. It was a setback to be sure, Boo was one of the few people Billie trusted to guarantee that all the investigative material came in on time and was logged, cross-referenced and chased up. She had quietly hoped that the emergency would be short-lived.

'Everything all right?' Billie asked, as Boo sped into view, shaving the usual millimetre off the wooden frame as she popped her head around the door.

'Not really. My sister's frantic again. It's my nephew, Kobi. He keeps going walkabout, skipping school, hanging around with a bad crowd. He's been gone a week now and the doctor's put her on antidepressants. I'm not sure if they're making her better or worse. She was hysterical when I got to hers. I had to calm her down, tell her that he's probably okay. He'll come back when he's hungry. Anyway, sorry, I just thought I would come in and catch up on the work I've missed.'

Billie felt alarm bells ringing. Boo hadn't been around for Ellis Darque's briefing, but if she passed on the possibility that Boo's nephew could be mixed up in county lines, she feared that her friend and colleague wouldn't sleep that night. The experience of having had a stalker in her kitchen would no doubt have freaked her out, despite Billie's attempts to make light of the event. Boo didn't need even more stress.

'It's ten pm.' Billie nodded at the clock.

'Pot calling kettle.' Boo grinned.

The door clattered open again. Billie realised that the current murders had spooked so many people that she clearly wasn't the only one keen to work on tonight.

Ellis appeared in view behind Boo. Billie smiled.

'Boo, remember on the last investigation, when you sent me to have a chinwag with that criminal Glenn Baxter?' Billie reminded Boo.

'Yeah. The one who probably ended up saving your life?' Boo chirped. 'That was all down to me, girl.'

'Well, you can meet him yourself now. He's had a wash and changed his name since then, so you're safe.' Billie pulled a cheeky face at Ellis, who took the jest without offence, stepping forward to shake hands with Boo. Instead, they both froze as though staring at ghosts.

'Ellis Darque, meet DS Beduwa Mensah. But we call her Boo, short for Boudicca. Her enemies claim she has blades on the wheels of that chariot of hers...' Billie trailed off. It was clear that neither was listening. Boo suddenly swallowed hard, then spun her wheelchair around fast, heading for the exit.

'Beddy...' Ellis called after her. But the bang and clatter of Boo shaving another few centimetres off the door frames in her haste to head out made it clear that she wasn't in the mood to exchange pleasantries. Ellis looked awkwardly towards Billie.

'I'm a detective. Let me guess. You already know each other?' Billie raised her eyebrows in question at the odd scenario. Ellis had even used his own nickname for Boo.

'Yeah,' Ellis replied, 'old friends.'

A final clatter could be heard along the corridor as Boo hurtled into the lift. The robotic voice announced loudly that it was going down.

'Could have fooled me,' Billie replied, wondering when she would get the full low-down on that story.

12

A WILDE NIGHT

'Nine people have now been confirmed killed in the recent hostage rescue in Columbia.' The radio announcer's best BBC voice cut through the darkness in the car, as Billie finally made her weary way home. The words also sliced through her heart. She swallowed hard. The death toll had gone up.

Had Max contacted Josta and Lola yet? Even if he had done so, there was no reason, from the couple's point of view anyway, to reach for the phone and share the news with Billie as a matter of urgency. They were both, of course, aware that Max had been a professional contact during her last investigation. But Billie guessed that neither woman had realised that the connection went much deeper. Didn't it?

Billie wondered if it was simply wishful thinking on her part. She for one, hyper aware of Max's passionate words on the subject of his dead wife, Natalie, hadn't dared share her own feelings. But he *had* alluded to an attraction to Billie, a pull that unfortunately he seemed determined to fight. Maybe Max himself wasn't aware, Billie mused, that she had been completely drawn to him from their very first meeting?

After recent events, Billie knew that she still had to battle against building emotional barriers to stop herself from being hurt, yet again. Maybe that made her seem disinterested? For a few seconds she let herself deliberate on the possibilities of the day before, when Max had called at her new home, holding a bouquet of flowers. What may have been the outcome then, had he not taken that urgent call and rushed away? Or if she hadn't done the same thing? More worrying, where exactly had he gone, and would he ever come back?

Billie looked at the time on the car dashboard. Midnight. Too late to ring Josta and Lola now, even on the pretext of checking that Lola had fully recovered from her strange robbery.

Billie was suddenly aware that she was about to drive close to Max Strong's house. She made a spontaneous decision, steering off the main road and onto the leafy lane leading to his smart Victorian villa. Billie smiled to herself when the handsome red-brick building loomed ahead. She had fought so hard against visiting this place at first, when the chief had assigned Doctor Max to be her shrink. That hadn't gone down too well, she reflected. She hadn't been able to get away quick enough. If anyone had told her she would be making a detour to the very same location and in the dead of night, back then, Billie would have told that person that they were stark raving crazy.

The street was silent. As she pulled up outside of Max's house, Billie could see that no lights were on, nor was his car parked on the gravel drive. Her heart sank a little. Somewhere in the back of her mind, she had hoped that Max would have returned home, been thrilled to see her, might even have invited her in. Billie reckoned that she could have covered her desperation to see him by claiming simply to be carrying out her public duty as a policewoman, bearing in mind the items stolen from Lola could have put his empty house at risk. That much was true anyway, Billie argued with herself, climbing out of her vehicle and crunching up the drive.

Tall apple trees on either side of the gravel-covered walk, cast dark shadows, the branches like outstretched gnarled fingers. Billie noticed that the security light by the front door, a motion-sensor type, hadn't kicked in as she had approached. Swallowed up now in darkness, she pulled out her ancient patrol torch from her pocket. Old police-beat habits die hard, she thought, and smiled inwardly as memories washed over her. Even when she had only been carrying tiny evening bags to smart events with her former fiancé, David, she had managed to stuff police paraphernalia inside. 'Ever ready' had been one of his nicknames for her and not because of their spontaneous sex life after all, Billie ruefully recalled.

A noise to her left, like a twig breaking, caused Billie to veer immediately off her trip down memory lane. Instead, she flashed her torch into the darkness down the side of the house. The light illuminated more mature shrubs framing the pathway leading around to the back French doors and walled garden that Billie remembered so well from her visits to Max's consulting room. A wooden gateway led out onto a side road, but it appeared to be firmly closed.

Billie shook away the feeling of unease that had crept up her spine. The noise had probably been caused by a cat or hedgehog. She gave herself a mental slap as she continued to walk around the side of the building, chiding herself that a few weeks away from murder investigations had twisted her mind and not in a good way, despite the enforced rest. Here she was imagining that every little movement in the night was about to lead to death and destruction.

Another noise, as though of feet on dry leaves, from immediately behind, caused Billie to spin around fast, shining her torch from left to right. A young urban fox froze in the piercing light from her beam before slinking away behind a bin, clearly in search of a fast-food takeaway tonight, rather than living nocturnal prey.

Billie swept her hair back, irritated at her spooked-out response. She wondered if her feelings of uneasiness were due to a delayed reaction to Josh Hallows having hurtled to his death at her feet earlier that day.

As Billie moved around the side of the tall red-brick house, she was suddenly aware of a dim light which wasn't coming from her torch. She switched it off. The darkness enveloped her like a black velvet cape, the only sound now was of the breeze, lifting strands of her hair and making something metal, like a watering can, rattle against brick. Billie squinted into the dark, wondering if the dim glow was caused by solar lighting, somewhere in the large, walled back garden?

She suddenly summoned a picture of that landscape in brilliant daylight, in her mind's eye. The first time she had viewed the peaceful garden oasis, was also the day that she had unexpectedly fallen for the criminal psychologist, as a magpie had flirted with him on the lawn. How he had assured her then that the birds were not always a portent of doom. He'd been wrong about that, Billie reflected, at least in her own case. She felt herself desperately hoping that he hadn't made another misjudgement so very recently, a deadly one at that.

Billie felt her way around the wall in darkness, her back pinned flat against the red bricks. Peering around the corner of the house, her heart started beating fast. She could see that the French doors were open, and the dim light was coming from inside. Had she caught a burglary in progress?

Billie quickly skirted along the back wall, her legs knocking against the large ornate pots of red geraniums positioned along the patio. Adrenaline was now surging through her bloodstream, all senses on high alert as she edged around the glass of the doors and crept inside. Max's consulting room was in darkness and appeared untouched. A very faint smell of lemony scent caught in the breeze, like a ghost of the owner tiptoeing through the room. Billie desperately hoped that wasn't the case, as she spotted the light source, spilling out from under a door to the left, which Billie imagined led to the doctor's private home.

She speedily and silently crossed to the door, took a deep breath, and then flung it open, shining her torch directly into the room.

'Police!' she called. 'Freeze!'

'Oh my goodness!' a female voice screamed, putting her hands across her face to shield herself from the piercing torchlight now directed on her. Odd because Lola Strong usually loved nothing better than to be in the spotlight.

'Oh dear. Sorry.' Billie dropped the torch and fiddled in the gloom for a light switch. No doubt Lola had simply been doing that mum thing, tidying and checking that everything was in order, and had lost track of time. The actress was sitting on the floor, wrapped theatrically in a colourful shawl, surrounded only by lit candles.

'I thought there was a break-in.' Billie blinked in the now bright light. 'You look as though you are having a séance,' she added to reduce the tension in the air, sighing a breath of relief as she reminded herself that ever the drama queen, Lola was never likely to present as a normal shampoo-and-set, apron-wearing mum. That was before she registered that Lola was surrounded by photographs of Max.

'I know he will come through to me if anything terrible has happened.' Lola looked at Billie desperately. Billie's stomach lurched at the thought.

'I'm sure Max knows how to look after himself,' Billie replied, trying to reassure herself as much as his mum. 'Is there any reason even to suspect that he's in Columbia?' Billie reasoned that everyone seemed to be simply jumping to conclusions as to his whereabouts.

'Who else but my darling son would be called upon in such a situation?' Lola was agitated and tearful. Billie wasn't sure if her demeanour was simply down to understandable anxiety for her son, straight after her recent robbery event, or if she was drunk. Lola was always colourful and as an actress, presented as a rather larger than life figure, but Billie had never seen her so down. Usually she was charming and gregarious, rocking that bohemian beauty despite her mature years. Billie could see Max's breathtaking features in her, the same profile and long dark lashes framing expressive eyes.

'He studied in South America; he was based there when he was in the army. He's definitely been there on one of his secret expeditions recently. I managed to get him to spill the beans with a strong drink one night.' Lola waved her arms expansively. Billie couldn't help smiling.

'So he knows his way around,' Billie replied, crouching down beside Lola, and surveying the photos from cradle to... Billie didn't want to finish that sentence, even silently.

'He first went there as a student to search for his father.' Lola dabbed her eyes with the corner of her fringed shawl. Billie's ears pricked up. She had simply accepted that Max had two mums. She hadn't given much thought to the mechanics of it.

'I was appearing on Broadway when Max was conceived.' Lola looked to the corner of the room as though looking for her spotlight, a Norma Desmond moment, lost in memory of her theatrical heyday. Billie shivered. She wished to God that Max would just walk back in the door right now. His mother was giving her the creeps.

'I got a standing ovation that first night. I was the toast of the town. My name in bright lights on 42nd Street.'

'Great...' Billie responded, as Lola turned to her as if for applause, whilst wondering whether it was wise to encourage the older woman, despite her interest now in how Max had come to exist.

'It was a one-night stand. I was carried away by the idolatry, the endless applause...' Lola continued. Billie heard the French doors bang, probably due to the breeze. She glanced over her shoulder. She had a long drive home and an early start in the morning. She decided to hurry the conversation along.

'I'm sure Josta understood.' Billie heard the words coming out of her mouth, doubting the truth of them, as she popped her head around the door and checked Max's office. It was still in darkness. The French doors appeared to have slammed shut.

'No, the show was a one-night stand. Not my affair. The critics never understood the subtlety of my performance, but the audience, they were standing, they appreciated it all.'

'So you met Max's father when you were out in New York?' Billie persisted.

'During rehearsals.' Lola nodded. 'Josta and I have always had a very relaxed relationship and I like to pick and mix my amours. In any case, she was obsessed with her superior at the mortuary at the time. She does sporadically tend to have all-consuming crushes on others. In this case, she was free to dissect their joint relationship with the dead without being shackled. It suited us both.' Billie was squirming now, deciding that this was way too much information.

'So Max's father was from South America?' Billie persisted.

'Philadelphia. The high-flying son of a well-to-do family,' Lola corrected. 'Josta and I had considered sperm donation, but in the end, we really hit the jackpot without resorting to turkey basters and all that paraphernalia.' She shuddered at the thought. 'You only have to look at Max, his beauty, intellect...'

Now you're talking sense, Billie silently agreed.

86

'Though his father was no oil painting. Luckily, Max inherited my bone structure. I found out I was pregnant when I got home, but by then the lights had gone down on Broadway and my stage-door Johnny had jetted off to a top job in his father's firm. Some multinational corporation. He had absolutely no interest in the baby, which suited Josta and I just fine at first. But then Max grew up and became an angry teenager, claiming genealogical bewilderment. He was determined to dig his daddy dearest out and Max being Max, he did just that. By this time, Spencer James Jnr III was managing director of the company. It was based in Columbia.'

'That must have been a difficult time,' Billie interjected. Having just experienced some shocking revelations about her own family history, her heart ached for teenage Max searching for his genetic history.

'It was an arduous experience for us all, not least his father, no doubt. Max enrolled in university in Bogotá and became heavily involved in environmental issues. Mostly, it seemed to me, aimed at publicising the destruction he claimed his father's company was causing to the rural economy and communities. Land-grabbing, environmental damage, etcetera. I guess a psychologist would see it as a desperate cry for attention, but Max was a very confused boy, with no idea what to do with his life back then.'

Lola started crying again. Billie decided it was time to lock up and move on.

'Is Josta at home?' Billie asked, putting an arm around Lola to help her up. She didn't think it would be safe to just dump Lola on the doorstep.

'Is Josta ever home?' Lola whined. Billie did want to point out that it was a case of pot calling the pan a burnt-arse but refrained. Right now, she was simply desperate to get on the road. 'She's much happier hanging around with the dead twenty-four seven,' Lola continued as Billie heaved her upright. She suddenly sunk into the side of Billie's body.

'I've always thought you were adorable, Billie.' She lunged at the detective in an attempt to kiss her. Billie sprang back, startled. Was Max's mum actually trying to hit on her? She held the woman at arm's length.

'Okay. Enough. Time to go home.' Billie hoped she was conveying her best firm police voice. She snuffed out the candles, switched off the light and practically marched Lola, as she would a criminal during arrest, out into Max's office.

'I left my handbag somewhere,' Lola whispered, realising even in her inebriated state, that she had overstepped the mark. Billie flipped on the light.

A red rose lay on the coffee table in the centre of the room. A card was attached. Billie hadn't noticed it on the way in.

'Did you bring that?' Billie was holding Lola with one arm as she nodded at the rose.

'I brought him some flowers, in case he came home,' Lola answered, waving to a bunch of mixed flowers arranged in a vase on Max's desk. 'He's always loved flowers,' Lola added.

'This one?' Billie scooped the card up and scanned the message.

Perhaps tonight will be the Wilde night, the words on the card read. Billie looked from the card to Lola. Had she been sending Billie the flowers? She was certainly a drama queen, but a stalker?

'Did you write this?' Billie was practically shaking Lola's arm.

'I feel sick,' she responded, staggering out of the French doors, and throwing up in the garden. Billie secured the doors, shining her torch ahead as she half dragged Lola to her car. The woman had started crying again. Billie resigned herself to getting no sense out of her that night. As she leaned over to secure Lola's seat belt, she touched Billie's arm.

'Billie, sweet–'

'Don't even think of it.' Billie decided that she had been through enough for one day.

'I just wanted to say that Josta used to send notes and flowers, to people... it might have been her, the rose and note on the table.'

'What are you talking about?' Billie felt a shiver down her spine. 'Why would Josta do such a crazy thing?'

'I mentioned her crushes... obsessions, including one of Max's teachers years ago. Josta kept ringing her up and sending flowers and poetic cards. Turning up constantly at events that the teacher went to. It was a strange love-hate thing. The more she was rebuffed, the more morose she became with her verse. Max got terribly teased at school. We were forced to move in the end and place him elsewhere for his education. I sometimes wonder if that's why he ended up training as a psychologist. These things do come back to haunt one...' – she trailed off – '... she *is* terribly fond of you.'

Billie was speechless as she rammed the car into gear. Her mind was engulfed in shock as she ran through her recollections, realising that Josta had prior knowledge of all the locations where Billie had been due to be present, when the roses and cards had been delivered. Surely her stalker couldn't possibly be Josta? She started inwardly arguing against the preposterous thought as she pulled out on her detour home. Probably the reason that she didn't notice the dark car, parked in the shadow of a tree down the side lane. Next to Max Strong's house.

The raven-black and star-spangled night played a symphony of noises, as Billie alighted from her car, having made it back to the beautiful and ancient seaside village of Alnmouth in record time. Billie loved the wind-chime tunes played by the sail masts of the boats, moored on the sandy shore near the mouth of the River Aln estuary.

The sound had, of late, rocked her to sleep in a sea-shanty lullaby, soothing away the horrors of the past. The boats rested far below the tall windows of her gaily painted new abode, at the point where her garden, having tumbled-down flower-filled terraces, ended with a blue painted wooden gate, leading directly onto the sand. It was her own version of paradise.

Beyond, the river widened as it spilled out into the wild and spectacular North Sea, fringed by high sand dunes. Necklaces of seashells and voyaging sun-bleached driftwood adorned the wide golden beaches. Billie could taste the salt skimmed from the waves on her lips, as the light breeze tugged at her hair.

She stood still for a moment, to experience the magic. Her shoulders relaxed. This was her happy place, far away from the urban areas where her working life was usually focused. A world away from murderers and drug gangs and crazed stalkers. She mentally thanked her sadly departed mum for leaving such a precious gift to her – peace at last.

Rosemary for remembrance. The thought skipped through Billie's head as she brushed past the scented rosemary bush on the approach to her door. So intent was she on hugging those precious memories of her mother close, that she sprang back in shock when a tall body loomed out of the darkness.

'Christ!' she cried. Her mind suddenly alert, adrenaline kicking in the fight-or-flight response. Billie spun around, ready to do battle. The flight side of the acute stress-reaction hormone never seeming to have worked for Billie. Her heart, however, was beating on overdrive.

'Sorry. I shouldn't have come.' Billie breathed a sigh of relief on recognising the voice of Ash Sanghera.

'Not if you were planning on giving me a damn heart attack. Jeez!' Billie playfully slapped her wingman's arm. He wobbled and she quickly caught him. She had forgotten his continued use of a walking stick since the terrible events of their last investigation together.

'I just didn't know where else to go.' He sounded exhausted. Billie unlocked the door and led Ash in. He looked dishevelled and sad, quite unlike the bubbly, bad-joke-telling friend and colleague who had solved a multitude of crimes with her in the past.

'What's wrong?' Billie rubbed his back. Ash was still having trouble recovering from the brutal assault that had been life-changing – for both of them.

'Jas chucked me out. Told me she's ending the marriage.' Ash looked like his life had come to an end. 'Can't say I blame her,' he added. 'She says she deserves to be with a real man. I spent last week in a trucker motel, then bumped into Derek Blythe last night in a takeaway and he let me doss down at his. But tonight, I had...'

'Why didn't you come to me straight away?' Billie was flicking on lights as she led Ash into her large lounge and sat him on one of the deep sofas.

'Bit out of order after everything that's happened. I'm desperate tonight. But I'll be out of your hair tomorrow, I promise.' Ash looked grey with stress and exhaustion.

Billie gave him a hug. They had been through a lot together recently and the situation had relayed home truths to each, delivered regretfully, with a fatal sledge-hammer blow. They had gone over the events of the last investigation several times now and Billie had finally come to terms with the past. She had hoped that Ash would also be able to move forward. Not least because she desperately needed him back at work, fast.

'You'll do no such thing.' Billie started pulling off his coat. 'I need some company. I'm rambling around in this big old place all alone. It gives me the creeps,' she lied.

'I'll have to find a flat or something, somewhere for the girls to stay when they visit.' Ash was clearly still in shock. He adored his three little girls, all Billie's goddaughters and one of them just a few months old.

'Don't do anything rash. I'll talk to Jas,' Billie offered, though she wondered if her input might make matters worse. She and Ash's wife had always had a close relationship, but now Jas seemed to blame Billie for her marriage difficulties, forgetting that the young detective had also lost out on the future that she had once considered to be rose-tinted.

'I don't think it'll work. Jas is right. I need to face facts, sort my life out.' Ash shook his head in dismay.

'Well, stay here until you do. Look, I've got six spare bedrooms for starters and I could do with a man about the house,' she added.

'Is that what I am?' Ash answered.

'Of course you are, stupid. Now stay put. I'll make us some cheese on toast.' Billie headed towards the big open-plan kitchen. Ash pulled himself upright again.

'Stay put. I'll do it. I'm not feeling that bad,' he quipped, showing a glimmer of his former jokey self. Billie's lack of cooking skill was legendary. A fast-burning career trajectory hadn't allowed for downtime spent slow cooking. She tended to live off takeaways.

'Great. Stay forever,' Billie answered as Ash hobbled over to the kitchen and started rifling the cupboards. Billie remembered that he had recently confessed that he had always wanted to be a chef. Things were looking up. She kicked off her boots and sunk onto one of the sofas, opening the pile of files from the office that she had brought back with her. She suddenly felt re-energised on realising that she had one of her best detectives right on hand, cooking up a storm, relishing the opportunity to bring herself up to date and get Ash's perspective on the recent murders.

'Oh my God... delicious.' Billie closed her eyes for a moment, savouring her late supper, as Ash laid two plates of food on the coffee table between them, amazed at how Ash could so speedily make the mundane seem so appetising.

'Tell Jas that. She hates my cooking.' Ash sighed.

'Well, all I can say is she doesn't recognise a good man when she's got one. Maybe it is time to move on.' Billie handed over the first file with Christy Callaghan's details in.

'You might be the new in-house chef, but I know something you don't about freshwater shrimp. The local ones.' Billie stuffed another morsel of food into her mouth.

'I'm all ears,' Ash answered. 'But I'll be checking you've got your facts right,' he added, already flipping through the paperwork with interest.

'I've missed you.' Billie smiled, swigging from the mug of home-made hot chocolate Ash had also served up. She meant it with all her heart. In her lovely home, with her best friend newly installed, the stresses of the past two days had finally started to slide away.

So it was that at three am, Billie lost the battle with sleep at the end of a long session discussing murder scenarios and reading statements. Ash hobbled over, gently laying Billie down and covering her with one of the soft cashmere throws draped over the back of the sofa. Billie caught his arm.

'And there's another thing...' Her voice was dreamy and faraway, more asleep than awake. 'I think I've got a stalker...' She trailed off. Ash turned the table light off, casting her into shadows.

'Ssshh, time to call it a night.' He stroked her hair as though she were one of his children. 'I think you're just having a bad dream.' He drew the curtains over the tall windows and headed over to the opposite sofa, and slumped down on it. Had he not done so, Billie's true nightmare may have been just about to begin.

Both had fallen into an immediate and deep sleep, so neither Ash nor Billie heard a figure creep away through the garden from a concealed viewing spot on the terrace, nor see the dark car making its way back out of the village, the driver having finally given up on any hope of visiting Billie home alone, tonight.

13

WILDE AS A CORPSE

In life, Josh Hallows had the body of a young Adonis. Billie imagined that he had cut quite a swathe on the football pitch, cheered on by admirers. He had been the school captain, head prefect, top of the class in maths. It appeared that everything he had touched had turned to gold. His parents, after all, had made it their life's work to set their beautiful boy on the path to success.

In death, he cut a more poignant figure. In less than twenty-four hours, the award-winning student warrior, who had stood up against school bullies, had fallen on the bloody battlefield of a children's playground. No amount of cutting and stitching by Josta would ever put the broken body back together again, not in the shape of the perfect boy that he had once been.

The autopsy had been gruelling. With a lot of work and dogged determination, Billie had now learned how to manage the stress-related flashbacks which had so overwhelmed her in the past. But despite her best intentions, she couldn't help a little stab of grief as she recalled the broken boy cradled in her arms the day before, the blood ebbing from his body. She chose to keep that memory. It would drive her towards finding the person responsible and making them pay, big time.

'Time for coffee, I think.' Josta finished up, leaving a mortuary assistant to wheel Josh Hallows off to a refrigerated body chamber.

Jo heaved a visible sigh of relief. She was ashen-faced and still having trouble, it appeared, getting used to the particular aroma of the autopsy suite. She had even been known to run off and throw up at the scene of a murder, a habit that Billie was happy to put up with for the time being, despite her one-time lack of love for the younger detective. She reasoned that the people she had to worry about were those who found nothing unsettling in surroundings such as these.

They trooped into the waiting room which displayed on the wall a single painting of a seascape paradise that for the resident tropical fish, could only be a pipe dream. Whenever Billie saw them, she wanted to orchestrate a tank break-out and ship the colourful creatures away to a coral reef shaded by coconut trees. There was as much chance of that happening as there was of Josh Hallows jumping off the gurney to announce that this had all been some schoolboy prank.

Billie's spirits lifted as her thoughts turned to Ash waving her off to work that morning, discarding the memory of his having nearly scared the pants off her last night. His arrival had given her the opportunity to talk through all three recent murders with the colleague and friend who she valued above all others. He might not yet be fit to return to work, but she had already benefitted from his insights at home.

'So let's get this straight.' Billie sipped her coffee. 'Christy Callaghan had chop injuries, with both sharp and blunt-force trauma.'

'Correct.' Josta munched on a biscuit as she spoke. 'Most likely an axe was the main culprit, but it's no mean feat chopping off a head, so other implements also appear to have been used.' She swallowed, rifled the biscuit bin again, took out a Jammie Dodger and bit into it. 'Signs are he was probably alive when his jugular was sliced open, but until his body turns up, I'm afraid I'm not able to issue you with a definitive cause of death.'

She offered the biscuit tin around. Jo excused herself and could be heard scampering along to the ladies' bathroom.

'And Sophie Grey had two stab wounds in her buttocks...' Billie took a biscuit and tucked in. Comfort eating.

'Yes and also in her leg. All from craft-knives, the type you can buy in any hardware store with retractable blades. Fiendishly sharp. In this case the two on her backside cut straight through her tracksuit and pants and may have been wielded by two different attackers. One blow was more forceful than the other and from a higher angle...' Billie pictured the hooded figures immediately behind Sophie Grey in the grainy CCTV footage. One had been taller than the other.

'The right side?' Billie was picturing the scene.

'Indeed. Both wounds would have made life jolly uncomfortable for her, had she survived. As I mentioned before, the knife wound on her leg was caused by her own weapon, secured down her left-hand sock. She may have reached for it, engaged the blade, whilst still bending and then been hoist by her own petard, as it were, on impact with the train. Would you like to run through the train-impact injuries again?'

'No thanks. I had nightmares about those last night.' Billie held her hand up to Josta, who smiled sympathetically.

'All three fatalities are the stuff of nightmares, I'm afraid.'

'So I can be confident in telling my team that we are looking for a blade and a claw hammer in connection with Josh Hallows' murder?' Billie shook her head in horror. She recalled the sickening sound as the back of the boy's head had hit the ground, right next to her, but Josta was confident that by then he had already suffered fatal blows to his skull.

'Absolutely. I'm afraid the poor boy shows evidence of both sides of the claw hammer on his skull. Those injuries most definitely were the cause of cessation of life. The blade wound to the chest is interesting, in that I'm of the opinion that the implement used was a pointed screwdriver. Fairly rare situation, though not unheard of.'

Billie sighed. She needed sugar. She rifled the biscuit jar and took out another biscuit.

'What a mess. We've got specialised help, an officer experienced in organised drug crime. So far, the hypothesis is that county lines gangs have moved into the area. Knocked off the competition in Jesus O'Brian and Christy Callaghan and used Sophie Grey amongst no doubt other kids to move the drugs around the country. Somehow Josh Hallows has gotten information that made him dangerous–'

'What tangled webs we weave, my dear.' Josta raised her eyebrows as she sipped her coffee. Suddenly, recollections of the night before swept into Billie's mind.

'How's Lola?' Billie asked, looking for confirmation on whether Josta's wife had been having some late life crisis recently, or perhaps that question applied to Josta herself?

'Sleeping beauty when I left this morning.' Josta smiled. 'Possibly that's all she needs, to catch up on a few zeds. She was fast asleep when I got back last night. I had a late one here,' she added, not imagining that anyone would find it odd that she seemed to prefer being in the mortuary alone all night with the dead, or perhaps lurking around her son's house, instead of being at home with her wife.

'Ma'am, I nipped back to the car, to get a new notebook.' Jo slipped through the door and almost stood to attention in that queer manner she had.

'Thanks for sharing,' Billie joked, accepting that she had to go with the flow as far as her subordinate's eccentricities went.

'And this was on the windscreen, ma'am.' Jo presented Billie with a single wild red rose. Billie took it, flicking over the attached card. *Wilde as a corpse*, the words read.

'Oh, my dear girl. Do you have a secret amour?' Josta teased. 'Anyone I know?' Billie thought of Lola's behaviour the night before.

'I sincerely hope not,' Billie answered. She kept any reciprocal jokiness out of her voice. Josta had left the room for a few minutes, just before the examination had begun, Billie recollected. If it did turn out to be the eminent criminal pathologist who had been doing this, and Billie had trouble even imagining that completely crazy notion, then she hoped that Josta had got the message loud and clear, that she was definitely *not* amused.

'Has Max turned up yet?' Billie said, changing the subject, at the same moment that her mobile rang. Ellis Darque was calling.

'Found a Cuckoo in a cage,' he began. 'Have I got your go-ahead to ruffle a few feathers?'

'A Trap House on our patch?' Billie was immediately alert.

'Yep, Amsterly.' Billie reacted with surprise. The location was a small market town surrounded by countryside. Not the sort of spot she would have expected to house a drug den. 'You're welcome to come along if you've got nothing more pressing on. I remember you like a bit of a party,' he cracked, referring to the first time Billie had met him, when he was undercover, and Billie had not been at her best. The result had been a major embarrassment on Billie's part.

'That's an invitation I can't refuse,' she joked back, giving a wave farewell to Josta as she moved out of the room.

'Reports of a vulnerable woman inside and at least one shooter on the premises.'

Billie picked up pace towards the exit, with Jo alongside her. The rose now dropped on the floor and trodden underfoot.

'Have you got the ARV?' Billie referred to the Armed Response Vehicle on hand for situations where firearms might be required. It would be heavily laden with equipment that brooked no refusal to entry, all with slang police names such as the Big Red Key, a battering ram to demolish doors and a Hooly Bar – a large iron bar with a spike on the end, used for smashing windows.

'Yep, got all the Gucci gear on board and a bag of boiled sweets in the glove compartment. What more could you ask for? Bring your stabby vest. 'Fraid you'll have to leave the sequins at home today.'

Billie smiled to herself. Ellis clearly absolutely loved the job, whether dangerously undercover living with criminals or in the firing line collaring them. Here was a man after her own heart. Shame that her own heart was aching for someone else. She thought of Max and shivered. She hoped it wasn't because someone had walked over his grave.

'Armed police. Step back from the door!' Billie had just given the nod to Ellis. The Big Red Key smashed down the flimsy door in a matter of seconds, before the heavily armed team bundled in. Hysterical screaming could be heard from upstairs. Billie hurtled up alongside an armed officer, as others with guns swarmed the rooms of the tiny house.

The screeches were coming from what Billie imagined was the main bedroom, though there wasn't room to swing a dead rat inside the small modern house on the new estate. For some reason, the '*Win a House*' competition, run by the local rag, ran through her mind. *Win a Rabbit Hutch* more like, she thought.

Across the bed, which filled most of the room, she could see a sprout of hair, twisted into an untidy topknot, poking out from white-knuckled fingers clenched over a bowed head. The female was hysterical. Billie quickly edged around the pink bedspread, finding Cilla Saunders, the dancer whom she had spoken to in the nightclub, on the day that Christy Callaghan's head had been found on the platter. She was cowering under the window. Billie hauled her upright, sitting her on the bed.

'Cilla. We meet again.' She felt sorry that it wasn't in better circumstances. Cilla had appeared to be pretty well-worn when Billie had talked to her only days ago, but now she looked positively wasted. Billie glanced to the neat MDF fitted drawers on the side of her bed. They were heaped high with the detritus of a drug marathon and by the looks of things Cilla wasn't choosy about the type that rocked her boat.

The ubiquitous drug-den rips of aluminium foil lay amongst fag ash and a small chunk of dope. A pile of pills to one side pointed to the smoking of prescription painkillers, but it was the pretty pink 'rose in a glass' ornament that worried Billie most. It looked very much like a test tube with a plastic rose inside. No doubt many grannies bought these as cute gifts for their granddaughters. After all, Billie recognised them as a staple product on display beside the till in garage shops whenever she paid for her petrol.

A sweetly kitsch piece of tat to the untrained eye, but also a cleverly disguised crack pipe, once the pink rose was removed. In its place, a shred of copper dish scrubber could be stuffed in the mouth of the glass, on top of the crack cocaine rock, before heating and smoking. By the manner in which this particular ornament was lying on its side, amongst the other clutter, Billie guessed that Cilla hadn't acquired the piece of whimsy to simply match the curtains.

Thundering footsteps and loud shouting continued for a minute around the house, as the armed police rushed from room to room. Cilla kept her hands pinned tight to her ears, shaking like a leaf. Billie gave her shoulder a rub. She didn't for one moment think that the poor woman was the organ grinder around here.

'Done a runner.' Ellis popped his head around the door. 'Neighbours said a pile of hoodies scattered out five minutes ago and did off on bikes. Haven't got a grass at base, have you?'

Billie immediately remembered Perry Gooch beating her to Sophie Grey's parents. A similar thought had passed through her mind then. She couldn't imagine that any of her core team would spill any beans, but she had taken on a vast swathe of extra officers due to the sudden pile-up of murdered bodies.

'Someone will swing if that turns out to be the case,' Billie answered sternly. 'Cilla, do you want to share the names of your housemates with us?' Cilla started to get even more agitated, shaking her head from side to side.

'I can't, I can't...' She started to sob.

'How long have they been here?' Billie persisted.

'I can't say.' Cilla caught her breath, tears now rolling down her cheeks.

Billie crouched down, so she was eye to eye with the seemingly petrified woman, holding both of her arms now, to stop her from falling forward, she was in such a state.

'It's all right, Cilla. You can say anything. We'll make sure you're taken somewhere safe, somewhere no one can harm you.'

'Like Christy was safe?' Cilla started wailing. 'If Christy Callaghan and Jesus O'Brian weren't safe, what hope is there for me?' she sobbed.

'You're renting here?' Billie looked around the room. It had the air of one of those places that investors bought in pretty country towns. Newly built, made of cardboard and ready to let out to the first person willing to pay the highest wonga. Cilla nodded, snot hanging from her nose. Jo passed her a tissue.

'Christy used to own it. God knows who it will go to now. Rent came out of my earnings and I did his ironing for him to make up the difference.' Billie wondered if that was the only additional benefit Cilla gave him. The poor woman may as well as have the words *Used and Abused* stamped across her forehead. It had clearly been going on for so long, in one form or another, that she didn't even realise that there could be any other sort of life.

'I can't afford anywhere else. They just followed me from the supermarket one day and took over.'

Billie guessed it was more likely that she had scored drugs from her squatters and they had spotted how vulnerable Cilla was. Maybe offered her a few samples for free.

'Why didn't you tell Christy?' Billie asked, wondering what the point was of being the personal skivvy to the local criminal gang leader if you couldn't call on him in situations just like this.

'I didn't like to tell him. He would have gone mad if he'd seen the mess...' She trailed off. Billie added the thought that Cilla was clearly in denial all round. It was almost as if she had forgotten that her former boss was also one of the big bad guys. That's what a trip down drugs lane could do to a person. Had the county lines gang used Cilla to find out when Christy Callaghan was at his most vulnerable? Had she inadvertently cleared the path for his killers to snuff out the life of the hand that fed her?

Billie could see that she wasn't going to get much more out of Cilla until she had recovered at least a little of her equilibrium and been assured of a safe house. She left Jo to take her in, as the armed guard moved out and the crime scene investigative team stepped forward, to see if anything juicy could be found to move their murder enquiries forward.

Ellis stood in the doorway of the small open-plan living room leading to a kitchenette. It was a dumping ground of old takeaway cartons, with spilled-out rotting food, overflowing ashtrays, filth, and disarray. It was clear that Cilla had long ago lost the battle to keep the house in good order. Instead, she had been like all Cuckoos stowed away in Trap Houses, a slave whose only use was to supply her jailers with whatever they needed, be that food, drug deliveries to fellow local junkies and often sex twenty-four seven.

'Left behind a pile of burner phones in their haste. Might get some intel from them.' Ellis nodded to a collection of phones scattered on the floor. Billie also spotted a heap of yellow plastic, pod-shaped items. The type that generally contained a surprise toy inside.

'Cilla didn't have kids, did she?' Billie looked around, wondering whether to call in the Social Services child protection officers.

A crime-scene investigator, fully gloved up and wearing protective gear, snapped one of the pods open. 'Reckon there's about thirty deals of heroin and crack in this one alone.' She nodded to the item. Billie's heart sank, wondering not least, what would have happened if an innocent child had got their tiny hands on it.

'I've seen mules come into prison with a whole lorryload of them in their guts.' Ellis sounded quite upbeat, as though affectionately recalling his times undercover in Her Majesty's prisons.

'Slip down easily and can't be spotted on the metal detectors on the way in,' he added. Billie shook her head in dismay.

'You look like you could do with a drink.' Ellis nudged her arm playfully. 'Haven't you got another party on tonight?'

Billie closed her eyes in horror then checked her watch. It was Derek Blythe's leaving do that night and she was supposed to be the one hosting it. Thank God she had asked Ash to step in and check her arrangements were all in order at the venue, aptly named The Cop-Out, a pub around the corner from headquarters.

'Come on. You can't let all this stuff take over your life. We'll give you a lift back in the tank, throw in a boiled sweet to get rid of that sour look. Play a few party tunes on the radio. Maybe you can work a miracle and turn into Cinderella on the way.' He gave her arm a playful nudge. 'You've got a face on you like a right old pumpkin at the moment,' he continued to tease.

'Less of the cheek.' Billie punched his arm jokily, chuckling. She accepted that he was right. She had to take care of herself if she was going to take care of these cases properly. Hadn't that been flagged up big time, during her endless counselling sessions? Once she had sorted out the late shift, she would get her glad rags on. Derek Blythe, her faithful team member all these years, was about to get a send-off he would never forget.

Unfortunately, as it was to turn out, neither would anyone else present that night.

14

A DEATH WISH

'Frankly, ma'am, I would rather eat my own spleen.' Jo blinked her myopic eyes in answer to Billie's query as to whether she was heading off to the party. Her shift had been due to finish an hour ago, yet she had politely ignored Billie's reminders to clock-off for the night. 'But I'm happy to stay late and help out here.'

She nodded to the hive of activity still going on in the buzzing office as the late shift cracked on with the work Billie had directed them to carry out. To be fair, everyone in the team knew that there had never been any love lost between the rookie detective and Derek Blythe and one thing Jo couldn't be accused of was hypocrisy.

Billie was quietly champing at the bit to carry on with the various leads that the team were following up too, but Derek Blythe had been a great supporter of hers. As head of the team, she should have been there at the start of the party which had already been underway for an hour. It was also her job to give the obligatory speech and hand over the traditional set of handcuffs engraved with the words *May the Force Be with You – Always.*

Not much of a reward for so many years of hard slog, but Billie had also chosen a separate gift – a rare vintage police watch, engraved with her personal thanks. If she didn't crack on, the party would be over before she got a chance to give it to him.

Billie looked around the room, running through her to-do list one more time. Cilla was snugly settled in her cell, too drugged up and terrified to be of much use to them this evening, but Billie was confident they could wheedle some info out of her first thing in the morning. Forensics had already started work on the haul from the Trap House. House-to-house enquiries from people living around the playground, in addition to witness statements from the train station and those associated with Christy Callaghan's nightclub were all being collated and cross-referenced. Despite Billie's assurances to the chief that she fully understood after the last investigation the need to maintain a healthy work-life balance, she would have been happy to bunk up in a sleeping bag in her office for the duration.

Boo was still tapping away on her PC. Billie kicked herself for not having caught up with her earlier in the day. For one reason or another, her friend and colleague was clearly out of sorts.

'Come on, party girl. Time to switch off.' Billie crossed over to Boo's workstation. 'Derek deserves a big send-off.' Boo kept her head down and carried on working.

'Rocket up his arse more like. I've always thought he was a misogynist bastard,' Boo answered distractedly, totally focused on her work. Billie was beginning to realise that her team didn't necessarily gel as well as she had always thought.

'You okay? Any word on your nephew yet?' Billie kicked herself for not having asked that question first thing. Boo finally stopped typing and put her head in her hands.

'Yep, they've found him. Local drug squad, that is.' She sighed. Billie rubbed her shoulder. That sort of news didn't bode well. It sounded like her nephew hadn't strayed too far after all from his home. 'Turns out he was running a nice little crack cocaine racket from a caravan hidden under a motorway underpass. He and his mates fancied themselves as real-life *Breaking Bad* characters. Pocket money my sis worked night and day to fund him with wasn't enough apparently.'

'Maybe he didn't realise what he was getting into...' Billie thought of Sophie Grey. Boo wasn't in the mood for excuses.

'He knew *exactly* what he was doing. Believe me, he wasn't just some innocent kid dragged in. He was about to start a chemistry degree at uni. Cambridge, at that, so he can't play the ignorant kid card.' Boo rubbed her face. 'That's his promising future down the drain. He's being held on remand and he's over eighteen, so technically an adult. Looks like he'll go down for a long stretch.'

Billie felt heartily sorry for Boo. She'd had to take more than her fair share of personal blows in life.

'If you need any time off...' Billie offered, her heart sinking at the thought. She wasn't quite sure how she would cope without Boo keeping everyone on their toes in the office, though she looked completely broken at the moment.

'No need. I'm not planning on visiting him anytime soon.' Boo couldn't disguise the anger in her voice. 'I'd rather catch up with my work, trying to stop drug-dealing scum like him.' Billie sat down next to Boo. It was clear that she was heartbroken.

'Don't be too hard on him, Boo.' Billie sighed. She remembered having met Boo's nephew at a family wedding just a couple of years earlier. He had been a nice boy then, as clean-cut and polite as Josh Hallows.

Billie had long ago realised that evil didn't always present itself in a red devil suit, breathing flames. Her own father was just such an example. She brushed the thought of him away and locked it in a little black box in the furthest corner of her mind. She thought she had already thrown away that rusty old key.

'He knew that if he just stayed on the straight and narrow, he was set for great things. Now he's only going as far as a prison cell. All actions have their consequences. It's about time people realised that.' It was clear to Billie that the pain that Boo had been keeping bottled up all day was starting to spill out.

'I mean, just look at the report I'm reading here!' She flicked her head towards her PC screen, making the beads on her hair braids jangle. 'Some bastard makes a pile of cocaine in South America and the fucking shrimps down the street end up stoned out of their heads!' Boo's voice had heightened now in fury. A sudden hush fell over the room.

Billie had a sudden vision of the stoned shrimps. 'There's a thought to conjure with.' She couldn't help giggling. Boo herself broke into a smile, though she was clearly still stressed.

'It doesn't bear thinking about though, does it? It's like a dance we are all doing together. One step the wrong way and there's a domino effect all around the world.' Billie glanced at the clock. She really had to go.

'So, talking of dancing, a good boogie is probably just what the doctor ordered. Come on, you needn't worry, I haven't arranged for any krill to be at the party,' she cajoled, 'maybe a few crab sticks but don't worry about them, they don't even have any crab in them. Plus, Ellis Darque was asking after you earlier.' Billie raised an eyebrow suggestively. 'Could there be a little love interest there?' she teased, desperately hoping to lift Boo's spirits.

'Could've been once.' Boo's face darkened. 'But that's well dead in the water.' She started typing fast again. Billie finally threw in the towel, accepting that the office warrior queen had seriously lost her mojo. It would take nothing less than a bomb to move her.

✳

'Murder on the Dancefloor' was blasting out on the jukebox as Billie pushed into the bar of The Cop-Out. It was heaving with various police types who had known Derek Blythe throughout his solid career in the force.

'Hey, if it's not the dancing queen!' Ellis, who had been propping up the bar, launched into his best John Travolta mickey take, pointing his finger at Billie. 'They're playing your song. Not going to get on the floor and strut your stuff?' he teased, referring to the first time they had met, when he had been undercover and she had been under the influence, giving the dad dancing some welly, to the same tune. Billie felt her face flush at the memory.

'I'm saving myself for the karaoke,' she answered, playfully shoving him out of the way. 'No doubt you've been practising your Macarena,' she jibed, grinning. 'Derek around?' She was keen to get the speech bit of the proceedings out of the way. Ellis shrugged.

'Probably out the back having a fag. Passed him heading that way when I was leaving the khazi just now. Not that I'm keeping tabs. Let's face it, he made clear at the briefing that I'm not top of his hit parade,' he answered.

'Showing your age, with a comment like that,' Billie quipped as Ash appeared from out of the crowd, clearly thrilled to be back in the swing of things.

'Thought you weren't coming.' He handed her a drink.

'Sans alcohol? I'm heading back to work after this.'

'Over my dead body.' Ash persisted in handing Billie the glass of wine. 'I'm designated driver tonight. Still on painkillers, so I couldn't drink if I wanted to.'

Billie finally relented, there were benefits, after all, to having a lodger. She hoped to God he would turn out to be better than her last one.

Josta's round smiling face suddenly peered through the crowd. She pushed towards Billie, deftly preventing her large glass of red wine from spilling. Billie's heart sank for a moment. She dearly hoped that she wasn't towing Lola tonight, or even worse, had a dead rose and crass card hiding in her pocket.

'Hi, where's the wifey?' Billie asked. Josta rolled her eyes.

'Gone off to visit some thespian friends, insisting that the show must go on.' She sounded less than impressed, but Billie could see a hint of relief in the forensic pathologist's eyes too. Billie stored the information, realising that she hadn't had any rose deliveries since first thing that morning. Maybe the stalking thing *had* been Lola having a mad moment, as a result of her drugging episode? Maybe she'd gone off to fixate on someone else, with her floral gifts. Perhaps her ramblings about Josta's past obsessions had just been a drunken flight of fancy from a woman who made a living, after all, as a drama queen?

'It might take her mind off things,' Billie commiserated, 'she has seemed particularly... fragile,' she added, wondering if it was obvious that she was fishing. Josta nodded in agreement.

'Barking mad, my dear, of late. I'm of the opinion that she's getting too long in the tooth for this acting nonsense, but to be honest, I've got used to my own company by and large these days. Much as I love her, a little bit of Lola goes a long way for an old woman like me who's got used to spending most of my days with the dead.' Billie quietly admitted to having some sympathy with Josta.

'Of course the return of the Prodigal Son has done much to lift spirits all around,' Josta continued as Billie's heart leapt into her mouth. The crowd seemed to naturally part for a second. There he was. Max Strong, healthy and handsome and way fit, standing right in front of her. Josta made herself scarce.

'Hey, Billie.' His voice was soft, like liquid chocolate. 'I hear you've flung yourself back into work. Amazing what happens around you in such a short space of time.' His lips curved in that slow smile of his, the one that made Billie's stomach churn.

'Is that right?' Billie questioned. 'Not only me it seems. Some people have flown to Columbia and back, climbed a mountain, hacked through jungle, fought armed kidnappers, and saved an innocent hostage.' She looked him straight in the eye.

'And some people have been dealing with a multitude of murders, so I hear,' he answered.

'Is that where you've been, South America?'

Billie could hear her voice giving away a note of desperation and mentally kicked herself for not playing cool. Max's eyes caught the light as he stared into Billie's own for a split second.

'You of all people understand, that if I told you the truth...' – he bent down and whispered in her ear – '...I would have to kill you.' Billie felt rumblings in all sorts of unmentionable places, as his eyelashes brushed her cheek, his soft skin touching hers for a split second.

It was at that moment the window beside them smashed, glass shattering loudly in all directions. The crowd took flight from the dance floor as a bottle landed on the space where Billie had been standing just seconds earlier. It rolled for a beat, stopped still and then suddenly burst into a blistering wall of flame. Pandemonium broke out.

Billie felt strong arms around her waist, whisking her aside and out of the door, the cold night air hitting her like a slap in the face. Josta had somehow got out before them. Billie could see her sitting on a low wall, having valiantly kept her drink intact in her glass. Screams filled the air as the fire took hold and people flew out of the exits. Max appeared again behind Billie, propelling her forward.

'Ash!' she shouted, turning, and pulling away with regret from Max's grasp.

'Billie come back!' he called, catching her wrist. She pulled him along with her as she shot back inside, immediately feeling the terrific heat. Ash was on the edge of the dance floor, kneeling on the carpet. As Billie and Max raced towards him, they could see that he was huddled over a young woman, who Billie recognised as one of the new interns who had joined her team to view CCTV footage. She was unconscious. Ash was attempting to put out the flames threatening to engulf her.

Billie spotted a fire extinguisher nearby on the wall and put it into action dousing the intern and the area around them, whilst Max lifted the girl over his shoulder and made for the door. Billie grabbed Ash's arm and helped him up. They moved out of the exit door just as a large lighting rig above the dance floor crashed to the ground.

The noise of fire engines and ambulances could be heard now, as Billie, Max and Ash worked as a team to try and bring the young woman around. She appeared to have taken the full force of the blast of flames. Max ran off again to help drag another injured partygoer out of the pub.

Billie could feel the heat, even from a hundred yards away, absolutely stunned at the intensity of the blaze in such a short time as the fire team moved in with their unique expertise. Two paramedics took over from Billie and Ash, rushing the intern toward a waiting ambulance.

Billie spotted Stan, the pub landlord, a former police-dog handler, being dragged out by Ellis. She ran over to help haul him out of harm's way, before remembering his beloved bloodhound, who had retired with him. The old wrinkly-faced dog named Kat had been known to offer entertainment to regulars, largely police officers on the way home from work, by giving enthusiastic attention to the pockets of random visitors, who might have a joint of dope they thought was well stashed deep in a pocket.

Billie had a special affection for the animal, having looked after her for a period during her time away from work whilst Stan was in hospital having a hip replacement. Handler and dog had grown old together, although Stan could beat Kat in a wrinkle competition these days. The huge bloodhound also had a few issues with arthritic joints and couldn't move so quickly anymore. Billie hadn't caught sight of her anywhere outside.

She raced for the open door nearest to the corner where she had last seen the dog, pulling her neck scarf up over her nose and mouth. Blinding smoke, irritating her eyes, made it almost impossible for Billie to see more than a foot or so ahead.

She felt her boots crunching on discarded glasses, only moments earlier full of alcohol, well aware that the liquid could only add to the blaze. The acrid smell of smoke and petrol almost overwhelmed her. She knew that she should alert one of the firefighters with breathing apparatus, to take over the search for the animal. But she also knew that Kat wouldn't be top of the list of priorities and she doubted the old dog would survive the wait.

Suddenly, she heard a whimper to her right, bent down and spotted Kat huddled under a table, shaking. Billie dropped to hands and knees and scampered across the floor, feeling shards of glass cutting into the palms of her hands, before reaching out and pulling the huge dog into her arms.

As she stood up, the smoke caught her throat, the smell and heat and noise disorienting her. She couldn't now see the way towards the exit door. Turning to her right, she moved forward, banging against the bar, burning her hand on a brass fixture. She jumped, almost dropping Kat, who began to wriggle in her grasp. Billie felt her breathing become laboured as she struggled with the dog's weight. She turned to her left. This time banging hard into a table, almost toppling over an upturned chair. She felt the dog sliding from her grasp. Beads of clammy cold sweat broke out on her forehead, despite the heat generated by the fire. She felt light-headed, dizzy, her legs starting to crumple under her.

Suddenly, strong arms wrapped around both her and Kat, spooning her from behind and propelling her forward. Her lungs felt as though they were aflame, as she was thrust out into the cool night. She took huge gulps of oxygen as Kat jumped out of her arms and, tail wagging furiously, scampered over to Stan, recovering on the wall by an ambulance. The two appeared thrilled to have been reunited. Her rescuer's arms tightened around her waist, the light, fresh lemony scent perfuming the smoke-filled evening air. He needed no introduction.

'Christ, Billie, I can't leave you alone for a moment. I sometimes think you've got a death wish,' Max whispered in her ear, laying his head momentarily against hers, before stepping back. Billie bent forward, hands on knees, still trying to catch her breath, whether from her rescue mission or the close proximity of Max, she wasn't sure.

Max crossed over to Josta without another word, seizing the glass of wine still in his mother's hand and taking a long swig. Billie looked around her. The sight of journalist Perry Gooch arriving on the scene, camera slung around her neck, harassing a young female PC, did nothing to alleviate her feelings of nausea.

Despite the momentary panic, the party guests, by and large being police personnel, had kicked into their well-practised emergency routines. As she walked around, checking on familiar faces, Billie's assessment was that most of the group appeared to be okay. However, returning to Ash, she found him on his mobile, appearing desperately upset.

'It's Jas,' he explained. 'The next-door neighbour says she's taken ill. The children are in a terrible state and the baby needs feed...'

'Let's go.' Billie grabbed his arm and headed for her car, as a camera flash lit up her face. As she took off at speed, spots of flash blindness making her blink, Billie couldn't help thinking that if Perry Gooch was the photographer responsible, then the journalist had only herself to blame if Billie ran right over her.

15

THE DEVIL'S BREATH

'She was like a zombie.' The next-door neighbour folded her arms, shaking her head at the scene of devastation. The home that until recently had been a cosy, happy family nest, appeared to have been ransacked. The living room, usually as neat as a new pin, had largely been turned over. The other rooms told a similar story.

Billie cradled baby Tani on her hip, feeding her a bottle of milk which she walloped back hungrily. Ash's older girls, Indie aged six and Happi, two years younger, were hunkering in to either side of Ash as he leaned against the wall. There was nowhere else to sit. All the furniture had gone.

'I said to her, "You never mentioned you were moving",' the woman explained, 'and she said, "I'm just giving these guys all my stuff".' The woman looked from Billie to Ash in amazement. 'She was helping them load the van as well. Brought out an expensive-looking camera and shouted, "don't forget this".'

'You gave them *my* camera?' Ash furiously demanded. His newly estranged wife had been looking around the room, her eyes appearing to track something only she could see. Billie made a mental note that her pupils were dilated.

'Yes, I gave them everything.' A dopey smile crossed Jas's face.

'But you didn't give the kids any tea?' Ash snapped. Billie held out her arm and caught his hand to calm him. The neighbour clocked it.

'Well, I don't like to pry...' the neighbour lied through her teeth, '...she said that you'd moved out. Never mentioned you had a new lady friend already, mind, but then *she* seemed very fond of the man doing the loading. Had the same drippy smile on her face, like she wasn't quite right in the head.' She nodded to Jas, who was sitting on the carpet propped up against the wall, wide-eyed but with a glazed look on her face. 'She said, and this is when I knew something was a bit off, she said, "Do you want to know where the kids' money boxes are?"' Ash looked fit to explode.

'Daddy, Mum's friends took all of our toys.' Happi was tearful. Ash pulled her close.

'It's all right, baby, Daddy's got you now.' Ash glared at Jas. She smiled back.

'I've got a headache.' She grinned at Billie.

'She's not keeping the kids if she's got men round, taking drugs,' Ash barked, absolutely livid, as Indie now started sobbing as well. 'I'll go to court.' He was about to go into full deprived-daddy rant.

'Let's keep calm. She looks like she may have been drugged.' Billie stared at Jas, who couldn't have been presenting less like her usually pretty, efficient mummy self. True, she and Ash had been through a big upheaval lately, but this was way out of character. Billie glanced at her watch and then to Ash.

'Ambulance needs to get a move on. I guess they're all over at the pub.'

'Oh my goodness me, I hope she's not inviting druggie types

round here. Brings the tone of the neighbourhood down.' The indignant neighbour had clearly decided to side with Ash.

'I don't think she's at fault,' Billie announced, putting down the finished bottle and rubbing Tani's back. When the baby responded by hiccupping a mouthful of vomit over her shoulder, she made a silent note to remember to use a burping cloth in future. So much for pretending that she knew what she was doing as far as kids were concerned.

'I've seen another case like this just recently.' Billie ignored the neighbour and spoke to Ash. She was thinking of Lola, as the ambulance swung into the drive, blue lights flashing.

'Ash, take the kids to my house. It's a safe place for the time being. Daddy's taking you to the seaside girls.' Happi and Indie responded with smiles of excitement at last.

'I couldn't...' Ash started.

'They've probably taken spare keys and maybe an address book.' Billie was thinking of Lola's situation. 'I'll go to the hospital with Jas. I'm sure she'll be kept in, at least overnight.'

Billie intended to have a word with Ellis. A drugs expert right on hand. If he didn't know what was going on, then no one would and Billie was determined to get to the bottom of these odd incidents, before someone else ended up with their photo on her murder investigation wall of horrors.

Billie kicked the hospital drinks machine for a second time. A bottle of water shivered in its holding but refused to drop down.

'Hey, I'll go and find an officer of the law if you do that again.'

Billie looked around, as Max wandered towards her, smiling. She knew that he had an office here at the hospital, should have guessed he would be working late, catching up after having been away. She wondered whether Josta had begged him to give her a lift to the party earlier, when he would probably, in truth, have much preferred to have been here all night instead.

'That's why I need to stay well away from you, Billie Wilde, you constantly seem to go searching for trouble,' he teased. It wasn't the first time he had reminded Billie of his doggedness in that direction. He had alluded to it when he had dragged her out of the pub with Kat the dog. Billie mused that the thought appeared to constantly play on his mind.

'You're one to talk, Columbian boy. Anyway, it's me who's been robbed.' Billie nodded to the machine, giving it a firm kick again. This time the bottle flipped down with a thud. She fished it out. 'Bingo!' She winked at Max. 'Watch and learn. Persistence pays off.'

'Are you all right?' Max was looking her up and down. Her hand did still sting from the burn in the pub, not to mention the shards of glass in her palms from the floor. She stuck it in her pocket. Playing the victim had never been her style.

'Still as mad as a box of frogs, doc, but hanging in there,' Billie joked. 'Actually, you remember Ash Sanghera, my wingman?' Billie asked. Max nodded. 'His wife has just been robbed today. I think she's been drugged up like Lola was.'

'My mother?' A look of alarm crossed his handsome features. Billie immediately realised that Josta and Lola hadn't passed that info on to their beloved son.

'Sorry, my big mouth.' Billie wanted to kick herself. 'But then again, I bet you haven't told them anything you've been getting up to in the past few days either,' she pointed out sheepishly.

'Jas Sanghera, is she all right? I only saw her this afternoon.'

Billie's ears pricked up. 'You weren't driving a removal lorry, were you?' Billie raised an eyebrow.

'Sorry?' Max frowned. 'I got back home just in time to make my consultation with her. That's confidential by the way.' He looked slightly startled at having shared the fact. Billie rolled her eyes.

'Well, just between me and you, she's having treatment in there.' She indicated a side room. 'Though thank God she's just nodded off. From what anyone can gather so far, she hasn't been physically assaulted, but she's certainly on something. Seems to be hallucinating and complained about being thirsty and having a headache in the ambulance.'

'And you say my mother has had a similar experience?'

'Lola,' Billie clarified. 'They took her address book and keys so maybe you want to change your locks at home.'

'Fancy a cuppa?' Max asked. Billie could think of lots of other things she would be preferring to do with him in the dead of night but decided that beggars couldn't exactly be choosers.

'Okay.' It wouldn't hurt to have a break and spend it staring into those big brown eyes. Only hours ago, she had feared that she would never get the chance again.

'Just a sec...' Max crossed over to a nurse coming out of Jas's room, took some notes from her and flicked through. As Billie recalled the sensation of his arms around her body as he had saved both her and Kat from being burnt to a crisp earlier, she could feel the pressures of the day evaporating already.

As they crossed to the lift, she momentarily allowed herself to drink in that fresh lemony scent, unique to Max, the bewitching smell that confirmed that he was alive and standing only inches away. The doors opened. As they entered, Billie leaned against the wall and closed her eyes for a beat, just to savour it, noting that she herself smelled of smoke and baby sick.

She opened her eyes in response to the touch of Max's hand,

brushing a tendril of hair away from her face. His fingers were smooth and healing.

'Tired?' he asked. 'From what I hear from Josta, you've been working non-stop.' His liquid chocolate eyes looked into hers. 'Don't forget you need some downtime too, Billie...' Billie wondered if that was a hint, as the lift doors slid open.

'There you are! Just the person I've been looking for.' Ellis looked from Billie to Max. 'Unless you're, em, busy, of course.' His eyes twinkled mischievously for a split second.

'No, not at all, this is Doctor Max Strong. He's a leading criminal psychologist,' Billie answered breezily, the words *the lady doth protest too much* running through her mind. She had been hoping to have a word with Ellis, so she supposed that now, with Max also present, it was time to get back to work.

'I've got that big bloodhound in the back of the car,' Ellis announced. 'Poor old Stan is being kept in for a few nights. Got some nasty-looking burns on him. Six of the punters have been admitted.' Billie wondered if one of them was the pretty PC she had seen him chatting up in the pub and that was the reason he was here. Ellis had no doubt broken a few hearts in his time.

'But no deaths?' Billie queried, wondering if there were about to be more unsolved murders added to her growing list.

'Not so far. One of them looking touch and go, mind you,' Ellis added as they went through the process of getting their drinks. 'Dear old Derek had hold of the dog to stop it following Stan into the ambulance. Stan was in a bit of a panic, asking him to look after it, you being so busy and whatnot.' Ellis Darque took a swig of his hospital coffee and winced. 'But your darling Dexie claims he's allergic to dogs, so palmed it off on me. I am too, the thing has been slobbering over me all the way here...' He blinked. Billie had noticed his eyes looked red and sore, but she had put it down to the effects of the smoke and fire. '... and

I'm staying at the hotel. They won't let dogs in,' he added. 'Just seen poor old Stan on the ward and he won't settle until he knows his dog's all right.' He looked Billie in the eye and grinned. 'He said it loves you.' He winked, marching off to find a seat.

'Seems you have a habit of provoking that effect, DSI Wilde,' Max whispered.

'Yep. Shame you can't confirm that with my former fiancé,' Billie answered, sure that Max was sending a joke in her direction rather than revealing his own inner feelings. *Chance would be a fine thing*, Billie mused, as Max smiled and shook his head in mock disapproval. He was well aware of her recent romantic situation.

'So you'll take the mutt then?' Ellis shook a bland biscuit out of a cellophane wrapper and dunked it in his drink. 'I managed to get back inside the pub and find its dog basket and a couple of cans of food. I hear you've got a big new gaff?'

'No problem,' Billie answered, 'as long as you don't mind me knocking your two heads together on the subject of drugs and robbery.' Billie ran through the facts that she had gathered so far on Lola and Jas's robberies.

'Been the odd case of something similar here in the UK.' Ellis dunked his second biscuit. It broke free and sunk into his drink. 'Also, a couple of tourists in Paris claimed that someone asked for directions. When they bent over the map shoved under their chins, the lost boys blew powder into their faces. Next thing they were off, happy as Larry, emptying their bank accounts at the cashpoint and handing the money over. No one is sure if the fairy dust thing's a bit of an urban legend though, certainly in Europe.'

'Sadly, I'm very familiar with it.' Max's face grew dark. 'In South America, particularly Columbia, exactly the sort of scenario that you've just described is widespread. Unofficial estimates of *burandanga* events are roughly 50,000 per year.'

'So what is it exactly?' Billie emptied out her own sad biscuit supper.

'A beautiful and dangerous flowering plant which grows on the Borrachero tree.' Max reached for his mobile phone and found a photograph of a stunning trumpeted flower which looked to Billie's untrained eye, very much like a lily.

'Known locally as the "drunken binge tree", it's been used for hundreds of years in spiritual rituals. In tiny amounts its seeds are converted into a mainstream prescribed medicine, scopolamine, used for seasickness. But criminals use the seeds from the fruit to create a drug that can be dropped into drinks, soaked into business cards, or indeed blown into the faces of unsuspecting people. It's tasteless and odourless.

'Once under the influence, the victim will appear, to others, to be totally aware of their surroundings, whilst in truth they are completely unable to control their actions or exercise any free will. They'll hand over bank cards, cash, valuables, help rob their own homes, agree to be sexually assaulted and even sign the forms to have an organ removed. Amnesia is a big part of the package, so afterwards they will have little or no memory of what happened.' Max looked deadly serious.

'And all of that can happen just by inhaling a puff of powder?' Billie needed some convincing.

'Yes, believe me,' Max answered. 'I've seen the effects with my own eyes many times. Most recently in the past few days. It's used in kidnappings quite regularly...' He trailed off, aware that Billie would put two and two together. 'If too much is used, say via several drinks in a nightclub, or on a vulnerable victim, it can be fatal.'

Billie thought of the recent deaths during the return of the hostage in Columbia that had been all over the news. Had this zombie drug, rather than mainstream weapons, caused any of those fatalities, she wondered.

'What is the name of it again?' she asked, determined to look up more information when she had a moment.

'Burandanga is the official name. But in Columbia, it is so feared that the locals call it the Devil's Breath.'

16

SAILORS TAKE WARNING

Red sky at morning, sailors take warning. The rhyme ran through Billie's head as she pulled back the curtains of her bedroom window, overlooking the Aln estuary and took in the breathtaking view. The blood-red sun had already half-risen over the sea, slashing the sky with gashes of pink and purple. Below, fishing boats sleepily nodded up and down as the tide lapped the golden sand.

A loud bark from below made her brain click into gear, despite the few hours of sleep that she had managed to capture. Billie had arrived home in the early hours with Kat the dog poking her large head out of the passenger seat window, ears flapping in the cold night air, face like folded velvet, as the giant pooch surveyed the terrain, so full of exciting canine exploration possibilities. Billie didn't know what Kat had been eating, but she had been compelled to wind down her window, causing her hair to have been blown into a tangled mat. *The things you do for love.* She smiled at the memory. With recent mad stalking events, it had been good to have the dog for company on the drive home.

Billie took the stairs two at a time, planning to head out for a quick run along the bay before work. The wide sandy beach was usually devoid of human life at such an early hour. For a moment she felt guilty, aware of the vast number of tasks awaiting when she got into work but reasoned that this ten-minute run allowed her to calm her mind and think clearly. After the stresses of late and warnings about burnout, she had finally accepted that she needed to stay healthy herself, in order to take care of her team.

Squeals of excitement now joined the barking. Billie laughed quietly, astonished at how much could change in life in such a short space of time. A couple of days ago, she had been a singleton living alone. Today she had acquired an entire family and a dog.

Kat raced over, madly wagging her tail, as Billie popped her head into the kitchen. Ash rocked the baby on his hip as he fed her, whilst Indie and Happi tucked into eggs and toast soldiers, stopping to sling their arms around the dog in between mouthfuls. For the first time since the hideous events of their last investigation together, Ash looked completely at ease.

Billie simply had to mention her destination, before breakfast was abandoned and she found herself Pied-Piper style, leading the whole group onto the beach as the sun finally broke free from its watery horizon. Having taken turns for piggy-back jogs up and down the sand, chauffeured by Billie, Indie and Happi raced off after the huge snuffling dog, announcing they had spotted hidden treasure.

'Okay?' Billie asked Ash, aware that he still had some difficulty walking too far whilst his injures continued to heal.

'Yeah. Sorry to land all of this on you.' He nodded to the children as Billie took the baby from him. She decided that the smell of salty sea and milky baby was the best way to start anyone's day, especially her own, so often full of death and destruction.

'You're kidding, right?' Billie kissed the baby's soft downy head. 'Stay as long as you like. But you'll have to feed the dog. It'll starve to death waiting for me to come home.'

'It's a deal. Precious time for me. Jas will start kicking off about having them back as soon as she's out of hospital.' Ash's face clouded over. 'But no way are they going to hers until I'm certain it's safe.'

Billie could see a custody battle looming. She waved her arm at the amazing vista. 'Well, right now you've got sea and sand and your babies are totally safe in this little paradise. Just chill out and enjoy the moment. Nothing is going to go wrong here.'

'Dad, we've found some treasure!' Indie shouted from further along the shoreline where Kat the dog was pawing the shallows and barking loudly. The girls were trying to drag a lumpy bundle towards the shore.

'Don't go in too far.' Ash gathered speed, always the attentive dad. Billie handed the baby back to him and then jogged ahead, joining the girls.

'What have you found, pirates?' Billie asked, pulling Kat back by her collar to avoid being drowned by the tidal wave she was causing, as the girls bent forward poking the bundle with sticks. Ash finally caught up with them.

'Whatever it is it stinks.' Ash wrinkled his nose as Billie's brain suddenly clicked into gear. 'Is it a dead seal or something?' Ash moved the girls back, in order not to upset them. It wasn't unusual to come across rotting seals on the beach, sometimes dead from natural causes, sometimes illegally shot by rogue fisherman, jealously guarding their hunting area.

Billie bent forward and hauled the bundle towards her, before jumping back in shock as the bedraggled form started to slide out of its sacking shroud.

'What is it then?' Ash asked, spotting the look of alarm on Billie's face. She glanced over to Indie and Happi who, to her relief, had already turned their attention to shell collecting at the base of some tall sand dunes.

'I'm pretty sure it's the missing half of Christy Callaghan's body,' she replied, reflecting that one really needed to treasure those precious moments in life, because in her experience, they had an awful habit of getting snuffed out in a flash.

17

THE LUCIFER LINE

'I'm sorry to have to tell you that Milly Lloyd died in hospital this morning.' For a team of people who weren't easily shocked, a stunned silence had fallen over the murder investigation room on hearing the news that the enthusiastic young intern who Billie, Ash and Max had dragged from the fire the evening before, had succumbed to her terrible injuries.

Billie glanced around. It would be an impossibly sad moment when the student's face joined the portraits of Sophie Grey, Josh Hallows and Christy Callaghan on their deathly walls of fame. Her workstation, where she had been diligently scrolling through hours of CCTV, now sat empty, below the one space free where her photos would have to go. If things went on like this, Billie pondered, they would have to knock through to the suite next door.

'She showed real promise too.' Boo seemed to be particularly upset by the news, having mentored the student. 'She thought that she might have found something on CCTV that we could link to Josh Hallows' murder and was pleased as punch. She wanted to run it by us this morning,' Boo added sadly.

'Okay.' Billie's ears pricked up at that info. Her personal

sense of sadness at the death of a young woman who had, albeit for a short time, been a member of her team, did not prevent her radar from picking up any intel that could possibly turn out to be vital. She was missing Derek Blythe already, desperately needing all of the experienced hands possible on deck to handle the ever-increasing workload.

'Although each of the murders we're dealing with right now are totally different in their modus operandi, my suspicion is that all of them are linked to the recent influx of county lines drug dealing in the area. The Molotov cocktail may have been in retaliation for our raid on the Trap House yesterday, where one of Christy Callaghan's employees was a Cuckoo. It might have been the case that they were using her for intelligence on Christy's movements prior to his murder, as well as her digs as a base for their dealing. We'll find out more from her today.

'Neighbours claim that her uninvited guests were older teenagers with unusual accents, staying for varying periods inside the house. Pre-teen local kids were constantly riding pushbikes in the street outside. We know that teenagers were also involved in Sophie Grey's death. Josh Hallows claimed to have info on the killers of both Sophie and Christy. Again, a teenage connection.'

Billie noticed Boo looking uncomfortable as she spoke, no doubt thinking of her own nephew, living in a different area but apparently involved in a not dissimilar situation. It felt to Billie that this sort of scenario was like a spreading disease infecting the whole of the UK and probably the rest of the world too, damaging once innocent childhoods forever.

'Ellis's assessment based on experience, is that the older kids involved at Cilla's might be far away now. County lines are successful because the children can be controlled and replaced, moved around to suit their handler. That is who we are searching for here. The big guys further up the chain.

'Ellis is bringing in some local kids, known as Tweenies in the county lines pecking order, who are known to have delivered drugs on their bikes. They fit the descriptions given by Cilla's neighbours of kids hanging around when they should be at school.

'It's worth a try but the chances are they will have no useful knowledge of the Youngers or Elders in the house. Even these refer to each other by nicknames and none of them would consider any of the other drug runners to be a friend. They operate along the lines of only having knowledge of what they individually need to know, and they share with no one else. It's a lonely and terrifying life. In most cases a slip-up means GBH or worse. As you're finding out, all of this combined makes it difficult to identify the perpetrators.

'We found the county line name and number on cards in Cilla's house.' Charlie Holden held one up. It looked like a business card. 'Number on here went instantly off the grid as we raided, but if we can find the brand holder of this, then we're quids in. We also picked up some BOGOF leaflets, listing various narcotics linked to this brand. Starting offers for the area, buy one, get one free, just like at the supermarket.'

Billie took the card and passed it around. 'Ellis Darque claims these will have been posted through the letter boxes of all of the local junkies, including all of Christy Callaghan's old customers. We need to keep our eyes peeled for other Trap Houses across our county, vulnerable people who might be targeted and Cuckooed. If we can catch a dealer in situ, he might just have a separate unencrypted mobile on him with a direct line to the guy who has set up the county line. Holy Grail scenario, I know, but shy kids get nowt, so let's keep our eyes peeled.'

'What's the name of the county line brand?' Boo craned her neck to see the card.

'Lucifer,' Billie answered. 'Well chosen as it turns out. This one really is the Devil's Line. Our job is to find the controller of Lucifer, get them locked away, then throw away the key, because personally, I hope that the bastard rots in hell.'

'Don't know nuffink, innit?'

Chip Little was the smallest of the so-called Tweenies identified as one of the kids hanging around Cilla's Trap House. He'd been nabbed whilst trying to make a getaway on a bike more suited to a kid twice his size. Billie wouldn't have been surprised if he had stolen it. Chip Little, at the grand old age of twelve years and three months old, had a record for petty crime twice the length of his stick-thin arms.

'Christopher, speak up and speak clearly, so that the officers can hear you,' the social services Appropriate Adult announced. Billie inwardly sighed. Proper procedure meant that a companion had to be present whilst a child was being interviewed, but instead of the intended effect of putting the kid at ease, Billie often found that those no doubt well-meaning individuals, often strangers to the child, had precisely the opposite effect.

'I am speaking clearly, innit?' Chip shrugged the woman's hand off his skinny shoulder. 'I don't know nuffink.'

Ellis slapped down three tiny plastic bags holding yellowish-white crystals.

'Found these in the rubber-handle grip on your bike. Are you saying you don't know what these are?'

'Where's my wheels?' Chip Little suddenly became agitated.

'So you admit that the bike was yours?' Billie chimed in.

'Where is it?' Chip tried to stand up. 'Course they're my wheels. Bought with my own notes, innit?'

'Didn't you borrow that bike from a bigger boy, Christopher?' the Appropriate Adult chimed in.

'Please don't try to guide the interview, madam. We want Chip's version of events,' Billie warned, musing that the sight of such a small boy in the police station could well be steering the woman into an attempt to offer him a way to wriggle out of trouble.

'Yeah, I got my own voice, innit?' Chip thumbed his chest in annoyance at the woman who sat back in her chair, tight-lipped and suitably chastised for her efforts. 'My old wheels were clappin'. I decided to buy big, man, buy sharp. Gives me a chance to grow into the ride. Just like my old woman used to buy my shooz big, innit? Room to grow. Careful with my own paper, man. Gotta budget.'

Billie glanced under the table. His skinny legs dangled down, feet not quite touching the floor. His trainers did look at least three sizes larger than she imagined his feet to be.

'So you're not the Mr Big of this drugs gang?' Billie kept a stony face, though she couldn't help being slightly charmed by the mouthy little character. Chip feigned an astonished reaction.

'I didn't know it was wraps of Sleet in there, man.' Chip folded his arms and nodded at the package, clearly aware of one of the street names for crack cocaine. 'I just do the deliveries. Fast boy, that's why I'm always in demand, innit?' he added.

'Well, you clearly knew that it wasn't pizza.' Ellis's voice was firm. Chip, in return, shook his head innocently.

'Could have been jelly beans, mister, for all I know. I was just doing my job.'

'Delivering drugs for the Lucifer line.' Billie stared hard at Chip. 'What do you think your parents will have to say about that?'

The Appropriate Adult sat up straight and interjected. 'The

boy lives with foster parents at present, officer. Father unknown. Mother is doing a stretch in jail.'

'Yep, so I'm the man in the house.' Chip nodded proudly. 'Will be that is, when Mum gets out of the pen.' He took out a wallet, rifled in it and lifted out a carefully folded receipt. 'See. That's the receipt for my wheels. Saved up.' Chip pushed the receipt over to Billie proudly. Billie glanced at the price. The bike hadn't been cheap.

'His school report records him as being rather accomplished in maths,' the Appropriate Adult added. 'That's on the odd occasions that he turns up.'

'I don't need no learning.' He reached into his jacket, pulled out a sheet of folded paper and smoothed it out flat on the desk. 'Look, here's my paper. Notes coming in, notes coming out. I aint got no mains...'

'What?' Billie looked to Ellis.

'Close companions,' Ellis answered. Chip nodded.

'That way I don't have no beefs, no enemies. Just hang around on my patch, waiting on my pusha, then being worksy, on the road with deliveries.'

'So you don't know the names of the other people in the house where Cilla lived, or any of the movers and shakers further up the line?' Billie looked through Chip's surprisingly neat incomings and outgoings sheet. She would have it photocopied, though most of the payments seemed to relate to the Trap House they had just raided and closed down.

'Nope. They don't tell me nuffink,' Chip answered.

'What are you going to do with all this money you've saved up then?' Billie could see that he'd accrued a tidy little sum. She hoped he didn't have a county line financial plan of his own, folded up somewhere safe, waiting until he grew big enough to back his business dealings with physical force.

'Put down a deposit.' Chip folded his arms and nodded, his mind focused on the future.

'On what? Another set of wheels? Moped maybe?' Ellis grinned at Chip. It was hard not to like the boy.

'No. Seen this.' He dug in his pocket and lifted out a folded page of newspaper, torn from one of Lance Harris's rags. The full page was an advertisement for new 'affordable homes' on one of the old playing fields sold off from under the feet of the kids who desperately needed just such a space.

'I'm going for one of these.' He stabbed the photo of a two-bedroom starter flat with his skinny finger. 'When Mum gets out. Gonna be our forever home, innit?' His face lit up at the thought. 'Gotta take care of the fam, when you're the man of the house, right? She'll be psyched.' Chip grinned, showing a row of surprisingly white straight teeth.

Billie's heart melted just a little bit more. She was desperately sad that this little boy was already well on the route to ruining his life, simply because he dreamed of living with his mum, safe in a stable home. The sort of situation that most families take for granted. Sadly, in Chip's world, the only way he could imagine getting there was by criminal means. Legally, with three wraps of crack cocaine in his possession with intent to supply, he was a fully-fledged drug dealer. A boy standing barely four feet and six inches tall. Not the picture that normally springs to mind when conjuring up an image of such offenders.

'These are up Hipsmouth way.' Chip held the page up for Billie and Ellis to see it more clearly. 'Snitch said any day there's gonna be a new Trap there. Bros are out going country lookin' right now–' Billie and Ellis exchanged glances. It was all they could do to avoid high-fiving each other. Chip realised what he was saying and clammed up mid-sentence. The Appropriate Adult shook his arm.

'For goodness' sake, Christopher. Don't go there, getting mixed up with drugs again,' she warned.

'No. I swear.' Chip was suddenly a picture of innocence. 'I'm on the straight from now on. Just gimme my wheels an' I'll do pizza deliveries, innit?' He looked from Ellis to Billie.

'Right, Chip.' Billie couldn't keep her stony-faced cop show up any longer. 'We're bailing you today. We'll sort out the details in a bit. I'm guessing that if you plead guilty at court then a Youth Rehabilitation Order will be imposed. If you stick to the requirements of the order, it can only help you in working towards that dream home.'

'Yeah, yeah. Where's my bike?' Chip carefully folded his newspaper dream-home cutting and pushed it deep in his pocket.

'It's with the lad who was with you when you were nicked.' Ellis was at the photocopier now, dealing with Chip's financial records. 'Your cousin. Said he'd take it to your gaff. It'll be there waiting.'

'I aint got no cousin!' Chip shouted, panic sweeping across his face. 'My bike's been nicked!' He wailed in horror, suddenly breaking down into sobs, like a six-year-old. The Appropriate Adult rubbed his shoulders as heartfelt tears hurtled down his chin, dripping onto his top. It was such an unexpected sight that both Billie and Ellis froze for a moment.

'Shit,' Ellis mumbled under his breath. 'He *said* he was his cousin...' Billie rolled her eyes, trying to hide a smile at his horror-stricken face. 'We're splitting this,' she whispered as she flicked on her mobile and scrolled through.

'Here's a new version of the one you've got.' She crossed to Chip, showing him photos of the shiny and expensive new bikes. 'Still want a red one, or are you going for gold this time? If I order today, you should have it tomorrow.' Chip cheered up immediately, perusing the bikes for sale before pointing to his choice.

'I'll take the gold with the go-faster stripes,' he announced finally with a wide smile. 'Sick. Make me go swift. Feds won't cuff 'n' stuff me no more, innit?' He gave a cheeky departing smile to Billie as the Appropriate Adult shooed him out of the door.

'You're not seriously expecting me to go halves on a top-of-the-range getaway vehicle?' Ellis shook his head, amused as the door slammed closed.

'We'll just have to live on baked potatoes until the next pay cheque comes in.' Billie chuckled. She didn't begrudge Chip Little his unexpected gift. It looked like such things were few and far between for the boy. She had seen from Chip's payment sheet that the Tweenies, who had the highly dangerous job of delivering drugs on the street, earned a pittance. He'd had to work long hours to build up his little nest egg.

'How much?' Ellis demanded in disbelief as he looked over Billie's shoulder whilst she completed the order. 'And they say crime doesn't pay.' He pretended to sound outraged. But Billie wasn't fooled, especially when he reminded her to include a range of safety equipment as extras with the bike purchase.

18

DISTORTIONS AND LIES

B illie leaned on the bonnet of her car, closing her eyes for a moment as she felt the breeze tug at her hair. She had just witnessed the autopsies on both Milly Lloyd and Christy Callaghan's torso, so was doubly grateful for the fresh air and green views all around.

Her head was still spinning a little from the smell and visual onslaught of the two bodies being dissected. One suffering the effects of fire, the other water. Whilst it was meat and drink to Josta, who tucked in with hardly concealed glee to the menu of possibilities before her, especially in the case of Christy Callaghan's missing piece of the jigsaw, ultimately it came down to the expected outcome. Christy had been alive when his head had been chopped off. Milly had been alive at the time she had been set on fire. Both deaths would lead to murder charges when Billie eventually got her hands on the perpetrators.

'Nothing from Cilla?' Billie was catching up with Jo Green. The younger detective was like a dog with a bone and although Billie would ideally have liked to have been the one interrogating the Cuckoo from the Trap House, she was at last taking heed of the chief's demands that she learn to delegate.

'Not a squeak, ma'am. She's proving to be a hard nut to crack, despite appearances.' That surprised Billie. She made a note to catch up with Cilla later at the safe house they had placed her in. She hadn't seemed like the sort to keep secrets. Billie finished the call, pausing for a moment to enjoy the sunlight warming her face, absorbing the welcome sound of children laughing in the playground next to the allotment, waving to the passengers on trains passing by, on the track which ran below the far end of the field.

'Hiya, Sleeping Beauty, missing me already?' Billie opened her eyes and smiled.

'You said it. Can't persuade you to come back on a short-term contract, can I?' Billie walked down a grassy slope towards Derek Blythe, who appeared from behind a bean frame on his allotment.

'You've got to be joking. Who needs the stress?' he asked. Billie had to admit he had a point. Dressed in T-shirt and shorts as he tended his allotment, he already looked years younger.

'At least you went out with a bang.' Billie lapsed into the dark humour all police officers fell into, in order to cope with the day-to-day horrors of their jobs. Her face darkened.

'Yep. My party's talk of the town today. Finally made my mark in the force in the last chance saloon.' Derek chuckled.

'But joking aside, Milly Lloyd died this morning.' Billie broke the news gently, not wanting to ruin Derek's first day of retirement. His smile fell, as he shook his head in sorrow.

'She was just a kid. Good job I've left. I would have had to find someone else to get my coffees,' he tried to quip, in order to cover the tears which appeared to well in his eyes. He rubbed his arm across his eyes as though simply wiping away sweat from his brow.

'She found some tasty stuff on CCTV by all accounts,' Billie continued, 'to do with Josh Hallows' death. I've got Boo going through it now. And Christy Callaghan's body's just turned up too. You're missing all the fun.' Billie hadn't totally given up trying to persuade Derek to think again about retirement.

'You're kidding me?' He looked shocked. 'You just keep all the entertainment until I've gone.'

'Got you this.' Billie took the specially engraved watch out of her pocket. 'I didn't get a chance to give it to you yesterday.' She handed the gift over to Derek, who looked visibly moved.

'Thanks. That means a lot... fancy a cuppa in the shed? I've got one brewing.' He flicked his head in the direction of the long shed at the far end of the allotment plot.

'Got any cake?' Billie questioned.

'Anything for you, dear.' Derek chuckled.

'You're on then.' Billie looked at her own watch and decided that she could do with a brew to pull herself together. She hadn't been able to get away quick enough from the mortuary today and was totally relieved to find that there were no flowers or card waiting when she reached her car on leaving. Billie lifted the latch on the gate and was just entering when an old man with a bent back hobbled along the grass.

'Derek Blythe, you don't waste time, lad. This your new lass?' he asked, smiling at Billie.

'DSI Billie Wilde,' Derek answered, 'she's my old boss in the force, Wilf. That's before I became a free man.' Derek chuckled again.

'A copper?' The old man looked Billie up and down. 'You're joking. They don't make them like they used to. You can arrest me anytime, love,' he added. *Quite the wag*, Billie mused.

'Have you told her about those kids on bikes hanging around here at all times of the night then?' Wilf asked Derek.

'She's murder squad, mate–' Derek started, before Billie butt in.

'Little kids or big kids?' she asked.

'Teenagers,' Wilf answered. 'Mouthy with it. I always come down here to check up on my leeks last thing at night. They're prize-winning. Don't want anyone doing any damage.'

'Don't worry, I'll keep an eye out for them now I've got time on my hands.' Derek rolled his eyes at Billie as Wilf headed on his way to his own allotment. 'He bloody sleeps with those vegetables of his, leading up to the Leek Show,' Derek complained. It was at that moment Billie's phone rang. It was Boo on the line.

'Are you on your way back to base?' Boo asked.

'I can be.' Billie pulled an apologetic face to Derek before she started to march back to her car. 'What's up?' She could hear the tension in Boo's voice.

'News. It's not good,' came the reply.

Student Burns to Death, whilst Police Party. The headline was printed in large letters on the front page of the evening edition of the *Herald*.

'Perry Gooch,' Billie snapped, flinging the newspaper onto the Formica table of the police canteen.

'Eat. You need sugar. It gets worse.' Boo nodded to a large slice of cake and a mug of tea on Billie's place. She took a bite, flicked to page two. A full-page photo of Derek Blythe, holding Kat the dog, stared out. *Retired police officer risks own life to drag dog and victim from the flames*, read the headline printed below it.

'Everyone who witnessed it said it was *you* who did that. Trust Derek Blythe to want to take centre stage,' Boo pointed out angrily. Billie relaxed a little, taking a swig of her tea.

'That's no big deal,' she answered. 'It's just a reporting cock-up. Anyway, I don't begrudge Derek his moment in the limelight. He deserves it, having missed out on his big goodbye party. If he'd been standing in the wrong place it could have turned out to be his wake.' Billie glanced at the front page again. 'It's this that maddens me.' She nodded at the headline.

'Wait until you see the centre-page spread,' Boo answered cautiously. Billie was unable to avoid the obscenity that sprang from her lips as she found the middle pages. Photos were arranged across both left and right and she was the subject of each and every one.

Head of Investigation More Interested in Chasing Men than Catching Murderers.

To Billie's fury, the first photo showed Billie outside of her new home, next to Max. He had brought flowers to place on her mother's grave, a former patient of his. The photo made it look as though they were on a date and he was handing the flowers to Billie. *DSI Billie Wilde in Secret Meeting with Dashing Criminal Psychologist*, ran the caption underneath the picture.

The next photo made Billie's blood boil further. It appeared to have been taken by Perry Gooch on her way out of the ladies' bathroom, on the night of the Community Awards ceremony. From the angle of the shot, Billie, dressed in a glamorous gown, appeared to have her head close to Josh Hallows as he whispered his knowledge of the first two murders to her. *Detective's Secret Liaison with A Young Boy, Caught on Camera. He was Mysteriously Murdered Less than 24hrs Later*, ran the caption underneath.

The third photo had been taken at the pub, just as Billie had arrived for Derek Blythe's farewell party, as Ellis had welcomed her with a quip and a silly dance. *Wilde by Name, Wilde by Nature, Dancing with a Mystery Man as A Young Girl Cries for Help.*

The final photo showed Billie rushing away with Ash on hearing news of Jas's robbery. *The Cop-Out. Leaving the Scene of Crime with a Fellow Detective, Rumoured to be Seeking a Divorce.*

Billie crumpled the newspaper up and pulled out her phone, furiously punching numbers into it.

'What the hell do you think you're playing at?' Billie had hit the phone loudspeaker in her race to vent her anger. The rest of the police canteen customers fell silent.

'Have you called to congratulate me on my fantastic news spread, DSI Wilde?' Perry Gooch sounded like the cat that had got the cream.

'Distortions and downright lies,' Billie answered forcefully. 'My team are working above and beyond on these cases. I won't have you discredit their professionalism in your joke of a rag.'

'The local people deserve to read the news and be briefed on how it affects them, officer,' Perry Gooch answered.

'Your readers rightly deserve the truth, not utter garbage dreamed up inside of your sad little mind.'

'Scandal sells, detective. If it doesn't bleed, it doesn't lead. Welcome to the real world. Our customers don't want truth. They want sex and drugs and rock 'n' roll. That's what I give them. Nobody cares if you are all dossing down on the office floor all night, because you are so hard at work you can't fit in home time. They want tittle-tattle and horror. I guess you're upset about your own centre-page spread. You might live like the virgin martyr, for all I care, but truth counts for nothing. Sleaze sells. End of.'

'Is that a fact?' Billie gave Perry Gooch a moment to answer.

'It's the truth, m'Lord.' Perry Gooch was on a cocky, confident roll now. 'Arrest me for it.'

'Straight from the horse's mouth. I've just recorded that on my phone by the way and I will be making sure all of the local TV and radio news channels are playing our cosy little chat tonight. Have fun down at the job centre, amigo.' Billie clicked her phone off.

A round of applause and cheers went around from the

listening police personnel in the canteen. Billie tucked back into her cake, winking at Boo.

'I'll get on to the news stations right now.' Boo grinned.

'Thanks. I'm hoping that's finally killed off the Gooch.' Billie finished her tea and stuffed down the last crumbs of cake.

'Now let's get back to work.'

'Ma'am, you'll never believe this,' Jo Green began, the moment Billie and Boo appeared in the doorway. She had never seen Jo look so animated.

'I already don't believe it. I've never seen you look so excited before, unless you're just suffering from wind,' Billie teased. Jo quickly reined in her show of enthusiasm as Billie joined her at her desk. The young detective immediately started running CCTV footage pulled in from the area around the pub from the night before.

A man suddenly appeared hazily in shot, looking decidedly shifty. He had a bottle in his hand. As he moved nearer to the camera he stopped, took a lighter from his pocket and lit a rag which appeared to have been protruding from the mouth of the bottle. As flames immediately started to lick up the cloth, he swung his arm and lobbed the bottle through the window, glass smashing everywhere. Then he sprinted off across the road.

'There's our man. Wish this was a bit clearer.'

'Your wish, ma'am, is my command,' Jo answered. Billie clocked the new, more confident air in Jo's voice, no doubt in part to Billie having been the one to have recommended her to the chief, for promotion.

'This is from a dashboard camera in parking mode. Driver handed it in just now. Bit miffed that the rest of her car is now a burnt-out shell.' Jo made a final click and a much clearer picture filled the screen. The man loomed clearly into view as he ran across the road and in front of the car, having started the blaze.

'You are joking...' Billie breathed out in disbelief. 'Run it again,' she requested, stepping aside so that Boo had a better view.

'Josh Hallows' dad?' Boo announced.

'Clear as day,' Jo confirmed, as the MIT team gathered around, and she played the footage for a third time.

'Time to pay daddy dearest a little visit.' Billie flicked her head towards the exit. Jo grabbed her jacket. 'Boo, can you ensure that this is preserved, copied and that Exhibits have the original?' she called over her shoulder, already moving off.

'Will do.' Boo looked uncharacteristically forlorn. 'After all, I'm not going anywhere else, am I?' She sighed heavily.

'That's one person I wouldn't have had top of my tick list as a killer. Good work.' The car turned into the street where Josh Hallows had grown up. Perusing CCTV was often a soul-destroying job and most of the team would have been happy to palm it off onto one of the interns, such as Milly Lloyd.

Billie felt sad that people were already talking about the student in the past tense. No one had been able to pinpoint what, exactly, she had discovered via CCTV just before her own death. Billie made a mental note to ask Derek Blythe to rack his brains when she next popped into his allotment for a cuppa. She hoped that Milly might have shared a juicy piece of intel with him, without his having registered the significance earlier.

'Do you think that Rick Hallows could be the Mr Big we're looking for, ma'am?' Jo pulled into the driveway of a large smart house in an exclusive side of town.

'Certainly looks like he enjoys living the high life, but I can't imagine him killing his son. Josh appeared to have been the apple of his eye.' Billie looked around the manicured lawns and smart garden furniture. Her own family home had presented a similar vision of middle-class English respectability. It had all been smoke and mirrors in her case, so who really knew the truth of what went on behind closed doors with the Hallows family?

'Also, most Mr Bigs have other people doing their dirty work.' She saw a picture in her mind's eye of Ricky Hallows hurling the Molotov cocktail through the pub window. There was no denying he had done the deed, but had Josh been trying to tell Billie that his father had been involved in the other murders?

The front door was already opening as Billie and Jo alighted from the car. Josh Hallows' mother stood at the top of the stone steps, a painfully thin, frail woman who appeared to be utterly bereft. She was twisting and untwisting a lace-edged handkerchief in her hand.

'Mrs Lydia Hallows? DSI Billie Wilde.' Billie showed her identity card. 'Can we come in for a chat?'

'I'm normally making Josh's tea at this time. He's usually coming home from school now,' was all the devastated woman could mutter, as Billie and Jo followed her along the hall into the living room.

The whole place was filled with the heady perfume of lilies due to the endless sympathy bouquets placed all around. Billie imagined every vase in the house had been called in to do duty. Jo started sneezing. She dug in her pockets for a tissue.

'Sorry. Hay fever, ma'am,' she whispered. Even Billie's eyes were smarting. The neat and tidy room was empty, save for that evening's edition of the news with the damning headline. Billie blocked it from her mind. At least Perry Gooch hadn't been sitting on the sofa with the bereaved parents today. She chose to be grateful for small mercies.

'Mr Hallows around?' Billie enquired. Josh's mum wiped away a tear trickling down her cheek with the scrunched-up handkerchief.

'He's not in, I'm afraid. Perhaps you could come back later?' Billie noticed an almost imperceptible guilty glance to the left from Josh's mother.

'We can wait. Has he gone far?' *On the run for example?* The words ran through her mind, unspoken.

'He's in the garden, doing some work. Anything to take his mind off things. I'll go and get him–' She suddenly started to bolt off in the direction of the back of the house. Billie's 'there's a rabbit off' detector, went on red alert. She was across the room in two strides and following fast in Lydia Hallows' footsteps with Jo close behind her. A long corridor opened out into a vast kitchen. Through the open door, Billie spotted movement at the very end of the long back garden, next to a shed.

'I'll go.' She blocked the grieving mother. 'DS Green, would you make Mrs Hallows a cuppa? I'll be back in a mo.'

She moved out through the back door, pulling it closed behind her. The smell of fragrant flowers was immediately replaced by that of smoke. It was coming from a bonfire that Billie could now see was being stoked by Ricky Hallows. He was turning into quite the pyromaniac, Billie noted.

The smoke had an acrid edge, rather than the sweet aroma of burning wood, leading Billie to quicken her pace. She was well aware that grief could affect people in all sorts of unexpected ways but bearing in mind the recent death of his beloved son, she couldn't really believe that his father had nothing more pressing on his mind than getting rid of random garden rubbish or toasting marshmallows around the garden bonfire. Could he, instead, be set on cremating a hot potato – crucial evidence, perhaps?

'Mr Hallows,' Billie started, before spotting a pile of appropriately named 'burner' mobile phones in the centre of the fire. She decided to cut to the chase.

'I'm arresting you on suspicion of arson–' she started, a split second before Ricky Hallows grabbed a shovel from the burning fire and swung it over his head, bringing it down hard on Billie. She shouted out with pain due to the unexpected ferocity of the attack and the excruciating heat of the metal against her hand, her reflexes having caused her to cover her skull a split second before the shovel made contact. Right now, she fought back, hanging on to Ricky Hallows' arm as she attempted to reach for her handcuffs, damning her injured hand for refusing to work properly.

Suddenly he kicked out hard with a heavy boot, knocking Billie's legs away from her on the uneven ground and onto the edge of the fire, before racing to the back fence and scrambling over. Jo, who had witnessed the attack, hurtled over to Billie, rolling her on the damp grass to put out the smouldering embers that were clinging to her jacket.

'Never mind me, put the bonfire out. Looks like he's trying to destroy incriminating materials.' Billie rolled onto her knees and pulled herself upright, before hurling her body up against the tall fence to give chase. She had almost scrambled to the top, before swearing in agony as her burned and mangled hand caught on a trim of barbed wire. Beyond, lay an open stretch of countryside, heavy with trees, Ricky Hallows was nowhere to be seen.

Billie dropped to the ground, radioing for backup to search for the runaway, before retreating to the house and propelling Lydia Hallows onto a kitchen chair.

'Right. What's the story? Either tell me now, or I'm hauling you off to the station. We can do it either way.' Josh's mum was almost hysterical now. Billie tried to calm herself down, despite her nerves being on edge with pain. On closer scrutiny, it was clear that the woman was extremely ill as well as totally distressed.

'Your hand, let me run it under water,' Lydia sobbed.

'Stay right where you are.' Billie wasn't taking any other chances with Josh Hallows' relatives, remembering that Ricky had also appeared to be completely harmless. She took a few steps to the sink and ran the cold tap over her throbbing hand as she spoke.

'We have CCTV footage of your husband throwing a Molotov cocktail through the window of the pub last night. One of my intern officers, a student only four years older than Josh, lost her life, so don't waste your sympathy on me. Think of her poor parents. God knows if anyone should understand their grief, you should. Now spill.'

'Ricky was upset about the party and so was I, when the police should have been looking for my son's murderer!' Her thin voice had an edge of defiance, through the tears. 'Just look at the papers,' she added.

'I wouldn't believe anything you read in *that* comic.' Billie damned Perry Gooch again, before remembering that news of Derek's private leaving do hadn't been public knowledge before the arson attack. Who exactly had given that information to Ricky Hallows?

'Who told him about the leaving event, which, by the way, was for an exceptionally long-serving and deserving officer? In fact, the same person who visited you with the news of Josh's death,' Billie demanded. Josh's mum twisted her handkerchief again, aghast.

'I see that now. He saved that dog and tried to save the girl...' Josh's mum started crying again.

'Did DS Blythe mention the event when he visited?' The thought came into Billie's mind as the only way that Ricky Hallows could have possibly been aware of the party. But she dismissed the idea even before she got an answer, deciding that even Dexie wouldn't be crass enough to mention his own leaving party at a time when he was breaking the news of their son's long goodbye.

'The note that came with the bottle,' Lydia Hallows whispered. 'I was in such a state when I found it on the doorstep. I just thought that one of the neighbours had left it as a gift.' She trailed off.

'The bottle with the firebomb in it?' Billie forged on.

'I had no idea.' She pushed the well-pummelled handkerchief up to her mouth as though to prevent herself from being sick. 'But Ricky was already in a terrible state and when he read the card that came attached to it, I think he just saw red–'

'A card?' Billie cut in. 'Do you still have it?' she demanded.

'Yes, um, Ricky dropped it on the floor as he rushed out.' She stood up and went over to the kitchen dresser. Billie followed. 'This is it.' Billie stopped Lydia Hallows from touching the card again. She reached for an evidence bag from her pocket as the writing started to come into focus, swallowing hard. She had seen the same scribble before, attached to wild red roses, rather than Molotov cocktails, noted the spelling of the repetitive word and its personal meaning to her.

A Wilde night is in store as murder police dance on your son's grave.

Your child's death already forgotten. His life means nothing.

The Wilde Wake will be in full swing tonight at 7pm.

Billie read the address of the pub clearly outlined below. A fire rose in her belly. She vowed that she would catch this bastard if it was the last thing she ever did.

19

MADMAN CRAZY BAD

'That looks nasty.' Max was entering the hospital, just as Billie was finally leaving, leading her to silently whistle 'Hallelujah'. There must be a god after all.

'Not as bad as it looks.' Billie had lied. The nurse had likened her left hand to a tin of badly opened corned beef, swollen and burnt, with additional shards of glass from the floor of the pub, already starting to fester. 'Nothing broken and I've been given piles of drugs. Everyone's taking them these days, don't you know?' she quipped. Not that she would be taking any of the prescribed painkillers. She liked to be in control at all times.

Having waited an hour to be attended to, she'd popped her head in on Stan to assure him that Kat was being well cared for. It seemed ages since she had shared that slice of cake with Boo.

'Fancy a cuppa?' she asked Max, not only because she wanted to pick his professional brains.

'Sorry, got a patient conference in five minutes.' He smiled. 'Anything pressing?' *I wish*, Billie silently answered.

'Just wanted a professional perspective on a specific sort of psycho I'm investigating.' Billie didn't want him getting ideas that she was making a play for him. She wasn't, was she? Damn it, she really *did* need some advice, her inner angel argued with her inner devil. Max's eyes lit up. As chat-up lines went, Billie mused, mention a psycho to a criminal psychologist and bingo, you were quids in.

'You know I'm always here to help you, Billie.' Max stretched out his hand and touched her arm. It felt like an electric shock, but she wasn't planning to let him see the sparks.

'Yeah, well, this time *I'm* not your psycho.' She referred to their original meeting when she had been sent for counselling and had fought tooth and nail against his suggestions.

'Got any expertise in stalkers at all?' Billie asked. Max's face darkened.

'You've got a stalker mixed up in your murder investigations?' he queried.

'Inadvertently, I'm guessing. Probably not linked to the murders at all but targeting one of the investigating officers...' Billie felt her face flush in annoyance.

'You're not the target?' he asked, his brow furrowing in concern. Billie shrugged.

'I'm told that my team nickname is Kevlar, so I'm pretty bulletproof. But any tips to help me catch the latest brand of crazy, would be appreciated,' she answered.

'There are many different types of stalkers, Billie, but they're notoriously difficult to stop. Sometimes interventions work for a while and then the stalking flares up at times of stress. You don't think that they were involved with the petrol bomb–'

'Forget it. I'll be fine.' Billie cut him off mid-sentence. She didn't like the look of absolute alarm on his face. Maybe he thought that she was too weak to handle such a challenge. Not like his still much loved and very dead wife who had hung around minefields in war zones, saving people. There was absolutely no competition with that, Billie reminded herself.

'Wait!' Max had speedily backtracked and was now blocking

Billie's exit route. 'If you are around tomorrow night, I have a regular group for women who are dealing with stalkers.' Billie shook her head in surprise.

'What? Like other people go to slimming clubs?' Billie answered, once again making a flippant remark on serious matters, lest anyone see a chink in her armour.

'You don't need to worry, Billie,' he answered perceptively. 'These are normal women, who are dealing with an extraordinary situation.'

'Lola told me about Josta and your old teacher...' Billie needed to know which of his mothers she had to be wary of, if either. He shrugged the comment away.

'Lola tends to overdramatise things,' he explained. 'Like, she's always lamenting to anyone who will listen, that I'm closer to Josta than her, despite my having inherited her genes.' His insight made Billie wonder if that idea could have made Lola wound up enough to persuade someone to firebomb a pub, with both of them in it? She shook the idea aside. She wasn't thinking straight. Truth was that she never could when Max was in her immediate vicinity.

'Josta simply had the sort of crush many people secretly have on someone unsuitable...' Max paused for a moment, looking at Billie. She flushed. '...It happened at a stressful time. Their relationship was at a low point and I got caught up in the crossfire. Straight couples don't have the monopoly on sporadically dysfunctional partnerships after all.' He smiled. 'I'm sure your stalker isn't my mother if that's what's worrying you.'

Billie sighed. Josta had been in The Cop-Out at the moment when the firebomb had burst through the window, hadn't she? Certainly, she had been inside moments before, though she seemed to have made it out to her seat on the wall quickly enough. Still, Billie decided, it was madness on her part to have been suspicious of such a dear friend in the first place. She guessed that her constant re-evaluation of relationships came down to her own family background.

'Unfortunately, your job means that you're very likely to have had dealings with someone with stalking tendencies. Maybe helped convict them for an unrelated crime. You are quite high profile, in court, in newspapers...'

Billie knew he was right; she'd already racked her brains on those types of contacts. It just creeped her out that whoever was following her seemed to know where she was going to be almost before she had thought of it herself, hence her suspicions about those closest to her.

'Come along to the meeting. You'll learn a lot – about stalkers and how to live with them, because believe me, some people have been stalked for all of their adult lives.'

'And they don't report it?' Billie frowned in disbelief.

'It's not as easy as that, Billie. Come along. It will be a real eye-opener.'

Billie felt the tension between her shoulders ease. Maybe she had been more spooked out than she had even admitted to herself by the stalking situation? One thing was for sure, after the appalling fire and resulting death of a young woman, she couldn't afford to laugh off the situation anymore.

'Okay then. I will.' Billie watched Max as he took out a pen and scribbled down the address, breathing in the hint of lemon cologne that signified his nearness to her, taking the opportunity to drink in the view for the brief moments his concentration was elsewhere.

'Thanks.' She took the piece of paper and attempted to walk off nonchalantly.

'Billie.' Max touched her wrist. 'We could have dinner together afterwards if you would like?' Billie did like. But she had no intention of reacting like a stammering schoolgirl.

'Cool,' she answered. 'Where?'

'How about my place?' Max looked her straight in the eye and held her gaze.

'Okay. See you tomorrow.' Billie shrugged as she agreed, walking casually away through the exit doors, whilst mentally screaming a loud cheer of delight and disbelief. Maybe this was the opportunity for them both to finally lay their ghosts to rest?

She was still going over the conversation, whilst trying to remember where she had stuffed the beautiful oyster silk underwear, meant to be worn on her wedding night that never was, when she unclicked the lock on her car door and caught the handle with her bandaged hand.

She pulled it away quickly. Her pristine white dressing was covered in dog dirt that had been smeared on the underside of the handle. Billie looked quickly around. There was no one who looked like a madman or a monster staring at her, but maybe her stalker had followed her here and been watching all the time?

As she opened the door, grabbing some tissues from the glove compartment to wipe away the pungent-smelling filth, Billie tried to reason with herself that, bearing in mind no rose or note had been delivered with this latest unwanted gift, it could have been the work of a member of the public, who had spotted her in A&E, recognised her from the damning newspaper report and made their own judgement on her quite clear.

But all the same, before climbing into the car, Billie checked the back seat and then locked the doors firmly behind her before driving away. There was something about this stalker that was seriously starting to get under her skin.

'I wouldn't,' Billie replied to the man holding out his hand as Billie swept through the doors of reception at police HQ.

'DSI Wilde.' The chief was standing next to the loathsome newspaper proprietor, Lance Harris, who Billie guessed had hotfooted it over in response to Billie's recorded conversation with Perry Gooch. Boo had texted Billie to say that it had been playing out all night on the local TV and radio news.

'Lance has come over to offer an apology for the spread in the paper. I explained that such stories can only act as a distraction to the investigations,' the chief explained. Lance Harris smiled, like a wily cat. It didn't reach his eyes.

'Apologies if today's editorial upset your equilibrium, DSI Wilde.' Lance Harris humoured the chief. They were probably regular golfing buddies. 'The staff member responsible has been dismissed with immediate effect,' he added.

'Only one?' Billie replied. He must have thought she was born yesterday. She was no fan of Perry Gooch, but the journalist would have had to get her tall tales past at least one editor and probably the proprietor himself, as he was here in town. A huge spread such as the one in that night's newspaper, didn't just jump into print without some high-level go-ahead.

'As way of making amends' – Billie noted that Lance Harris was glancing towards the chief not her – 'we're planning to launch a competition with a bursary as a prize. "Fund a bobby to make it onto the beat". A great tribute to the young lady who sadly didn't make it. Name the award after her... Myra was it, or Mabel?'

Billie couldn't believe that the chief was falling for the utter garbage coming out of the man's mouth.

'We'll run a centre-page spread. Explain how she harboured a dream from childhood to join the force and fight crime. Interview her grieving family. Show that through our bursary, her spirit will live on. I'm sure it will draw a lot of sympathy from the public for the police.'

Thereby getting more mileage from the tragedy. Billie silently fumed. She wanted to punch him in his smarmy face – with the hand still reeking of dog dirt. Instead, she started heading for the stairs. It was bad enough to have crap on her hand, she wasn't in the mood for a particularly odious lump of talking shit to be anywhere near her shoes.

'I've told Mr Harris we'll join him for drinks tomorrow night. We can talk over the campaign. Make sure that we're all on the same page this time,' the chief called after Billie.

'I'm busy,' Billie argued. It was true, but even if it hadn't been she would rather have put her own eyes out with sharp sticks than take up the chief's offer.

'That's an order, Billie. Six pm sharp. Delegate any clashing duties.' His face brooked no argument, even from his darling goddaughter. Billie damned him, then swore aloud as she reached the top of the stairs. The thought had just hit her like a brick that she was meant to be having her dream date with Max tomorrow night.

'Fuck!' she swore again to no one in particular.

'Is that an offer or has something upset you?' Ellis wandered over to Billie, appearing amused at the sight of her marching along in full strop mode. 'We've been waiting for you with bated breath. Guess who we've got in custody, desperate to whisper sweet nothings in our ears?'

'Ricky Hallows?' Billie's spirits lifted immediately.

'Got it in one.' He looked at his watch. 'In five minutes, if you're ready.' He pulled a pained face. 'Better wash your hands first though, ma'am.' He nipped his nose then grinned as he walked off. Boo had been watching from her workstation.

'Has he not outlived his usefulness yet?' Boo nodded towards Ellis as he disappeared through the door. Billie wondered what exactly had gone on between those two in the past. She really enjoyed having him around. He was fun, not bad-looking and totally brilliant at his job.

'Don't be so hard on him, Boo. I think he cheers the place up.' Billie perched on the side of Boo's desk.

'I can get you a bunch of flowers for the room if that's all you want.' Billie thought of the dead flower deliveries of late. They definitely didn't bring out her jolly side.

'Any intel on the card sent with the bottle to Ricky Hallows yet?' Billie asked.

'Nothing so far, other than to point out that it isn't handwriting. It's computer generated and the paper is bog standard. No prints.' She shivered. 'It looks like the same person who left the note with the rose, in my kitchen.' Boo was suddenly distracted, reaching for a perfumed room spray on her desk and squirting it in Billie's direction. 'What sort of burn ointment are they using in hospitals nowadays?' Boo wrinkled her nose.

'Hand me the medical box.' Billie unwound the soiled bandage and dropped it in a bin. Boo found a suitable replacement in the emergency container kept in her cupboard, before meticulously wiping the wound clean and starting to re-bandage Billie's hand.

'Looks painful,' Boo soothed, as she wound the bandage.

'Your relationship with Ellis?' Billie chose to misunderstand. 'It sure does. Perhaps some healing is required.' Boo continued to wind and pin the bandage on Billie's hand, before she finally spoke.

'We worked together. Way back when I had legs. Undercover, investigating extremists then, rather than drug dealers.' Billie had always been full of admiration for Boo's strength of character. Now she realised that her UCO training was probably responsible for her being able to operate even under the toughest of conditions.

'So what went wrong?' Those sorts of relationships were often closer than marriages, Billie reflected, her mind turning to Ash for a moment. She could feel the sadness radiating from Boo.

'Yep. We always had each other's backs. But then one day, we didn't...' Billie was about to ask more, when Jo popped her head around the door.

'Ready for you in the custody suite, ma'am,' she called.

'Off you go for your close-up, Mrs DeMille.' Boo nodded to the door. 'Excitement's that way.' Boo looked back at her work and continued typing.

Billie had no option but to drop the conversation, for the time being anyway. But she decided that the sad Cinderella persona didn't sit well with her normally upbeat friend and colleague. Boo was making it clear that she wasn't having a ball anymore. Billie headed off down the corridor, determined to turn her back into the feisty warrior princess that the team knew and loved so well.

'What you speaking on, madman crazy bad?'

Billie raised her eyebrows and looked at Ellis. He was running an earlier taped interview with Razor, one of the Drill gang members featured in the video performance on Sophie Grey's mobile, before they headed in to interview Josh Hallows' father in person.

'Pray tell, what are you insinuating, my deluded friend. Are you stupid?' Ellis kindly offered in translation. The young man wasn't looking as cool now that he was ensconced in a police interview suite, rather than posing on the street with his mates.

'It's mostly no comments thanks to advice from his brief, but he did have the odd moment of clarity. Might be one or two juicy bits of intel...' Ellis ran the tape forward. Frankly, Billie had never been great at languages. Though she had managed to keep up with Chip Little earlier, she felt fortunate to have an Undy, as Ellis and his colleagues were known when they were undercover on the street, alongside her. They made it a key part of their jobs to be fluent. After all, their lives depended on it.

'Skunk bitch. Patty. Sooljah of the Beast,' the Drill star spat out. Even Billie understood that he wasn't complimenting poor Sophie Grey.

'He's claiming that Sophie was clueless. Working for someone called the Beast. Name fits the Lucifer line brand. Might be our man,' Ellis explained hopefully. 'Could also be that he's simply trying to distance himself and lay the blame on a rival dealer,' he added, running the footage forward again. 'This bit might be interesting...'

'Her old man licky, licky with the snow and the crazy weed. Wasteman! Bitch lurk. We chirp some at the rents.'

'That may as well be Martian-speak.' Billie shook her head, befuddled.

'He's basically arguing that he simply talked to Sophie at her dad's house when he was doing a personal drugs delivery and thereafter, she tagged along.'

'Drugs delivery to *Sophie's dad*?' Billie couldn't believe what she was hearing. 'You are joking!'

'Heard it from the horse's mouth. Seems that he can't get enough of cocaine and marijuana. Our friend, Razor, isn't a fan of his.'

'Think we'll be visiting our distinguished keyboard player first thing.' Billie looked at the clock. Another late night. 'But time to hear what our other favourite daddy has to say, first.'

❄

'Sorry about your hand.' Ricky Hallows, dishevelled and distraught, looked up at Billie as she entered the custody suite and went through the preliminaries to the interview.

'Frankly, I'm more concerned about the agony that you inflicted on Milly Lloyd leading up to her death.' Billie got a sudden glimpse of the seriously burned young intern lying on the hard ground of the pub car park, when the countdown to the tragic end of her life had already begun. It was followed by another, of her already half cremated body being carved up in Josta's mortuary. 'Not to mention the eternal torment to her parents.'

'You don't need to tell me about pain!' Ricky Hallows writhed in his chair. 'I might as well be dead myself. What's the point of going on without my beautiful boy?' He started to cry. Billie pushed the tissue box, always in the middle of the table in the custody suite, towards him.

'Are you also known as the Beast, Mr Hallows, running the Lucifer drugs line, by any chance?' Ellis Darque didn't waste time with niceties. Ricky Hallows looked absolutely astonished.

'What do you take me for?' he answered, aghast. 'I don't know anything about drugs. Why don't you try and find the killer of my boy, instead of asking me absurd questions?' He looked at his defence solicitor for support.

'Because you're a killer of a girl, as I've just outlined.' Billie began to think that the lights were on, but nobody was home with this man.

'I didn't mean to hurt anyone...' He held his forehead in despair. 'But when that note came, I just saw red, and the bottle was literally handed to me on a plate.'

'Any idea who gave you that?' Billie persisted. She knew his wife's version of the story. Now she wanted to see if his tallied.

'The wife brought it in. It had just been left on the step... we thought by one of the neighbours...' He trailed off.

'Nice neighbours you've got, mate. Do they regularly pop round with Molotov cocktails? Mine just knock to ask for the odd cup of sugar,' Ellis chipped in.

Ricky Hallows blinked, as though the enormity of his actions was just now sinking in. Billie concentrated on his reactions. Had her stalker been responsible for a normally sane man cracking at a time of immense stress, or was the person sitting across the table putting on a performance worthy of an Oscar?

'You're an engineer, Mr Hallows?' Ellis cut across Billie's thoughts.

'Yes,' Ricky Hallows answered. 'Josh was hoping to follow in my footsteps. It's a solid career,' he added, not quite realising that he had no chance of ever returning to it, as a result of his crime.

'I believe you've worked in South America?' Billie had to hand it to Ellis. He hadn't been putting his feet up whilst she'd been out of the office. He'd done his homework.

'Yes, Brazil... a couple of times.' Ricky Hallows shrugged. 'But I don't see what–'

'So you'll be aware that South America is one of the biggest exporters of cocaine in the world?'

'It's also a major exporter of oil and I work for oil companies, not drug cartels. Are you lot still drunk? No wonder the paper felt the need to alert the public! When are you going to apprehend the killer of my boy?' Billie warned herself not to rise against the accusation.

'Can you explain the pile of pay-as-you-go phones that you were intent on burning on your bonfire yesterday? The type of burner phones, if you'll pardon the pun, that are used extensively in county lines drug dealing?' Billie's voice was steely. Ricky Hallows looked at his solicitor in exasperation.

'I was having a clear-out. Do you know what it's like to have one of your family murdered and another suffering from a terminal illness?' Ricky Hallows bent over the table towards Billie, angry and agitated. She decided not to go there with an answer, out of respect for Lydia Hallows, her frailty now explained. She had no doubt who would win the competition between the two of them for most family members murdered, however, and it wasn't the man glaring at her right now. 'I needed something to take my mind off the horror of it all,' he added.

'That doesn't explain the number of phones you seem to have accumulated in a family of, what? Three people?' Ellis kept up the pressure.

'My wife asked me to clear them away. We'd encouraged Josh to set up a little online business selling kids' stuff. Games, gadgets, phones. Gear that teenagers want. It started off as a school project in his business studies class. He won an award for making the most money with his online sales idea.' He hung his head sadly.

'Josh was always a winner. The wife went a bit crazy to be honest, emptying his stuff out when he's still not cold in a grave... said I had to face it, he's never coming back. She's had trouble dealing with the latest prognosis and now this...' The big man started crying again. 'My darling boy. I didn't want her to throw all of his things away. Maybe I thought that a miracle would happen, that it had all been some sort of mistake and that he'd turn up on the doorstep, say, "Where's all my stuff?" She's always tidying... highly strung... kept nagging me, even before she became ill. Then when the bottle and card turned up, I don't know, I just cracked.' He was suddenly silent for a moment. 'That poor, poor girl.' He shuddered, a look of utter horror on his face.

'What do you think?' Billie asked Ellis, as they wound up their interview and Ricky Hallows was led back to his cell.

'Doesn't strike me as our man, to be honest. Just a guy who's gone out of his mind with grief. I've got a kid myself and if I'd thought the cop shop was in party mode when her killer was on the loose, I'd probably firebomb the gaff as well. Especially if some wind-up merchant was egging me on with a readily primed firework,' Ellis answered. 'You notice the spelling on the note, right?'

'Yep. I'm well aware that my name was on the firearm that killed her.' Billie should have guessed that such a detail wouldn't have got past him.

'Well, you've got one major fruitcake to worry about there. Got rid of any dicey boyfriends recently?' Ellis teased.

'Yeah. But I managed to get him murdered, so unless he's coming back to haunt me, I can tick that one off the list.' She walked away, leaving Ellis totally dumbstruck.

20

NEVER BE TOO CAREFUL

It was nearly midnight when Billie walked through the almost empty corridors of Police Headquarters and started down the curved staircase towards the exit. She had considered asking Boo if she could doss down at her place again, rather than start on her long journey home under some of the darkest skies in the world, but Boo was now long gone, it seemed.

'You must be the last two left.' Daz, the security guard, rattled his keys as Ellis appeared from the lower corridor.

'Just making sure all the interview tapes are shipshape,' he called to Billie. 'Look at the time. If you're not careful, you'll lose those glass slippers, Cinderella.' He pointed to Billie's hefty combat boots, as he pulled his hood up and his scarf around his face.

'Feeling the cold?' Billie asked. She recalled that it had seemed quite mild outside earlier.

'Can never be too careful in the vicinity of the cop shop,' he answered. Billie was well aware that he had only recently been undercover on next door's patch. She guessed it made sense to take extra precautions. She suddenly thought of her stalker and shivered, wondering whether she should, perhaps, take a leaf out of Ellis Darque's book herself?

'I've got a fake moustache and beard in my bag, if you don't think you've done a good enough job,' she teased, as they approached the exit door, alluding to the fact that only his eyes remained uncovered.

'Kinky.' He chuckled. 'Playing the man about the house tonight?' he quipped as they split and went in their separate directions.

Billie couldn't understand why Boo had such a downer on Ellis. She, for one, was enjoying the easy camaraderie and upbeat air he added to the investigation. He was a grafter too. She would happily jump at any opportunity to have him on her team full time.

'Are you all right?' Billie could see a young woman wearing a hooded jacket, loitering by the bottom of the stone staircase leading from the exit door.

'Yeah. Just wondering if you could post this on your noticeboard, please? I'm looking for work as a nanny. Uni holidays,' she added, smiling.

Billie noticed the girl's large amber eyes and tawny afro, thinking that she was probably the most stunning beauty that she had ever set eyes on. She took the hand-printed card from the girl and ran back up the steps, asking Daz to pin it on the staff board outside of the canteen. The hours worked by most of the police teams meant that someone was certain to take up the offer.

'Thanks.' The girl smiled as Billie ran back down the steps. Billie couldn't help noting again that she was a real eye-catcher, even dressed down in the uniform of every student.

'I'm sure someone will give you a job. Everyone neglects their kids in this place,' Billie joked. 'Need a lift, Maya?' Billie asked, having clocked the girl's name, Maya Sands, printed on the advert. She felt slightly uneasy about the youngster roaming the streets at night alone.

'Cool. I just live at the top of the town,' she replied, as Billie led the way to her car.

'Hang on.' Billie got a tissue from her pocket and wiped the door handles. She wasn't about to fall for the dog shit scam again. 'What are you studying at uni?' she asked, so that she wouldn't be forced to explain what she was doing and why.

'Law,' Maya answered, as Billie opened the passenger door. Maya climbed inside and buckled up her seat belt. 'Well I will be. I'm starting at the end of summer.'

'Don't go for the policing side of it. Or you'll end up working these hours,' Billie answered as she climbed behind the wheel, nodding to the clock in the car which lit up as she started the engine. It was past midnight now.

'I wouldn't mind. My dad was in the force,' Maya answered. Not on her patch, Billie guessed. She couldn't think of anyone she'd ever known who could have passed on such perfect genes to the youngster. 'He hasn't been around for a long time now,' Maya whispered with a note of sadness in her voice. Billie felt for her, having recently lost her own father.

'My dad was a cop too. Gets in your blood it seems.'

'Well, I'd like to make a difference,' the girl answered shyly. Billie reckoned the youngster could probably make it as a top model if she wanted. It was nice to know that not every kid wanted to be an online influencer or TV celebrity. 'I've already got childcare qualifications so I can earn money whilst I'm studying,' she added.

Within ten minutes, Billie had dropped Maya off outside of the house that she had pointed out that she was staying in. Waving goodbye, Billie felt like a breath of fresh air had swept through her life, as the young student had chattered excitedly about her university plans. The upbeat feel of youthful new beginnings was welcome, after the tragically early demise of three of the murder victims that she was investigating. Billy watched in the back mirror until the girl had safely turned in to the pathway of the house. Her phone rang. It was Ash.

'Hey, sorry to ring so late, but if you are on your way back, might you stop by a night garage and pick up some milk?' He sounded exhausted, the baby crying in the background.

'No problem. On my way now,' Billie reassured him. 'Kids taken it out of you today?' she queried, well aware that he still wasn't back to full fitness after his recent extensive injuries. Billie reckoned that leading a murder investigation was much less stressful than managing three small kids and a giant bloodhound.

'It's just that the hospital has been in touch. There's been a case management review.'

Billie had a quick recollection of Max's mention of that same subject when she had met him at the hospital earlier. Had it been about Ash's wife, Jas? He *had* confided that she was a patient of his.

'Everything all right with Jas?' Billie asked. By the tone of her friend's voice, it didn't sound like good news.

'They want to send her to a place to recuperate...' Ash started. 'I never really mentioned, with everything else that was going on...' Ash hesitantly continued, aware that he was treading on painful ground for both of them, '...but after the baby, Jas suffered from terrible postnatal depression and, of course, my behaviour didn't help.'

'Ash, I've told you. There's no point in beating yourself up forever.' Billie sighed. 'We've all got to move on.' She had suffered more than most after all, but they had no option but to shuffle forward.

'Well, they think this latest episode, the drugging thing, has exacerbated her post-partum psychosis. She needs to go into a unit for treatment, so I've got the kids for a while longer.' He sounded worried.

'Well, that last bit is good news,' Billie reassured him. 'You can all stay for as long as you want,' she added. Ash and his kids were the closest she had to blood relatives after all. She loved having them around.

'Thanks, but I'm not sure I can manage, that's the thing.' Ash sounded pained. Billy thought of her new friend, Maya, looking for work as a nanny.

'I've got an idea. I'll run it by you when I get back. I think I might have found the answer,' she replied.

Billie turned the key in the car engine and drove off. Had she glanced back she might have caught sight of Maya, peeping around the hedge of the random house at which she had asked to be dropped off. She stepped out onto the pavement and walked away.

21

LIFE DECEASED

'I believe that this was the piece playing when she died. He just keeps on repeating it,' the woman whispered, as she opened the door from the huge hallway into the vast lounge of Rupert Grey's home. Billie presumed that this younger woman was the first violinist who had replaced Sophie Grey's mother in his affections. 'I'll fetch some tea,' she added quietly, padding away down the hall towards the kitchen.

'Pretty woman and talented, too, by all accounts.' Billie filled Ellis in. The usual preconceptions of the mistress in such scenarios, bored her rigid. Ellis peeped into the lounge and caught sight of Rupert Grey.

'Yep. Punching above his weight there,' Ellis agreed. 'Maybe that's why he's on the charlie,' he added.

The musician was playing his magnificent grand piano in front of the huge window overlooking Durham Cathedral, eyes closed, lost in thought. The poignant notes of the haunting piece of music filled the room as Billie and Ellis entered.

'Pavane pour une infante défunte.' He opened his eyes; they were brimful of tears. 'Pavane for a Dead Princess.' He looked from Billie to Ellis. 'You do know these were the last notes that she ever heard.'

'I do.' Billie had gone over the traumatised station piano player's full statement. However, by the time she had arrived at the tragic crime scene, a radio in one of the cafés was blasting out 'Be Young, Be Foolish, Be Happy', whilst Sophie was still lying in pieces on the tracks. Billie had demanded that they turn the damn thing off. She thought it best not to mention that. Let him live the fantasy of his daughter's tragic but romantic death – for a few more moments anyway.

'Got a little princess of my own,' Ellis said. 'Just a toddler, but I feel for you, sir.' He shook his head sadly. Billie remembered him on their very first meeting, recounted that he had gone so deeply undercover that his young daughter hadn't recognised him anymore. Nor had his wife. She had ended their marriage.

'Sophie was a magnificent pianist herself,' Rupert Grey added. 'The scum who did this should be wiped from the earth. Low lifes, taking such beauty from the world.' Billie had an uneasy feeling that at some level, despite being genuinely heartbroken for the loss of his daughter, Rupert Grey was getting high on the drama of it all. Once a performer, always a performer, she reflected.

'Sure thing,' Ellis confirmed. 'Total scum. We're onto it, sir.'

Billie took out a photograph of Razor, the Drill artist interviewed by Ellis the night before.

'Do you know this man, Mr Grey?' she asked. He glanced at the photo, blinked hard and then answered.

'Dear me, no. He doesn't look like the sort who mixes in our circles.' He sniffed as though a bad smell had been waved under his nose.

'Who's that, darling?' His new amour arrived carrying a tray of green tea and delicate macarons as though Billie and Ellis had called around for a soirée. Billie stepped in front of Rupert Grey, in order to prevent any chance of his affecting her reaction.

'This man.' She held up the photo, remembering she hadn't asked the young woman's name. 'Sorry, you are?'

'Ilaria. Rupert's partner.' The woman smiled as she offered the refreshments. Both Billie and Ellis declined.

'We think he might have known Sophie,' Billie continued. Ilaria placed the tray on the coffee table and looked at the photo, reacting with shock.

'But, darling, I think we *have* seen him–'

'Don't be ridiculous!' Rupert Grey snapped. Ilaria looked taken aback.

'I just thought...' She trailed off.

'It's very important that you tell us if you've had any dealings with this man or any of his associates.' Billie's voice was firm as she looked from one to the other of the two lovers. 'The information could help us find Sophie's killer and also help protect other innocent children.'

'Of course we haven't. He looks like a ruffian!' Rupert Grey's face flushed with anger, or panic, Billie wondered. Hard to tell, with low lifes.

'Ever taken drugs, Mr Grey?' Ellis finally gave in and scoffed a pink macaron from the plate as he perched against an arm of the sofa.

'History is full of outstanding musicians who used drugs to stimulate creation of some of the world's most famous pieces. It's not like Berlioz was down in the gutter robbing people when he used opium to create "Symphonie Fantastique".'

'That's some comparison, Mr Grey.' Billie raised her eyebrows.

'So you've never had a drink, DSI Wilde? You were plastered across the newspaper with a big glass of cheap-looking plonk in your hand yesterday. I didn't see any self-judgement with your choice of drug there.'

'Just answer the question.' Ellis's voice grew stern.

'I mean, who decides these things? Taken under controlled situations I believe that drugs can unleash inspiration. There's no harm involved. Not that I expect those of you in the *Gumshoe Gang* to comprehend the lives of those of us who are born to make magic.' Billie had heard enough.

'I understand the plight of children who have had their lives devastated having been coerced into county lines involvement, in order to deliver drugs to people just like you. Your daughter, Sophie, was one of those children. Where did her chance to make magic go? Up your nose perhaps?' Billie had finally wiped the superior look off Rupert Grey's face. Ellis took a swig of his cup of green tea and grimaced, regretting his second thoughts on accepting the refreshment.

'In fact, it might just be that she lost her life carrying cocaine or hash that would eventually make its way right back here to your door. You don't get an opt-out just because you can tinkle a few ivories,' Ellis added, still wincing with the taste of the tea. He nabbed another macaron to compensate.

'Tell them what you know, Rupert!' Ilaria suddenly sprang into action, no longer the genteel little mouse. 'I've seen that man here, hovering around the garden. I know you've had dealings with him. Think of Sophie!'

'She's talking nonsense. I'm phoning my lawyer.' Rupert Grey marched across the room. Ilaria only looked torn for a moment before she rushed across to the piano and lifted the lid.

'It's here.' She waved to a large bundle of drugs in a clear bag hidden inside, much to Rupert Grey's horror.

'I don't think Berlioz stashed it under his piano, mate, that's not quite how piano tuning works,' Ellis quipped.

'It doesn't work anyway,' Ilaria spat out, 'though I know he secretly thinks it makes him a tiger in the sack. He's just a sad old man, who, I'm seeing quite clearly now, would sell his own daughter to the devil. You're not the person I want to make music with, Rupert. I'm done with you!'

'Ilaria...' he started, as his lover grabbed her bag and headed for the door.

'Back off. All actions have consequences, Rupert!' She slammed the door behind her, with Billie silently cheering her on. The girl was smart as well as being able to play a mean violin.

'She's got it in one, Tiger.' Ellis nodded towards Ilaria removing herself from the situation as fast as she could along the street outside, as Billie formally arrested Rupert Grey for possession of class A drugs. 'Still, there are some great prison bands these days and you're already in with a few Drill artistes. The world could be your oyster,' Ellis added cheerily.

Billie's phone suddenly rang. It was Jo. She had been in court first thing that morning, where Ricky Hallows had been charged with murder.

'Mr Hallows was released on bail this morning, ma'am. Brief pleaded diminished responsibility. Said his mental functioning was impaired at the time of the offence. He'd been getting treatment for depression before Josh's murder.'

'Still, bail is rare even on a reduced plea to manslaughter.' Billie frowned. 'Rare to nearly unheard of.'

'His legal representative argued exceptional circumstances. Doctor's note confirmed that Lydia Hallows has only a matter of weeks left and Ricky Hallows is her sole carer, now Josh has expired. District Judge agreed, ma'am.' Jo relayed in her very formal style, quite jarring to Billie after the cheeky Cockney camaraderie of Ellis Darque. 'She lost her own son only last year, after a school bullying issue, so I imagine she was feeling particularly sympathetic, bearing in mind Josh's award for helping kids in a similar situation.'

'Fair enough.' Billie couldn't help having some sympathy for the man and the judge as well, come to that. She couldn't remember her schoolmates fighting hell for leather or dropping like flies after falling out, when she was growing up. 'Though there could have been an argument for remanding him for his own safety. There are lots of angry drinkers with scorched eyebrows out there.'

'Me for one,' Ellis muttered, as he led Rupert Grey out to the police car. Billie followed.

'Indeed, ma'am,' Jo replied. 'The judge might be thinking the same thing once she's had time to reflect. Member of the public rang in an hour ago. Ricky Hallows was found hanging from a tree in the same play park where Josh died. Just had confirmation of life deceased.'

'Are you all right, ma'am?' Billie wasn't one to let her feelings show, but the sight of Ricky Hallows, proud father, being cut down from a tree branch only inches away from the spot where she had held his dying son in her arms, just three days earlier, had almost caused her to lose her equilibrium, which would have counted as a crime worse than death in police circles.

'Could be worse. Might have had my heart set on the swings today.' She clung to police gallows repartee instead, nodding to a toddler in full tantrum mode, as he and his granny were barred from entering the park.

Five dead bodies in one week. All were calling out to her to fight for them. Ricky Hallows had died of a broken heart and Milly Lloyd, because his heart had been broken. Josh Hallows had died because he believed he knew who murdered both Sophie Grey and Christy Callaghan.

Was she losing her touch, having been away for weeks? Should she have pinned Josh down immediately, made him give her the names, before ensuring his safety? Had she let down his father in the same way, by not taking her stalker seriously? Because she was willing to bet her life that had a Molotov cocktail not been delivered to his doorstep with a note from her stalker attached, he would still be alive and kicking right now.

It was time to stop pretending that being trailed by a maniac was simply all part and parcel of being a high-ranking police operative. Did she think it would be seen as a weakness for her to take such things seriously? Was she going to continue trying to live up to the myth of her perfect father, the former police chief, for the rest of her damn life?

'Penny for them, ma'am.' Jo broke into Billie's mental self-flagellation.

'Just wondering if I could have put a stop to things before they went this far,' Billie admitted out loud.

'I thought that for years after my mum hung herself,' Jo confided. Billie mentally kicked herself for being so self-absorbed. She had forgotten that the scene could hold its own special horrors for her junior officer, bearing in mind her own tragic family history. 'But whatever the truth is, we can't bring them back, so we just have to do our best going forward,' Jo continued.

'Thanks, you're right. Let's move.' Billie squeezed Jo's arm in a show of solidarity. As they left the park, Billie was aware of a flash of gold from the corner of her eye. Suddenly Chip Little, doing a wheelie on his new big golden bike, raced into view.

'Like the new ped?' He grinned that wide white smile of his. Billie couldn't help returning a chuckle. Chip Little, despite his criminal proclivities, was like a ray of sunshine beaming down on a dark day.

'Wow, that arrived quickly!' Billie made a mental note to check her bank account.

'If you need a ride, I'm your man. Got room on the back.' He flicked his head to the bicycle seat, still wrapped in cellophane, which was too tall for him to actually sit upon.

'I'm good, thanks. You didn't see anything in the park over there?' Billie asked. Chip glanced over to the police activity and shook his head solemnly.

'The bones? Didn't see nuffink, Mother Fed. Got my eyes straight on the road to success. That's a promise.' He did another wheelie, obviously thrilled with his new bike.

'You look like you can handle wheels,' Jo piped up. Billie could see that the little cheeky chappie was working his magic on her too. Her voice was less formal and considered. 'I'm in the local roller derby team. We're starting a kids' club. You look like you could do some damage.'

'Sounds like your fishing?' Chip looked interested.

'Hard contact and the players wear cool threads.' Jo reached for a card in her pocket. 'I'll be there tonight. Come and see the action.'

'Proper. Sounds like a plot.' Chip caught the card in his hand as he whizzed by, giving Billie a wink before he raced off up a side street.

'Looks like you've got yourself a friend there, ma'am,' Jo observed, as they headed for her police car.

'I think I've got myself a stalker as well,' Billie finally confided, as they got in the car and pulled out into the traffic.

'That bunch of dead roses at Sophie Grey's dad's?' Jo queried. Billie nodded.

'I've had one of those myself, ma'am.' The young officer continued along the route back to town, not noticing a black car, as it overtook several others, tucking in behind them on the road. 'Found out about my family I guess,' she added, referring to the criminal fame of both her brother and mother. 'Got threatening letters and phone calls. Someone even set up a scam website in my name...' She trailed off, concentrating on the traffic. It was thinning out now that they had turned onto the coastal route, where the narrow road was snuggled against a sheer cliff at one side and the rocky seashore, far below, on the other.

'I used to get horseshit sent to me, rather than roses,' Jo recalled, with a small smile. Billie remembered the dirt on her own car door handle and felt her hackles rise in annoyance.

'So how did you deal with it?' Billie was astonished at the number of negative activities which Jo had somehow managed to deal with in her life.

'Dr Strong runs a group for women who have been stalked.' Billie felt her heart lurch at the mention of Max Strong.

'Right. He invited me to go to that tonight,' Billie answered.

'You'll find it useful,' Jo continued, 'you would be amazed at just how many of us there are. We helped support each other. Still do. A lot of them are in my roller derby team now. We can blow off steam together there. Show off a bit of girl power and have some fun. Safety in numbers, I guess.'

'Didn't you think to report it?' Billie asked, incredulous.

'I'm sure you're aware I haven't always been flavour of the month at work, ma'am, and judging by the stories of the other girls, the force don't take it very seriously. It's hard to convey the situation to someone who hasn't experienced it. Just explaining that a particular person is continuously lurking outside of the house or ringing the phone then putting it down or finding notes on the doorstep with cryptic messages that prove they've been watching. It sounds trivial. The officers generally laugh it off as just the ramblings of neurotic women.'

Billie wondered if that was why she had failed to share her own stalking experiences with the team. Had she been so intent on proving that she was one of the 'boys' that she had brushed her own stalking incidents off as trivial, something only a weak woman would take seriously? If that was the case, she felt even more responsible for the death of Milly Lloyd. She couldn't help thinking that things might have been different had she acted straight away. Instead, she had been suspicious that her own deliveries of flowers and notes had been the work of Lola, or Josta. The sad, slightly deranged offerings of a neurotic woman. A wave of shame washed over her. Brainwashing was a funny thing, she realised.

'Is your stalking still going on now?' Billie was infuriated that so many women seemed to have been affected by stalkers. Jo shrugged.

'It just stopped one day. Not long ago. I guess my stalker got bored and latched on to someone else.'

'I'm going to ensure that mine is retiring full time,' Billie vowed, looking out at the scenic view. 'Well done for trying to interest Chip Little in your roller derby club.' Billie realised that she had sometimes been lax in encouraging the younger officer. 'I think that's what the lad needs. A feeling of belonging and somewhere positive to work off all that energy.'

'It's good for releasing pent-up aggression, ma'am,' Jo answered.

'Sorry if some of that has been directed from me,' Billie replied, remembering the times she had thought of Jo Green as The Grass, her arch-enemy, whereas she had, in reality, turned out to have been Billie's lifesaver. 'You're an impressive detective. That's why I put you forward for promotion. You were the best person for the job. Even if we did get off to a shaky start.'

Billie had never seemed to find the right moment to put the record straight on her feelings towards the younger policewoman, but after Ricky Hallows' mental health had led to the harrowing scene that they had both just left, she was well aware that there really was no time like the present to speak such truths.

'All in the past, ma'am. Thanks for the vote of confidence. It means a lot.' Jo kept her eyes on the road, though she did blink quickly once or twice.

A loud screech of brakes behind made Billie glance sharply into the passenger mirror. A dark car loomed up frighteningly close as they rounded a curve in the road. Billie's heart leapt in her chest. It looked just like the vehicle that had appeared to have been following her on the day of Josh Hallows' murder. With a sudden and sickening crash, it made contact with the back of the police car, sending it careering sideways across the road.

'Shit, we're going over!' Billie shouted, as a startled Jo fought and failed to right the vehicle from the impact. Suddenly the car flipped and slid down the cliff face, smashing against rocks as it did so. She was aware of the glass of the windscreen shattering as the vehicle dropped under the water with some force, slippery seaweed flooding into the car like a tidal wave.

Billie struggled to release her own seat belt along with Jo's, as she gasped for breath, engulfed in the salty surge of brine, trying to pull her junior officer after her, out through the smashed windscreen, the force of the water having blocked their escape via the doors. But Jo hadn't moved, her eyes were closed, specs knocked sideways by the waves, lying at a funny angle. Billie fought to break more glass to widen the exit, the sensation in her lungs making her feel that they might be about to explode. Bubbles started to wave up to the surface from Billie's mouth as she started to lose the battle. She felt herself sliding downwards, feeling her grip loosening on the framework and then... nothing.

22

WIDOW'S WEEDS

'Is she alive?' Billie decided that the sight of Max striding at speed along the corridor, in her direction, stress etched across his handsome face, was probably well worth almost getting drowned for. She lifted her forehead from the wall where she had been leaning against it, still slightly suffering the after-effects from her unscheduled swim, though she had firmly refused the offer of a bed, in order to be thoroughly checked over.

A nurse had quickly rebandaged her burnt hand, even more mangled now, from windscreen glass shards and salt water. Other than that injury and a few scratches and scrapes here and there, she was relieved to have survived pretty well unscathed. She was simply waiting to wave Jo off to the operating theatre, to have a few broken bones mended, before she headed back to work.

'Hi.' Billie smiled. 'Don't come too close, I might still have a few stinging jellyfish in here somewhere.' She ran her fingers through her damp corkscrew curls, finding the odd remaining piece of seaweed within the tangle. Max looked down. A puddle of water was forming at Billie's feet from her soaked clothing.

'Jesus, Billie. I nearly had a heart attack when I heard. Is Jo Green okay?' he asked a passing nurse.

'Just preparing her for surgery now. Nothing we can't mend.' The nurse gave Max her most charming smile and carried on her way.

'That's good news.' Max sighed. 'Billie, you're going to catch your death...'

'You sound like my mother.' She rolled her eyes. 'Maybe both of them.' She smiled. He was well aware of her recent family revelations.

'Or both of mine.' He grinned. 'Come along to my office. I've got a change of clothes in there. Sports stuff. Something might be useful. Save everyone thinking that you have incontinence issues,' he teased.

Billie squelched alongside him. Following doctor's orders was making her feel better already. As they entered, Max closed the door to his office behind him.

'Take your clothes off,' he ordered. Billie blinked. She'd had some late-night thoughts on this very subject, whilst dreaming of being in his vicinity, but none had panned out quite like this.

'Just wondering if that's an order, doctor?' she teased mischievously. He looked up, catching Billie's eye and shook his head with a grin.

'Maybe later,' he counter-flirted, 'but right now, I'm off to get us some coffee. Back in two minutes. There's a towel in here and some other stuff. Have a root around.'

As he left, closing the door firmly behind him, Billie peeled her soaking clothing off and wrapped herself in the soft fluffy white towel that had been folded on a shelf inside of Max's cupboard. It smelled, as he did, absolutely intoxicating.

She sat down for a moment, suddenly feeling tired in the warm room, such a safe haven after her cold, dangerous shock of a swim. She closed her eyes for what felt like a matter of moments. When she opened them again, Max had already arrived back, two steaming cups of coffee in his hands.

'Are you sure that you don't want to get checked out, Billie? I've just heard the details. It sounds like one hell of an accident.' Billie gratefully took the mug of coffee from him, curling her legs under her, suddenly feeling exposed.

'It wasn't an accident. I've been followed by that car before. It's my stalker.' Max's face grew dark.

'I'm guessing then that he falls into both the resentful and predatory categories.' Max sipped his coffee. 'I don't want to scare you, Billie, but in my experience that combination is the most dangerous of all.'

'You don't need to tell me that, after what just happened.' She sipped her coffee. 'So how many different classifications of stalker are there, in your wild world of psychology?' She pulled her towel around her more tightly as Max's dark eyes fixed on hers.

'Well, there are five recognised individual categories, with some crossover on occasion,' he started to explain. Billie rolled her eyes and sighed.

'So mine has crossover issues too. Trust me to end up with a double nutcase.'

'By far the main cohort are the rejected stalkers, people who have had an intimate relationship with the victim, have been rejected and then seek revenge. So, if you've maybe had an intimate relationship with anyone, then dumped them recently?' He raised an eyebrow in question.

'Nope. Still in my almost widow's weeds, doc.' As was he but based on the atmosphere in the room right now, that sad joint status was likely to be changed for the better tonight.

'Then there is the intimate stalker who is deluded that the victim is a willing romantic partner...'

'Count that one out as well.' Billie thought back to the messages. 'I haven't exactly been receiving love letters.'

'The incompetent stalker, usually linked to those suffering from mental-health issues – but we can rule that out, by the looks of things.' Max scratched his head. 'And then the fourth and fifth categories, both of which appear to be relevant to your situation. Resentful – the type who may simply imagine that they've been unfairly treated and retaliate by inflicting suffering. We can probably tick that box.'

'Well I have no doubt that many of the cons that I have helped prosecute feel pretty aggrieved,' Billie agreed.

'Finally, predatory stalkers.' Max paused for a moment before continuing. 'I'm afraid predatory stalkers are almost always preparing a sexual attack, Billie. You seriously need to watch your back.'

'That puts me in a difficult position.' Billie put her mug down and stood up. 'I'm carrying out multiple murder enquiries with, from today, yet another member of my team down. So, what am I to do? Have someone follow me everywhere I go, just on the off-chance that I have someone following me everywhere I go?'

'I would recommend yes, you should, bearing in mind what has just happened.' Max was looking seriously worried.

'No way. What do other women in my position do?'

'First of all, you're fortunate that you will be believed, because most of the group of women I see who are dealing with stalkers have trouble convincing the police it's really happening.' Max echoed what Jo had been saying.

'Incidents are looked at in isolation without joining the dots together. The torment is mostly psychological, and these stalkers are very good at manipulating their stories. I've even got a woman in my group who insists that she has been stalked by a police officer. Imagine coming to your station without any physical injuries and convincing the desk sergeant of *that*?' Max shook his head in frustration.

'When this investigation is over, I'm going to make sure all that changes,' Billie said firmly. She headed over to the cupboard and started looking through the clothes on the shelf, pulling out a soft sweatshirt and tracksuit bottoms.

'I don't doubt it.' Max had a smile in his voice. 'At the moment, the courts treat stalking very leniently. Once arrested, the stalker can appear very presentable and sound very plausible in the dock. As a result, they rarely receive custody of any length, where there would be a chance for them to receive a full course of treatment. As soon as they get out, they invariably start again. With most of the women, it's a case of not being able to change the behaviour of the stalker, but instead change the way that they react to it. Learning coping mechanisms to allay panic attacks, for example. Sadly, many of the victims spend the rest of their lives having to watch their backs.'

'There's not a hope in hell that I will be doing that.'

Billie dropped the towel and started pulling Max's clothes over her head, so incensed by the idea, that she forgot for a moment that she was absolutely naked. Max appeared to have some difficulty in tearing his gaze away, even as Billie was quickly swamped in sweatshirt and bottoms that were several sizes too big.

'Ready for the catwalk,' he quipped, handing Billie a bag to put her wringing wet clothing in. Billie handed Max her empty mug in exchange.

'Sorry, I can't make the stalkers' club tonight; I've got a work meeting that I'm not allowed to miss. But is supper still on?' Billie decided that she was no longer in the mood to beat about the bush. 'A table for two will do. I won't be bringing any bodyguards with me.' She hammered her feelings on the situation home. Max couldn't help laughing at the sight before him.

'If you're coming in that outfit, then how could I possibly refuse?'

23

SEEN A GHOST

'The pressure's really on.' Billie made the situation clear to her team. 'The chief wants this all wrapped up asap, especially after the negative news coverage.' She hoped that the hateful headlines would ease off now that Perry Gooch had been sent packing.

'We're currently one person down whilst Green gets put back together, so we need to push to our limits.' Billie wondered yet again if she could pull some strings and persuade Derek Blythe to come back, even if only until the end of the investigation. She missed his down to earth, pragmatic approach to work, though she had to admit she would have a hard job on her hands to convince him to return. Dexie had looked as happy as a pig in muck beetling about on his allotment.

'Ellis and his team are out at the main train stations, looking out for kids who are travelling alone, heading to our patch and showing the signs of being drug runners, just like Sophie Grey. Chances are that Trap Houses are going to start popping up all over our region, now the county line floodgates have opened in the area. We may have to set a trap of our own, in the hope of getting up close to the dealers and in with a chance of someone spilling the beans as to who the Beast really is.'

Boo bit her lip. Billie wondered if she was thinking of her nephew, who had been so recently caught in the act cooking up drugs.

'Any luck with the CCTV footage that Milly Lloyd flagged up in connection with Josh Hallows' murder in the park?' Billie asked. Boo shrugged.

'Nothing showing up yet, except for a dark car that appeared to have been slowly circling the park and which seemed to speed off straight after the attack on Josh...' Billie crossed over to Boo who was bringing the footage up on her PC. '...might be something or nothing,' Boo added. Billie bent close and squinted at the hazy moving picture. It looked like the car that had followed her on the day of Josh's murder and also the one that had just rammed her and Jo over the cliff. Could her stalker have also been involved in Josh's death? She had just told Max that she hadn't thought her stalker was involved in the drug-related deaths. Could she be wrong about that?

If the car had sped off, then the driver couldn't have been the same person who had left the rose on the passenger seat, Billie pondered. If possible, she was keen to keep her personal stalking problem away from the minds of the team when they had so many homicides to focus on, but had she somehow missed a vital clue because of it?

'Good work.' Billie patted Boo on the shoulder. 'Let's get this footage cleaned up. We urgently need to bring the driver of this car in. It looks like an old Merc. I can tell you all that in addition, it looks like the car that just sent Jo and I on our dice with death.'

Billie caught the shocked reaction from the assembled staff members. She guessed the car number plates would be false, but she still damned herself for not having been more alert when the car had loomed up behind them. 'If that *is* the case, then perhaps the murderer is taking dangerous steps to prevent us from catching them, so stay alert, gang.'

'Save that CCTV on a memory stick, Boo. I'll give you a lift to the digital forensics lab. I'm on my way to interview Cilla again, in her safe house. See if I can get her to spill any further beans.' Boo had that cooped-up look once more and Billie guessed she would jump at the chance of a change of scenery, even if it was only a couple of blocks away to another police building.

'I've been wanting a word with you.' Boo had waited until they had entered the lift together before speaking. 'This county lines business has really gotten to me,' she started.

'I guess it hits home, with your nephew having been mixed up in the whole drugs nightmare,' Billie sympathised. It was tough for her seeing so many young lives wasted. She couldn't imagine what it must feel like for Boo, knowing a young family member, at eighteen years old, would be heading for the hell of an adult jail. Such an event couldn't help but have a vastly negative result on the rest of his life, so recently focused on Oxbridge success and a glittering future.

'I can't bear to just sit and watch it happen.' Boo sounded distressed.

'Well, the work you are doing here–' Billie started, before Boo cut in, ready with her argument.

'Is just glorified filing and bossing around.' Boo looked pained. 'Oh yeah, I know somebody needs to make sure everything is logged and checked, but it's just not me. It's never been me. I used to be in the thick of the action.'

Billie rubbed her friend's arm. She guessed that having Ellis on the scene had brought back memories that Boo had hidden away, after the incident that had caused her to lose the use of her legs.

'I want to go undercover.' Boo had stopped the lift between floors.

'What?' Billie ran her fingers through her hair.

'Set me up in a Trap House somewhere.' Boo was suddenly animated. 'Believe me, I was one of the best UCOs in the force.'

Billie hesitated to answer, the vision of a filthy Trap House, druggies and guns ran through her head along with the fact staring her in the face, that Boo was now confined to a wheelchair.

'But that was before, Boo,' Billie started, her head spinning at the thought.

'I'm the perfect UCO *now* for this job. Don't you see?' Boo's face was alive with the possibilities. 'The dealers find a vulnerable person...' She pointed to herself. Billie laughed.

'You, vulnerable?' Then she realised that Boo was right. No one would guess in a million years that a lone woman using a wheelchair, perhaps trying to score a bit of dope, was actually an undercover detective.

'You'd have to dress down a bit,' Billie joked, trying to deflect the focus of the conversation.

'Easy, and my wheelchair can be rigged with sound equipment, camera – who the hell ever knows what all the bits on a wheelchair are there for, except someone who sits in one?'

'How would you get out quickly if trouble kicked off?' Billie still needed persuading even though the idea had caught her imagination. She'd certainly have trouble getting it by the chief without some persuasion. Boo deftly unclipped her wheelchair footrest and held it high.

'Lethal weapon.' Boo let the lift continue on its way.

'That's true enough,' Billie conceded. She'd been whacked on her ankle by Boo's footrests enough times, as she whizzed by at speed, to know that particular piece of equipment could do some serious damage.

'Please think about it,' Boo pleaded, with a stare that Billie knew brooked no argument. The lift doors opened onto reception.

'Your guest is here, DSI Wilde,' Daz the security guard called over. Maya stood up, smiling. Billie waved. At least that was one thing that had gone right today. Ash and the girls had met Maya via video messaging, and she had taken the job as nanny to Indie, Happi and baby Tani. Billie planned to drop her off at home on the way to Cilla's safe house.

'Meet the newest member of my menagerie,' Billie joked to Boo. 'Maya's moving in for a while to look after Ash's girls.'

Billie glanced from Maya to Boo. She was looking at the young student, absolutely dumbfounded. Maya held out her hand.

'Hi.' She smiled. Boo still didn't move for a second.

'What's wrong? You look like you've seen a ghost.' Billie nudged Boo.

'Sorry.' Boo remembered her manners. 'It's just you reminded me of someone, from a long time ago,' she answered, a troubled look on her face. She didn't seem able to take her eyes off Maya as she shook her hand. The three continued through a side access door to the car park where Billie's car was waiting.

'Here, Maya, put your bag in the boot.' Billie clicked her electronic key that opened the trunk. Maya swung it up. Then screamed. It wasn't empty. A curled-up figure lying in a pool of congealed blood filled the luggage space. The lifeless eyes of Chip Little were staring straight at them, a terrified expression frozen for eternity on his sweet young face.

'Stabbed, I'm afraid.' Josta crossed the car park to Billie. 'More times than could possibly have been necessary. I've cooked chickens bigger than that wee boy,' she added. 'Seems to me our killer actually enjoys the cut and thrust. I'll have to confirm the blade when I get the child back. It appears to be about eight centimetres long. Went clean through one of his legs, the mite was so thin. Damn shame. I remember when Max was that age.' She shook her head in sadness as she wandered off to oversee the body being transferred to the mortuary vehicle.

Billie wiped her eyes. A vision of Chip Little showing off his ability to do a wheelie on his brand-new bike had just cycled through her mind's eye, hence the unexpected tears. She tried to concentrate on the evidence rather than the memory of a unique young personality needlessly snuffed out.

The murderer appeared to have a range of tools at their disposal. Or it could well be that several different members of the county lines gang were carrying out the killings, including other kids. This was turning into an utter nightmare.

A waving hand caught the corner of Billie's eye, beyond the taped-off area. A welcome sight: Ash. Billie so wished her wingman was back at work, especially with Jo out of play too. She hardly ever got to see him now that he had moved into her place, not having had a chance to spend much time at home recently.

'How's Maya doing?' Billie asked. The young girl had certainly screamed loudly enough when faced with the body of Chip in the boot, but that was to be expected. Billie had called and asked Ash to come and pick her up, due to the unforeseen circumstances.

'Great.' Ash heaved a sigh of relief as he waved to the park across the road, where Maya was entertaining his children, along with Kat the dog. From the squeals of delight in the distance, she seemed to have passed muster all around. 'Hardest job in the world looking after kids. I would do anything to be well enough to come back to work but...' He sighed, nodding to the stick he was still forced to use from time to time. 'I'm missing my mates, the banter...' He looked longingly over to the murder scene.

'I might just have the answer to your prayers.' Billie hooked her arm into his as an idea took shape. 'And mine as well.'

'You're wanted,' Ash alerted Billie. Josta was waving her over again, to the boot of the car, from which Chip had just been transferred to the mortuary vehicle.

'Seems our murderous friend left a little calling card.' She indicated a printed card, the type which was now familiar to Billie. It had been positioned under Chip's body. *Trapped Rat. Wilde talk costs lives*, it read.

Billie felt anger surge through her body. This time there could be no uncertainty. Her stalker knew that she had met with Chip Little and had retaliated, therefore they were *definitely* linked to the county lines murders.

Her shadowy follower was trying to control the investigation, but Billie had no intention of being manipulated. Especially not by a cold-blooded killer. 'I won't rest until I collar the evil beast,' she vowed.

24

TURN THE OTHER CHEEK

'This is utterly ridiculous!' Billie was still arguing with the chief constable as they approached the penthouse suite in the smart hotel overlooking the seven bridges of the River Tyne.

'You've made your views crystal clear, Billie, but as you will learn, success in this game is as much about pressing the flesh, as crack police work.'

The chief's words of wisdom did nothing to pacify Billie. Had it not been for the fact that even Boo had insisted that she couldn't possibly accompany the chief to this ridiculous meeting with slimy newspaper owner Lance Harris, swamped in Max Strong's sports kit, she would still have been wearing it. Instead, Boo had come to the rescue yet again, with a blue shift dress that she kept at work for quick-change getaways to social events.

'But we've got another murdered child, and Chip Little was left in *my* car,' she argued furiously, trying to stop her mind wandering to the young boy with his thousand-megawatt smile, lest tears sprang into her eyes once again. She had already used up half of a toilet roll in the ladies at work when thoughts of the vulnerable little soul's horrific departure from life had engulfed her. 'The only flesh I want to press is that of the maniac carrying out the killings.'

'So you've delegated, Billie. The team is hard at work. You don't have to be at everyone's beck and call all day long. You can't change what's happened, especially when you're working with homicide, but the reason you had all of those counselling sessions after the last time, was to change the way you think and respond to it.'

'So how on earth does anyone mentally reframe their thoughts about the murder of a twelve-year-old child, spinning it into a fun mind game?' she huffed. The chief smiled, indulging her tantrum. Billie reined herself in a little, aware he would have probably taken disciplinary action against her outburst had she not been his godchild. She tried to remind herself that she couldn't argue against nepotism one moment and then try to use it to wheedle out of things she didn't want to do the next. 'Just grab a glass of wine and chill out, my dear,' he answered.

The door to the swish penthouse suite swung open. Lance Harris smiled his lizard-eyed welcome, as Billie glumly followed the chief into the huge suite with vast windows overlooking the twinkling lights, strung like a necklace along the river.

'Enchanting to meet you again, DSI Wilde.' Luciana Martinez loomed into view, holding out a perfectly manicured hand. 'I hear that you've had a quite, shall we say, challenging day?' Billie looked at the chief. She could have sworn that they had put a news blackout in place over Chip Little's murder.

'You were extremely lucky to have survived such a terrible accident,' Lance Harris added. Billie now understood what they were referring to. She had almost forgotten about the amphibious vehicle incident, save for checking in that Jo was making a good recovery. She shrugged.

'I'm surprised you didn't have one of your intrepid

journalists abseiling down the cliff to take a few snaps for the paper,' Billie replied. 'They seem to get everywhere these days.'

'A beauty like you should enjoy the limelight more, DSI Wilde.' Lance Harris chuckled as he poured champagne and handed the glasses around. 'In any case, as I assured you earlier, that particular employee has been dismissed.'

Billie was under no illusions that the newspaper proprietor was even remotely sorry for the sensationalist spread. The double-page photo shoot of Billie with various alleged amours, was open on the huge glass coffee table.

'You have interesting taste in men, DSI Wilde.' Luciana Martinez perused the damning news report. 'This gentleman' – she pointed to Max – 'is devilishly attractive, don't you think?'

'He's a criminal psychologist, often called upon for police consultation,' Billie answered defensively. 'This photo was taken when we were discussing a client that we had both shared.' That much was true, she mused, the details would have made another sensational spread, of course. How Lance Harris never got wind of the full story behind the last investigation, she would never know.

'Dr Max Strong,' the chief confirmed. 'I can totally recommend him, if you find you have any madmen in your midst.' He chuckled. Billie flashed a disparaging look at him, remembering that she had first met Max when the chief had sent her for counselling.

'So the A-team is at work.' Luciana Martinez smiled, indulging the chief. 'Alas, all this street crime' – she wrinkled her nose in distaste – 'there is no way of controlling it. One must simply control the way one thinks about it.'

'Such as?' Billie really felt that she'd had enough of the fashionable psychology that everyone seemed to be spouting these days, as though it was some new set of laws created by ancient gods, freshly unearthed on stone tablets.

'It involves the little people.' Luciana Martinez sipped her wine.

'Exactly. Children are dying–' Billie started on a rant, before Luciana Martinez cut over her.

'No, you misunderstand my words, superintendent.' The beautiful doctor spoke more slowly, as though English wasn't Billie's first language. 'People lower down the food chain. Lowly people. They aren't like us. They live in a world we can't change so we really don't need to waste our precious time worrying about them.' Billie felt that she might be about to explode.

'Well, frankly, if I took that attitude, I couldn't sleep at night,' Billie snapped back.

'You can't sleep at night, Billie,' the chief butted in. 'That's why I brought you here tonight.'

'What?' Billie looked from one to the other. They were smiling at her.

'We'd like to offer you a job.' Lance Harris tried to top up Billie's glass. She moved her hand away. 'My newspaper empire is expanding into South America. Doctor Martinez will be my partner. We already share many business dealings.'

'More rags?' Billie questioned. 'But what about your precious environment, Dr Martinez? How much of the rainforest will be felled for you to simply make more money? I don't want to be rude' – Billie turned to Lance Harris – 'but I don't think the world would miss your brand of news.'

'I like your spunky style.' Luciana Martinez flashed her expensively created white teeth. 'Your chief' – she looked flirtatiously from under long false lashes at Billie's godfather – 'has accepted our offer of becoming head of security.'

'What?' Billie whirled round in shock.

'It's true, Billie. I'm due to retire this year. I've given up trying to stop an endless tidal wave of crime. Can't control it, that's for sure and I think that's hit home with you, too, by now. But I can control the way I think about it and I've concluded that it would be great to take on a new challenge in an exotic country, with wonderful company...' He waved his hands at Lance Harris and Luciana Martinez. 'I'd like you to come with me.' Billie thought she must be hearing things.

'Me?' Billie was shocked.

'I assure you we pay our security staff extremely well, DSI Wilde,' Luciana Martinez confirmed. 'I would like you to be my personal bodyguard. I think we complement each other. You will make a good impression at the events I'm required to attend.' She looked Billie up and down. 'You will have a generous clothing allowance, of course. I am leaving in the morning. Perhaps you want to meet your... colleague, Max Strong, to say a fond farewell? I can drop you off later in my car–' Billie ignored her, spinning around to face the chief.

'Are you crazy? What about the situation here? This county lines thing will only get worse, unless we put a stop to it.'

'You will never put a stop to it.' Lance Harris shrugged. 'But I'm sure some other plod would jump at the chance to step into your shoes. Don't waste any more time worrying about things you can't control. Start enjoying the better things in life.'

'Exactly.' Luciana Martinez clinked her champagne glass against Billie's. 'Turn the other cheek.' Billie slammed her glass down.

'You said it,' she answered, speedily heading for the door. 'I'd rather be guarding the Chip Littles of the world, than you lot.' She slammed the door behind her and stormed along the corridor, punching some numbers into her mobile.

'Boo?' She had come to a decision and there was no going back. She no longer had any intention of resisting her own truth. 'There's no way we can go on simply mopping up, not when kids are dying. We need to get down and dirty.'

'So you'll agree to me going undercover?'

'Let's do it.' Billie ended the call. Luciana Martinez could stuff her Sermon on the Mount Beatitudes. Someone was responsible for the deaths of Sophie and Josh and Chip as well as the adults on her patch of the world. She was determined to seek justice. Time to go on the offensive and dump any idea of turning the other cheek.

25

CRAZY BELIEFS

'Sorry, am I too late?' Billie tried to hide the butterflies in her stomach as Max opened the door dressed in an open-necked white shirt and jeans. She argued with herself that the feeling was simply down to lack of food intake, not the fact that he looked totally gorgeous and utterly relieved to see her.

'Who doesn't love a midnight feast?' He bit his lower lip, then smiled that crooked smile of his that made Billie's insides lurch once more.

It wasn't that she'd never had a sex life in the past – God knows, the last inquiry confirmed her devastating childhood horrors in that area. Intensive counselling had thankfully put paid to the harrowing flashbacks from that time. However, the revelations about David, her former fiancé, had done nothing to bolster her confidence about being hot in the sack.

Once his secret other life had been shockingly revealed, it had hit home hard that their particular vanilla brand of sex hadn't been top of his room service menu at the many hotel bedrooms he'd frequented without her. She wondered if Max had entertained dozens of lovers since his wife's gruesome demise. The way every female looked at him, she would be amazed if he hadn't, whereas David had been her one and only proper lover.

'Shame you've changed. I quite liked your earlier ensemble.' Billie realised that he was jokingly referring to his own borrowed clothes, but the look he gave her as she stepped into the hall, wearing Boo's figure-skimming shift dress, told a different story. Billie thought about announcing that she still wasn't rocking any underwear, the Chip Little situation having left no time to nip home and ransack the house for her posh pants, but thought better of it. Not wise to be too presumptuous after all. He might really have just been inviting her to his home for supper.

On the drive over, she had already convinced herself that she had blown their date big time, turning up so late. She'd been so incensed by the shambolic drinks episode with Lance Harris, that she'd raced back to headquarters and been hard at work, determined to put her plan into action, then suddenly looked up and realised that instead of just a few minutes, hours had passed.

'No bodyguards?' He peeped out into the street, before closing the door.

'No stalkers either. Made it here all by myself.' Max led her along the main hall to a door opening wide into a huge kitchen den with a table set for two.

'So, madam, dinner is served.' Max waved her in as though she were royalty. Truth be told, a weight seemed to have been lifted from her. Maybe it was because she had decided that from now on, she was going to be true to herself, act on her own interpretations linked to events, rather than listening to so called experts who kept urging her to simply put a rosy glow on everything. She wasn't willing to take that view when kids were being killed all around her. It was called being her own person, dammit.

'Something smells delicious.' Billie sniffed the air. He had obviously gone to some trouble. A beautiful white damask cloth covered the table. A single candle was lit in the middle.

'Sancocho de Pescado con Coco. Fish and Coconut Stew to you. That's about the limit of my cooking capabilities.' Max grinned.

'Sounds Columbian. Picked up any of the ingredients recently?' Billie raised an eyebrow.

'Always the detective, DSI Wilde. I have been to Columbia many times; I will admit that much.'

Billie remembered her conversation with Josta on the subject when they had been worried sick that Max might have been involved in the hostage situation.

'And what did you learn there?' Billie remembered that Lola had told her that he had studied at the university.

'That there is no simple battle between good and evil. That there are worlds within worlds, forces at work that none of us can comprehend and that actions have consequences. Often which we can never foresee.'

'That sounds a bit deep, and I've just decided that I'm done with psychology-speak,' Billie teased. 'I was merely wondering if you found any good hotels?'

'Thinking of a holiday there?' Max frowned.

'I was offered a job in Columbia today. In security.'

'Working in security in Columbia is like signing your own death warrant,' he answered, looking concerned.

'Isn't that what you've been doing?' Billie countered. Max paused as he served the food.

'I speak with some knowledge on the subject,' he finally conceded. 'Please don't go there, Billie. You would have to set aside everything that you believe to be right. Be willing to understand that the good guys aren't always good, and the bad guys aren't all sporting scars and looking like villains. You would have to be on your guard twenty-four seven.'

'I'm up to scratch with that already. It seems most of the bad guys I'm searching for at the moment, are schoolkids. It's breaking my heart,' Billie admitted. 'What on earth has the world come to, when drug lines all the way from South America are ending up on estates here, killing our kids, even polluting our rivers? Maybe if I took the job just for a while, I could get to the root cause...' Max caught Billie's hand, stopping her train of thought. His eyes glittered in the candlelight.

'You'll end up dead, Billie. I couldn't bear it if someone else I–'

He was interrupted as a key could be heard turning in the front-door lock before it banged open. Josta could be heard huffing in and marching along the hall. She appeared in the doorway.

'Oh, I am sorry, dears. Just thought I would pop in on the way from work, Max. Devil of a time getting that poor wee mite settled in for the night.'

She spoke of Chip, the young, newly-deceased gang member, as though he had been a living child who she had just read a bedtime story to. Billie considered, as she quickly removed her hand from Max's, that perhaps Josta had done exactly that. Though Max's mum had just wrecked a magic moment, she couldn't feel aggrieved. Billie always felt a huge responsibility for the murder victims for whom she tried to get justice. She was grateful that, especially in the case of children, Josta always treated them with the utmost sensitivity and respect. Billie couldn't believe that she had recently harboured doubts about her.

'Oh that's hit the spot.' Josta sighed as Max, rolling his eyes good-naturedly at Billie, poured his mum a large glass of wine. She pulled a spare chair up to the table.

'Max, this table covering. Did you take it from the airing cupboard in our house? I've never known you to make the effort. He must want something from you, Billie, my dear.' Josta winked at Billie. Max flushed pink much to Billie's amusement.

'I just couldn't find a clean tablecloth, what with being away...' he started in full Pinocchio fashion, sipping his wine at what Billie guessed was his best attempt at nonchalance.

'You still haven't, my dear boy.' Josta ran her hand over the white material. 'This is the family laying-out cloth–' Max spluttered into his drink, whilst Billie shot back from the table. 'The last person on here was your dear departed grandfather. Bowel cancer did for him. I remember him laid out right there' – she prodded the centre of the tablecloth – 'as dead as a duck.'

'Oh my God!' Billie couldn't help giggling at Max's outburst. He started to swiftly remove the items from the table. Josta, totally unconcerned by the shroud laid out in front of her, simply rolled her eyes.

'Men, my dear.' She smiled benignly. 'They need a woman to keep them straight. You've also left a bunch of those red roses from your garden in the porch. No water. They'll die if you don't get a vase. In fact, they look half dead now.'

Billie's senses sprung to high alert.

'What red roses?' Max looked annoyed now. 'Mother, it's gone midnight, you turn up here talking nonsense about the table covering... I don't have any red roses.'

'In your garden you do, dear chap.' Josta knocked back her drink, rolling her eyes at Billie again. 'He leaves it to Lola and I to sort out his shrubbery.'

Billie wasn't laughing now. She got up and headed back into the hallway. A large bunch of dead red roses were propped up in the porch next to the closed front door. She hadn't noticed them when she had come in.

'See what I mean, dear?' Josta had followed, with Max

behind her. Billie spun around to face them both, just as Max's mobile rang. He answered it, listened intently and then started walking back into the kitchen den, his face deadly serious. Josta yanked up the flowers. Billie didn't see any note attached this time. The choice of reasons why didn't bear thinking about, but Billie couldn't stop her mind racing through them.

'I might as well put these straight in the bin,' Josta announced, opening the door. Billie could see a dark car parked in the street. It looked like a Mercedes. She felt her stomach tighten.

'That car...' she started. Josta followed Billie's line of vision. 'Do you know who owns it?'

'It's an old thing that Max normally keeps in his garage,' Josta answered. 'I dropped him off at the airport in it the other day. His car is having some repairs done and mine was blocked in at work. We all tootle around in it now and then. Lola has been using it too, whilst she's been at home. She's a terrible driver. Looks like she's had a bump in the thing. She'd be better off manning a tank.' Josta chuckled, as she stepped out to dump the flowers in the dustbin. 'I thought she was using that car to visit her friends, but it looks like she's gone by train and forgotten to park it back in the garage. She's not been herself at all recently.'

Billie blinked. Was it even the car that had slammed her over the cliff? Mercs weren't exactly rare vehicles, after all. Billie folded her arms, ready for some serious interrogation. Like finding out the definite times and locations of everyone who had the use of that car recently and where exactly *was* Lola right now? Max emerged from the dining room.

'Those flowers,' Billie started. His eyes were dead as he cut across her.

'I'm sorry. I've got to go. I've just had bad news about a friend.' He rubbed his hand over his mouth.

'Which friend is that?' Josta bundled back in again, her usual affable self.

'Jamie,' Max answered, reaching for his jacket.

'Jamie Squires?' Josta turned to Billie. 'Jamie's his friend from army days. Lola said that she wheedled out of you that Jamie boy went along on your recent South American excursion?' She smiled in a conspiratorial fashion at Billie. 'Those boys are as thick as thieves.'

'Well, not anymore, mother.' Tears welled in Max's beautiful dark-brown eyes. 'He's dead.'

26

SWEET CRUMBLING TOMBSTONES

'You're having a laugh!' Ellis had made his feelings clearly known. He wasn't in favour of Boo going undercover, not at all. 'I've been around the block a few times, but even I wouldn't risk dossing down in a Trap House. Are you crazy?' He paced up and down the murder inquiry office.

'Nearly,' Billie answered. 'So are the rest of the team. They want to do anything they can to catch this killer and as you know Chip said that the Lucifer line is moving in to Hipsmouth, so they're going to be looking for a Cuckoo's nest. We won't get another opportunity to lead them to our own Trap House.'

'With Beddy inside? No way!' Ellis retorted.

'Last time I checked, it was me running this show.' Billie climbed off the corner of the desk where she had been perched and faced Ellis down.

'Yeah? Well, I seem to remember that you called in *my* specialist knowledge and I'm advising big time, it's a *no* to her going into a house full of crackheads.'

Truth be told, Billie had paused to have a few second thoughts herself, in the long night during which she had tossed and turned, thinking about Max, his suddenly deceased friend, the mysterious bunch of roses in his porch and then the car that had been parked outside of his house. Had someone followed her to Max's home, watched her enter and then slipped the flowers inside? The idea seemed preposterous, but the only other options involved madness on the part of either Josta, Max or increasingly absent Lola and she didn't want to allow her thoughts to linger in that sort of direction, yet again, for long.

Chances were, she had finally reasoned to herself at five am just before her alarm went off, that Lola had simply gathered the blooms from the garden on the day that Billie had visited earlier in the week and forgotten that she had left them there. She hadn't exactly been bright-eyed and bushy-tailed when Billie had encountered her in the dead of night at Max's house, after all.

As Ellis paced the floor moodily, Billie's deliberations turned back to Boo, just as she suddenly appeared in the doorway, make-up free and wearing stained clothes that looked like charity shop rejects. Her swish beaded braids had been removed, leaving a fuzzy short afro and her shiny chariot-like wheelchair had been replaced by a decidedly lacklustre model. Boo looked like an entirely different person, which had been the idea after all.

'Are you still happy to go ahead with this? Ellis is strongly advising against it.' Billie swallowed hard. Right now, Boo did look incredibly vulnerable if trouble should kick off. She seriously hoped that she wouldn't live to regret her decision to put her dear friend in such a precarious position.

'Ellis Darque isn't my boss.' Boo flicked a disparaging glance at him. 'He never has been. He's well aware that I know how to take care of myself.'

'Really?' Ellis marched across the room, making clear his distress at the sight of Boo.

'What do you mean by that? Because I use a wheelchair, I'm not as capable as anyone here?' Boo challenged menacingly.

'You know I always rated you, Beddy, but things are different now... you are different,' he added softly, touching the arm of her wheelchair. Boo flicked it sideways so that he lost his grip. She was as in control of her chariot as anyone could be of their allegedly able-bodied movements.

'That's true enough. Things *are* different. This time I've got a crack team behind me offering support,' Boo answered. Billie could see the effect her reply had on Ellis.

'In my office, now.' Billie looked from one to the other. She had to get to the bottom of this animosity before they put the plan into action. Billie needed Ellis to be at the top of his game. She was under no illusion that Boo's life could depend upon it. Boo and Ellis, heads turned away from one another, crammed into Billie's tiny office.

'Shut the door,' Billie commanded. Ellis complied.

'Why do I feel I've wandered into the middle of a domestic here?'

Neither Boo nor Ellis answered for a beat.

'If you can't work as a team, then this idea is off the slate.'

'Good,' Ellis answered. Boo reacted angrily.

'Good for you. No one else. Let's face it, you couldn't exactly work as part of a team last time, could you?' Boo spat the words out. Ellis flushed.

'I did my job properly. Wasn't my decision to pull me out of the operation,' he answered, flashing a guilty look at Billie. She sighed.

'Is that right?' Boo shook her head. 'You shagged one of the targets, that's why you were taken off the job. Can't remember that being in the job brief. Could have done with an extra pair of hands when the wall came crashing down on those of us who actually stuck to the game plan.'

Billie felt the temperature drop in seconds. Ellis hung his head, without replying. Boo glanced sideways as though realising she had gone too far. Billie remembered that Boo had lost the use of her legs when some rioting environmentalists, way back, had got overexcited protesting on a wall, trying to stop bulldozers starting work on a new motorway.

'Look, I'm trying to bang a killer to rights, not offer marriage guidance. What happened in the past, stays in the past on my watch. Is that clear?' Billie felt like a headmistress telling off two naughty schoolchildren that were secretly her favourites.

'Ellis, you can't go in all high profile to a Trap House at Hipsmouth. It's only a few days ago you were working undercover on next door's patch. Sod's law someone from Jesus O'Brian's lot would clock you and then the game really would be up. Boo's got all the right credentials and we've located a ground-floor flat on an estate. It's just come up, with ramp and accessible bathroom. It's not going to make centre spread of the *Ideal Home* mag. In fact, no self-respecting cockroach would willingly doss down there, but it fits exactly with Boo's reason for being a new face in town. We're secreting microphones inside, under the guise of being local council employees checking accessibility before the tenant moves in.'

'You do know that female Cuckoos are regularly raped?' Ellis was more subdued, but clearly felt that he had to make the point.

'So I tell them I've got a colostomy bag.' Boo spat the words out. 'They'll believe it, even if it is a load of old bollocks. Amazing how scared and ignorant people can be of disability.' Her words were barbed. 'Happens to be my secret weapon, whatever *some people* might think,' she added.

Billie sensed the passion between them. It wasn't the same relationship at all that she and Ash had when they worked together, but she was in no doubt whatsoever, as sparks flew between the two, that they would watch each other's backs to the death if need be. She felt safe to continue.

'We've taken on an empty industrial unit across the road from the back door of the target house, so no one will take much notice of a new IT business setting up shop there. That's our cover and it means we are literally a few feet away and able to monitor at all times.

'Ellis, I want you to oversee the operation from there, whilst Boo is inside. Jo has been released from hospital and is coming back tomorrow. Against everyone's advice, particularly mine, but she's determined to pitch in. Not much good at sprinting yet, but she's going to be positioned opposite the front door next to the late-night convenience store, ostensibly begging. She's on crutches right now, so she's playing a right little Tiny Tim. She'll relay back to us any intel on people heading your way from that angle.'

'And look at my James Bond kit.' Boo couldn't help grinning at Billie as she lifted her armrest to reveal wires inside of the empty metal tubing.

'The wheelchair is a really useful prop,' Billie said to Ellis, who despite his misgivings could not avoid taking an interest. 'It's rigged up with sound and video gear, so we can monitor everything that goes on. The aim is to get intel on those higher up the chain, the Beast being the golden ticket. Boo, if you can access any phone numbers that can take us straight to him, rather than simply the kids doing the donkey work, we'll be laughing.'

Billie could tell that Ellis was grudgingly impressed with the preparations so far.

'Okay. I'm in.' He looked up at Billie. 'But I don't want her hanging around in there more than a couple of days tops. Teenagers are tricky enough at the best of times. You've got to understand, a kid high on some of the shit in a Trap House, possibly playing the big guy with a shooter in his pocket, won't behave like good citizen Josh Hallows. He'll be a total raving lunatic.'

'Okay. We'll get in and out as soon as... I appreciate that you've got Boo's welfare at the heart of things, Ellis.' Billie tried to bring Boo around. She was still avoiding eye contact with Ellis.

'You can be certain of that. Always.' He glanced sideways at Boo. Billie noticed Boo swallow hard. She suddenly felt like cupid, but she decided to hold back on the arrows for now.

The very thought of pointed weapons when her nerves were on a knife edge over the plan was almost enough to kill her enthusiasm stone dead.

A knock on the door offered a welcome break in proceedings. Ash popped his head in, pulling a silly salute.

'Ready to serve, ma'am.' He grinned, then looked at Boo. 'Taking over your hot seat, seeing as you're going out all dressed to impress,' he joked. Boo couldn't help chuckling. The whole team had a soft spot for Ash and Billie could see lots of smiling faces in the office beyond, thrilled to be welcoming him back to work. He was the only person Billie would have trusted to do Boo's job as well as she did whilst she was working undercover, and it would gradually ease him back into the cut and thrust of things. He shook hands with Ellis, as always, the cheeky charmer.

'If it's you taking over my job, I might have second thoughts,' Boo joked back.

'Don't worry, I won't be rifling your address book for hot guys. You've always had terrible taste in men.' Boo glanced at Ellis. He looked to the floor sadly.

Billie was pleased that Ash had decided to be upfront about the fact he was attracted to men. No doubt it had come as a big shock to the team and Billie in particular, when his secret life had been uncovered so tragically during the last investigation, but everyone was simply pleased and utterly relieved that he was still alive.

'Just one little thing, boss,' Ash added, as he pushed the door further open. 'The nanny's an absolute sweetheart, but she's allergic to the mutt, so I've had to bring it in.' Kat the Dog bundled through the door, scattering papers from Billie's desk as she rushed over to give her slobbering greetings. Ellis suddenly started sneezing. He reached for his handkerchief.

'Jeez, it's like a lunatic asylum in this place today. You'd get more peace in a Trap House.' He headed out, blowing his nose. Billie was happy to take that as a tentative stamp of hard-won approval. Even Boo was smiling now as the dog bounded over to her. The moment of light relief was welcomed – especially as Billie was due to head off to another meeting. This was one that she was seriously dreading.

There was no good place to impart the worst news of all. But of all the bad places, the visiting room of HMP Shilum was probably the pits. The walls were a glossy pink, which reminded Billie of a particular revolting penicillin medicine she had been force-fed in her childhood. Formica tables were scattered around the airless room, which smelled of cheap bleach. The only decoration on the walls were posters warning of dire consequences if people didn't obey all of the rules.

Hannah Little hadn't obeyed any of the rules. But then, her drug-addled parents hadn't taken enough interest in her to spell them out in the first place. She had been a schoolgirl mum, who had scrimped and scraped to feed her first couple of kids, when both of their dads had gone AWOL. By nineteen, she'd turned to small-time shop theft when the twins had come along. Their dad, who had taken great, if momentary pride in getting his latest girl pregnant, had already found another amour to impregnate before the stork had delivered.

She was only twenty-one, the date in years gone by when youngsters finally grew old enough to be given the key to the door, when she was thrown out onto the street by a landlord at the end of his tether, turning to heroin to dull the pain of having her kids taken away. Unfortunately for Hannah, the meagre wraps of heroin she had dealt, to buy a cot and nappies for baby Chip, who was by then well on his way, had resulted in a three-year jail sentence.

Chip had been special though. His mum had already been banged up when she had given birth to him, allowing Hannah to learn the joys of being a full-time carer at last, albeit under the watchful eye of prison minders, for the first eighteen months of Chip's life. The two had forged a strong bond.

At eighteen months old precisely, Chip had been whisked away from his mum, as the rules decreed, to continue his life with a string of foster parents until Hannah had sat out the rest of her sentence.

Billie could never quite understand how the tiniest cogs in the criminal world, like Hannah Little, got the most forceful sentences. She had once caught a dangerous arms dealer and been infuriated to watch him get a single year in an open prison. But then he had been a rich Caucasian man with influential connections, rather than a poor homeless woman with mixed-race grandparents.

Neither mother nor son had ever quite recovered it seemed, from that early separation. Even when reunited, Hannah had continued a pattern of heading in and out of prison and Chip had regularly been taken back into care. In the outside world they had struggled to master the life skills necessary to recreate the secure world that they had once enjoyed in prison.

'This was the place I first said goodbye to him,' Hannah finally said, finding her voice a minute or two after Billie had imparted the news of Chip's death. 'First place I said hello as well. Gave birth to him in the hospital wing here. This was the only proper family home we had.' Billie ran her fingers through her hair, her heart breaking that this dank prison was as good as it ever got for Chip Little.

'Thought he would be all right this time though. My friend, Cilla, said she'd look after him.' Billie's ears pricked up.

'Cilla Saunders who used to work in Christy Callaghan's club?' Billie leaned forward.

'Yeah, until she set up in business herself. Said she'd keep Chip busy. Make sure he stayed out of any trouble.' She sniffed. 'I should never have believed a word that bitch ever said.'

Billie blinked as she took in the information. She was beginning to think that she shouldn't have believed a word either. Hannah Little got up and wandered off towards a prison warden who had appeared at the door.

'Hey, Betty, you'll never guess what. My little Chip's gone and copped it. Bummer, eh? Maybe we can have his funeral service here? He would have liked that.' She turned back to Billie. 'I'll be due some compensation, right? Criminal injuries board are gonna pay out big time for this.' Hannah Little gave a sweet smile showing a row of teeth like crumbling tombstones.

Billie could take no more. Clearly Hannah Little wasn't as ignorant of how to work the system as she liked to make out and that Billie had been keen to buy into. It was a matter for debate whether a mother who had been such a failure at looking after her child, had the right to make money out of his violent death, but as Billie strode out of the building, she had murder firmly on her mind. *Somebody* was going to pay for this.

❄

'She's talking utter bollocks.' Cilla Saunders flicked the ash off her fag onto the beige-carpeted floor of the safe house. 'Hannah Little is off her skaggy head, everyone knows that.' Billie detected a harder edge to Cilla than she had presented earlier, as the heartbroken club employee and caged Cuckoo in the Trap House.

'So you weren't looking after Chip?' Billie persisted. Cilla shrugged.

'Chip, Flip, Stick – she had so many of the little buggers at different times, all with the same sorts of names. Last time I saw her, she was being carted off. I was coming into Big Bargains, that store on the corner of the high street, as the coppers were marching her out. Caught nicking a joint of meat.'

'Perhaps to feed her kid?' Billie answered.

'Feed her habit more like. She'd jump at the chance to swap her kids in return for a wrap and when I saw her, she was well on the rattle. Maybe she did say to keep an eye on one of them, but if I said yes, I was just being polite. Far as I know, all her little runts are in care.' Billie tried to keep control of her temper.

'So you didn't know that Chip Little was one of the Tweenies outside of the Trap House, when you were inside, or that he was ferrying deliveries to users in the neighbourhood?'

'How the hell would I?' Cilla was indignant. 'I was trapped in all the time, fearing for my own life, wasn't I?' Billie now felt sure that she'd been taken for a mug. The crocodile tears at the drug bust had simply been an act. 'Tell you what' – Cilla flicked her head to a framed photo, one of the few personal items in her hastily arranged witness protection abode – 'made sure my lad was brought up right. Done well he has.'

Billie looked at the photo of Cilla's son, the entertainer she had mentioned on the day Billie had been presented with Christy Callaghan's head on a plate. Pennies were beginning to drop. He worked on the ferry from Amsterdam in the Netherlands – one of the main wholesale locations for cocaine.

'That right? Is his success down to crime, rather than strumming a mean guitar on choppy waters? Maybe proceeds from Christy Callaghan's dealings, or your own?' Billie glanced out of the window. Ellis and a couple of his team had arrived at the door.

'What you talking about?' Cilla appeared dumbstruck as Ellis walked in.

'Warrant to search the premises.' He waved the piece of paper as he marched into the room and started opening cupboards. Billie checked her watch, calculating that it shouldn't take long, bearing in mind Cilla had only been resident for a handful of days.

'Please yourself. I'm not staying locked in here, like I'm the crook in all of this…' Cilla marched towards the door. 'I didn't want to stay in this dosshouse in the middle of nowhere anyway.' Ellis ousted a bucketful of cleaning cloths out from under the kitchen sink.

'Bingo.' He grinned at Billie, holding up two plastic bags. 'Big rock and a bundle of brown.' He indicated a quantity of crack cocaine and marijuana.

'This is a set-up. I'm not staying here to be insulted.' Cilla made to grab her coat from a peg in the hallway.

'No you're not.' Billie grabbed Cilla's arm. 'Remember that nice little cell we let you stay in the other night? We haven't even changed the sheets. Cilla Saunders, I'm arresting you for being in possession of class A and class C drugs, with intent to supply.' Billie unhooked the coat from its peg and handed it to Cilla. 'I'm guessing you won't have to worry about the next roof over your head for a while. Bit of luck, you might end up dossing in a cell right next to your old mate, Hannah Little.'

27

DEEP FRIED MARS BARS

'Look at us. It's like a day trip to Lourdes,' Boo joked as she sat beside Billie in an accessible vehicle with a specially designed 'Community that Cares' graphic on the bodywork. Jo Green was positioned behind, with her crutch placed across her knee.

'Well, let's face it, we're praying for a miracle. All we need is for the drugs mules to move in on your Cuckoo's nest and give us a lead to the Beast. Job done. Then we get you the hell straight out of there.' Billie was dressed as a local volunteer, hair stuffed under a peaked cap, wearing jeans, hoodie and trainers, in the hope that she would appear to be simply helping Boo to move into her new home. A random collection of suitably shabby furniture and assorted clutter filled up the back space of the van. Billie glanced at her two companions, both about to put themselves into extremely dangerous situations. She felt a tight knot of tension in her belly.

'It's not too late to pull out, either of you. Have I made that clear?'

'Only around a thousand times,' Boo teased.

'Jo, I'm sure you should still be in hospital, rather than hunkering down in a shop doorway.'

'Feeling fine, ma'am. It's just a minor fracture in the ankle department and a few hairline cracks and bruises here and there. I only wish I had been able to make it to the kid's roller derby last night–' Billie cut her off, knowing what she was getting at.

'Don't start on a guilt trip.' Billie knew that Jo was quietly devastated about Chip Little's fate. 'Josta reckons that he was deceased long before the time of your roller derby meeting.' Billie tried to push away memories of the autopsy of Chip Little the day before. Even the hardened forensic pathologist had been forced to turn away, grab a tissue from the countertop and give her nose a hefty blow, when Billie had explained the importance of the carefully folded pieces of paper found in his pockets. Billie reflected that at least his mum would have the benefit of the boy's life savings, on release from prison, just as he would have wished. Bets were off as to how many days it would take her to inject it up on a major drugs trip, rather than Chip's dream of a forever home.

Billie pulled into a parking bay on the main road.

'Are you warm enough in that?' Billie turned around, looking at the old puffa jacket, woollen hat and tracksuit bottoms that Jo was wearing.

'Give it a rest.' Boo laughed. 'You sound like her mother.'

'Let's not go there, ma'am.' Jo gave a small smile. She and Billie were well aware that the young detective's maternal history was a minefield. Now definitely wasn't the time to tiptoe through that disaster area.

'Break a leg then.' Billie used the ancient theatrical good luck expression, high-fiving Jo, before the young detective carefully slid out of the back seat and hobbled on her crutch towards the shop doorway immediately opposite Boo's soon-to-be new home.

'She's got some guts that girl,' Boo said to Billie as they watched Jo get into position.

'Goose calling the chicken plucky.' Billie put the van into gear and moved off again. 'But you're right. I underestimated her before. Couldn't live without Jo on the team now.'

As Billie did a circuit around the small busy market town, turning into the back lane leading to the Trap House, she felt a sense of unease. It was nothing to do with the possibility of being tracked. She had now fully briefed the team on all of her stalker's activities. Today, Billie had moved out of base in a car with darkened windows, before being transferred to the undercover van. A backup vehicle was following behind, just to check whether she was somehow still being tailed and if so, they could nab the driver. So far, no sign. Being short-staffed, Billie tried not to remind herself that it was an extra safeguard that she could well have done without instigating. But after finding the message with Chip Little's body, there was now confirmation of a direct link between her hunter and the Lucifer line.

She'd discounted Josta as a suspect once and for all, not only because the thought of her being linked to a major drugs ring was totally preposterous, especially when Billie recalled having witnessed Josta's rebuke of Luciana Martinez days earlier on that subject, but also because she would have had to have been an award-winning actress to have reacted as she had at Chip's autopsy. She hadn't shared any of her earlier suspicions in that direction with her team, thank goodness. The implications were too horrific to even contemplate.

Billie had asked for Cilla's son to be picked up at the ferry terminal, on arriving back from his latest working trip to Amsterdam. Perhaps he had a dark car and a history of stalking? She damned herself for not having sussed out Cilla earlier.

'You will make sure to keep communications with Ellis open?' It was an order not a question. Billie glanced out of the van, to the right. The blinds were closed on the window fronting IT Solutions, the dummy name of the firm that they were using as a front to set up surveillance opposite Boo's back door. She knew that the team were all in place inside, ready and waiting should Boo be successful in enticing the Lucifer line dealers to move in.

'You're not still worried about that, are you?' Boo rolled her eyes.

'You did question his professionalism...' Billie trailed off for a couple of seconds, seeing Boo bristle as the subject was brought to the fore once again. But she needed reassurance. 'So, of course it's in the back of my mind. He seems shit-hot to me, but I don't want him disappearing from *this* job all of a sudden.'

Boo sighed, shaking her head. 'Look, it was *my* fault that he was taken off that undercover operation,' she finally revealed.

'I thought he was caught shagging one of the targets?' Billie protested.

'Yeah, but they were environmental activists, not drug dealers. They were trying to save the planet. God knows, you don't get nicked for that now, you get a medal. Some of the target group were good people. It was a challenge not to genuinely like them. Difficult not to get involved.' Boo's voice was full of regret. Billie could see the difficulties, especially now that climate change solutions were such a big vote winner with governments right around the world.

'I was the one who shopped him.' Boo glanced at Billie. She looked relieved to have gotten the fact off her chest at last.

'Does he know that?' Billie's mind started racing. She needed Ellis to be focused on Boo's welfare, with no thoughts of revenge clouding his judgement. Boo shook her head.

'Nope,' she answered, crestfallen. 'It was tricky. I was sharing a flat with the person he was seeing. I was pretending to be her best friend for God's sake! So you could say that I stabbed both of them in the back,' she added.

'But you were doing your job,' Billie reminded her. She felt there was something more to the fall out. 'Were you and Ellis ever, you know, a couple?' she asked. Boo shook her head. Billie wasn't convinced.

'We were close partners in the team. Maybe, I dunno, yeah, if I'm honest, there was a bit of jealousy on my part. Ellis had shown interest in us being more than just work colleagues, shall we say. But there were too many complications on my part. I was still married, unhappily, but suddenly we were on that job and I wasn't in a position to do anything about it, so...'

'Then the accident happened.' Billie understood the situation now. Boo smiled grimly.

'Guess you could call it divine retribution.' She put on a brave face. 'He tried to come to see me several times after, but I couldn't face him, I felt so guilty. I think he believes that I blame him, but I don't. I condemn myself, for what I did. If I hadn't put in the damning report, he would have been watching my back when the wall fell down.' Boo rubbed her face, as though she was trying to wipe away hurtful memories.

'Well give him a chance this time.' Billie ran her fingers through her hair, trying to keep calm in response to the information and think clearly. 'I'll wager my life on the fact that he's fully on your case with this job.'

As she checked that the coast was clear, then jumped out of the van ready to get Boo settled in her little home of horrors, Billie hoped desperately that her assurances would prove to be correct.

❋

She felt as though she had been poisoned. Even by Billie's low standards, the convenience-store pie that she was ramming down her throat tasted way past its sell-by date. It was late afternoon when she had finally left Boo's Trap House, having made absolutely sure that her friend was okay. Even with Boo's endless reassurances, it had still been difficult to leave her alone there, like baiting up a hook with a juicy piece of meat, waiting for the sharks to come circling.

Billie had taken the vehicle around to the back of the store, in a car park open to a green scrubby area, where she was sitting now on a mound of grass. Word was that, in recent days, youths with out-of-town accents had been hanging around the convenience store's loading and rubbish area, dealing drugs. Intel had also been received that texts had been sent out to regular drug users with opening offers from the Lucifer line. It was a good guess that the new faces were looking for a suitable Cuckoo's house to use for their base.

From the blacked-out windows at the back of Billie's van, she had a clear view of the area and in the next few minutes, as the weak sun of late afternoon finally blinked into early evening, the plan was for Boo to make her way around to the loading area in order to try and attract the teenage drug runners, by playing the part of a junkie attempting to score. Billie was using these last few minutes of low daylight to suss out all the exits and entrances to the area, in order to ensure that Boo was completely protected.

'Auntie Billie!' a young voice squealed in delight. Billie flicked her head around, to see Ash's two older girls running across the grass towards her, balloons clutched in their tiny fingers. Maya, manning baby Tani's pushchair, with all manner of bags and coats dangling off the handles, walked close behind grinning from ear to ear. Normally the sight would have lifted

Billie's spirits, but now as she flicked a glance back towards the loading bay, she desperately willed the sweet little group to turn and walk the other way.

Billie stood up, wiping her hands on her jeans, still keeping her eyes on the convenience store loading area as Indie and Happi flung their arms around Billie's legs in a hug. She bent forward and kissed each on the top of their heads.

'Well, what a surprise!' Billie smiled, as Maya joined them.

'We've been to the circus!' Indie skipped around on the grass, waving her balloon for Billie to see. Out of the corner of her eye, Billie spotted a youth slip out of the back door of the store. His hoodie was up, scarf pulled high over his nose and mouth as he tucked himself into the corner of the loading bay. Happi reached her arms up for a hug. Billie lifted her onto her hip, using the movement to step back. The youth was taking a phone call.

'There's a little kids' circus on in town. They've had a great time,' Maya said. 'Hey, thanks for everything,' she added, peeping down to check that the baby was sleeping soundly. 'I haven't had a chance to say it before, with you being at work non-stop.'

'I did warn you. That's the thing about this job. No normal hours... in fact, I'm working right now...' Billie hoped that Maya would take the hint. Out of the corner of her eye she could see another youth now joining the first. The sun was beginning to sink rapidly beyond the horizon. Any minute now, Boo would be making her way out.

'No worries. We're heading for the bus home.' Maya took Happi from Billie and strapped her into the seat behind the baby in the double pushchair, giving Billie a chance to keep her eye on the loading bay. A downtrodden individual with the odd speedy gait of a user on 'the rattle' and desperate for the next fix, appeared from around the corner and headed towards the loading bay.

'This isn't a great place to be after dark,' Billie advised, realising she would never have given that sort of advice in relation to this pretty town before today. County lines seemed to be spreading like a cancer, even to usually sleepy out-of-the-way places like Hipsmouth. *Is this the sort of future that awaits Indie, Happi and Tani?* Billie dreaded the thought. She shivered.

'Got it,' Maya said to Billie but she was glancing over her shoulder. Another buyer was entering the loading bay area. Billie realised from Maya's knowing look that she was aware of exactly what was taking place there. It was a sad fact, Billie reflected. In her youth a convenience store loading bay simply loaded grocery produce. Life had seemed uncomplicated in so many ways then. Maybe she was getting old.

'Come along, Indie. Put your coat on. We're going on the bus.' Maya poked in one of the bags and lifted out the warm jacket. Billie was pleased that at least one thing that she had arranged was going to plan. She gave the girls farewell hugs, eyes trained all of the time on the now steady stream of buyers making their way to score what she was certain, would be Lucifer line drugs.

Maya was about to walk away, much to Billie's relief, when a large sheet of paper slid from her bag and fell on the grass. Billie swept it up and handed it to her.

'Thanks.' Maya took the paper and then stopped. 'Actually, I know this isn't the right time, but I need to come clean...'

'Sorry?' Billie had already turned towards the van. She could get a better view from the darkened back windows in the vehicle and give a running report to Ellis, positioned two streets away in the undercover operations room in the industrial unit, watching Boo's back door.

'The other night, when I was waiting outside on the steps. I wasn't just looking for work...' Maya started hesitantly.

'Right.' Billie had only half of her mind on the conversation. There was a hidden camera fitted in the back door of the vehicle and if she could only get into position there, she could be capturing vital evidence.

'I was looking for my dad, the policeman I mentioned.' Maya turned the wayward sheet of paper over and handed it to Billie. 'Do you know him?' Billie stared at the photo, swallowing hard.

'I thought you said that you had lost your dad?' Billie stammered in puzzlement.

'Well, I have lost him. He left Mum before I was born. When she died a few weeks ago, I found this photo in a box. I've discovered that he might be working in this area now.'

Billie wanted to congratulate Maya for having all the makings of a good detective. She had been spot on.

'I guess he'll have less hair now,' Maya joked. *She's right there*, Billie silently agreed. She handed the photo back.

'Nope. Sorry,' Billie answered. She was – truly sorry. She'd had some family identity issues of her own in the past, but now was not the time to answer truthfully. Definitely not the moment to break the news to the girl, that the father she longed to meet, was right now less than two hundred yards away as the crow flies. Ellis Darque needed to be totally focused on the job in hand, not a mind-blowing meet-up with a daughter he might not even be aware of.

At that moment, Boo wheeled around the side of the supermarket, about to turn into the loading bay. Billie needed to move, not least because even though Boo was fully disguised, six-year-old Indie knew her as Auntie Boo and liked nothing better than to have a spin in Boo's wheelchair at full pelt, on off-duty team get-togethers. If the child clocked her, then the game was up.

'See you back at home. The bus station's that way.' Billie waved Maya back in the direction they had come from, turning and heading towards the van. Quickly checking that the little party were homeward bound, she slipped inside, clambering over the seats and into the empty back area. She clicked on her mobile and focused the camera.

'She's made contact. Two youths... a third one has just joined the group. All wearing dark jackets, hoodies pulled up and scarves covering their noses and mouths.' She clicked away as she spoke.

'Okay, nice work. Thought we might be sitting here all night waiting for a welcome party,' Ellis replied. *Little does he know how close he's come to a family reunion.* Billie pushed the thought to one side, as Boo turned back from the deal she was making, having been careful to play out the agreed script of sadness, lonesome living and the need for a little regular illegal something to calm her 'condition'.

'She's offered the carrot on a stick. Made clear that her gaff is just around the corner...' Ellis relayed to Billie, from his position listening via Boo's hidden microphone.

'On her way back now,' Billie confirmed as she watched Boo slowly trundle into the momentary light spilling from the back of the store before turning at the corner and disappearing out of view. The three youths stepped forward into the light. Billie clicked away with the camera as they paused to talk for a moment and then moved off, following Boo's route.

'I think they're going after her,' Billie announced, quickly exiting the van from a side door and making her way across the car park in the dark. She wanted to make sure that the team were on the right track and that the gang weren't simply going to mug Boo and run away with her wheelchair to sell for scrap metal. She wasn't sure if she was truly relieved or not when the three youths fell in line either side of Boo and started up what looked like jokey banter. 'Yep. They've caught up with Boo.' Billie had the microphone and mouthpiece attached to her ear.

'Got them chatting away. The girl hasn't lost it,' Ellis relayed in admiration, listening in remotely to the conversation via Boo's rigged wheelchair as Billie kept back in the shadows and followed them along the side of the convenience store wall onto the front street. 'Here we go. One of them has just asked to use the toilet in her house, saying the store facilities are closed for cleaning...'

Billie watched as the group crossed a road and then headed for the front door of the flat Boo had made her temporary home.

'They're going in,' Billie relayed to Ellis, as Boo unlocked the door and the youths pushed into the lobby in front of her. She slowly followed as Billie ran her fingers through her hair wanting desperately to tag behind, in order to ensure Boo would be okay. The door banged shut.

'Right. Got them this side,' Ellis answered. 'So far so chilled. They're having a look around.'

Billie turned back, dropping a few coins into the dish of a beggar by the cash machine outside of the small supermarket's front door. She stooped down as she did so.

'You all right?' she asked Jo. 'I'll go and get you a cuppa and a sandwich under the pretence of being a good citizen.' Billie added.

'Thank you, have a good day,' the younger detective answered, probably for the first time ever not using the title ma'am, as she usually did, in answer to Billie. She was burrowed down in a ratty sleeping bag, keeping an eye on the windows of the flat straight ahead.

'Thanks, missus. Looks like all my birthdays have come at once.' She nodded to Billie a few minutes later when she emerged with a takeaway cup of machine-grim hot chocolate, a sandwich curled up at the corners and a dried-out cupcake sealed in cellophane. Billie gave a small smile as she handed the sorry dinner over, before walking on.

'Okay. They've just announced that they're moving in full time. Rifling through the cupboards for grub,' Ellis said to Billie via her earpiece. 'Good job we stocked up on crisps. And biscuits. Boo's telling them they're from the food bank. Needless to say, they're not in a sharing mood with their host.' Billie's stomach tied in a knot. She was desperate to minimise any risk. She turned and retraced her steps, giving the impression to anyone interested that she might have lost her way. Jo was unwrapping her sad little cake. Billie bent down in mid-stride for a quick word.

'Now they're inside you can knock off and take a few days' sick leave. That's an order,' she whispered, before continuing to walk around the side of the store towards the car park, without looking back. Her mobile phone rang. She clicked it on.

'Billie, are you all right?' Her heart leaped. It was Max. 'So sorry about having to rush off the other night,' he added.

'Sorry to hear about your friend, Jamie,' Billie commiserated. 'It sounds like his death was unexpected.'

'That's why I'm ringing.' Billie sensed tension in Max's voice. 'He died due to an overdose of burandanga – Devil's Breath,' he clarified, though no clarification was needed.

'Josta mentioned he's been with you recently in South America...' Max still hadn't confirmed the location of where he had recently travelled, but Billie didn't doubt that she was correct.

'There are concerns that his death was in retaliation, for recent events.' Max didn't try to argue. 'Another of the team mysteriously died yesterday, too, and some family members have been affected by ugly incidents involving the Devil's Breath.'

'Like Lola?' Billie asked.

'And Jas Sanghera,' Max replied, 'probably mistaken for a friend rather than a patient, if someone had watched her leaving her counselling session with me at my home.'

'So you're saying a South American death squad is in the country?' Billie could hear the astonishment in her own voice. The idea sounded like something in a boys' storybook.

'Possibly, or perhaps contacts working in the UK, carrying out orders. I've made Josta take a few days off. She's gone to stay with a friend.' He sounded tired. 'Billie, I'm worried about you.'

'Me?' Billie had reached the van. There were several people she was also worrying about tonight, but she didn't count herself as one of them.

'You were pictured with me in the newspaper. Anyone would have thought we were more than just colleagues.' He said the words tentatively.

'I think we won the argument that the reporter was clearly writing rubbish,' Billie answered.

'I'm ringing from a payphone at a service station. I'll be staying in Cumbria,' he added, 'in a little out-of-the-way hotel I know. Just for a couple of days, until we get more intel on the incidents. I'd feel better if you would join me here.'

'Tonight?' Billie blinked hard. Had she heard correctly? Had Max just invited her to run away with him? An incoming call tone started to cut across the conversation. Was Ellis trying to contact her?

'I'm in the middle of a huge investigation,' Billie started, 'sorry. I really have to go right now.' The call tone continued. Someone was being persistent.

'I know how important that is to you, Billie, but your life is important to me too—'

'Look, I'll ring you back,' she cut in. *Talk about choosing the worst time to ring.* 'I've got an urgent call coming in.'

'I'll send you the name and address of the hotel—' he started before Billie was forced to cut him dead and take the call waiting.

'Sorry,' Billie answered.

'Thought you must be fixing up a hot date,' Ellis teased. *Little did he know*. Billie's mind raced as she tried to switch back to full work mode.

'Is Boo all right?' she asked.

'Doing well,' Ellis answered. 'They're demanding pizzas. There's a takeaway up the street, so Boo's just left on gofer duties. Give you a chance to see for yourself.'

'Ham and pineapple,' Billie ordered at the counter, before slouching down in a seemingly nonchalant fashion on a seat next to Boo, sitting in her wheelchair, in the far corner of the takeaway.

'I hope it's your undercover alias ordering that abomination of a pizza.' Boo chuckled.

'I'm guessing caviar is not on your menu either,' Billie argued.

'Three pizzas and three deep-fried Mars bars,' a girl announced, bringing the order over to Boo and placing them on her knees. Billie grinned. 'What did I tell you?'

'And what does that tell you?' Boo answered, raising her eyebrows.

'That they already have furred arteries at around fourteen years of age?' Billie questioned.

'Pay attention.' Boo took the brakes off her wheelchair. 'One of the pizzas is the haggis special,' she offered.

'There's a Scottish connection,' Billie guessed, now toying with the idea of ordering a deep-fried Mars bar herself. The sweet delicacies may have originated over the border but had caught on like wildfire in the takeaways of north-east England.

'Nearly. I spotted a train ticket that fell out of one of their pockets. Looks like they've just hopped it from Berwick way,' Boo answered, highlighting the most northern town in England, where the country bordered with Scotland, forty miles north. 'Not your usual county lines urbanites.' Billie frowned.

'Neither was Sophie Grey.' The child had started her journey in Durham, fifty miles south. 'No word on the Beast's identity yet?' Billie enquired hopefully.

'Nope. We're still at the polite niceties stage,' Boo quipped. 'Love to sit here chewing the fat, but I've got to get back to my druggie boys.' Boo's face shadowed for a split second. 'Two of them are carrying blades and the third one a gun. He was sitting at the table splitting heroin and cocaine, making up wraps when I left. Guess it's tea on the knee tonight.' She winked.

Billie wasn't fooled. Things were starting well, and she was grateful for this moment of light relief, but one wrong move and Boo was indicating that there would be serious consequences. Time to get back into character.

'I'll have a word with Derek Blythe. His allotment's up that way,' Billie whispered as her pizza was handed to her.

'Good luck with that,' Boo answered. 'He puts on quite a show for you, but from my viewpoint, he gave up any serious detective work a long time ago.' Billie could see that Boo wasn't going to forgive him easily for taking the front-page story claiming to have been the hero of the firebombed pub, but Billie still had a soft spot for the hugely experienced copper. Given half a chance, she would still welcome him back with open arms.

Billie followed Boo outside as she turned her wheelchair to the right and headed back down the road, like a human packhorse.

'She's on her way,' Billie relayed to Ellis, before her mind turned to Max once again, all alone in some romantic hotel just an hour or so west, in the UK's beautiful Lake District.

'Just got a message relayed for you from base. Urgent,' Ellis answered. 'On behalf of the chief. He wants you back there for a meet-up immediately.'

'You're joking?' Billie responded.

'Messenger said he couldn't get you on your moby and he's in a meeting for the next thirty minutes, so not to ring back. But it's a red alert in connection with this stuff. Don't worry. As soon as you see Boo re-enter the Trap House, we'll ensure that she's safe. I'm not in the mood for any crazy surprises tonight,' he added. Billie's mind returned to Maya and her search for her dad. *Little does he know how close he's come to the surprise of his life*, Billie couldn't help thinking.

'Damn him.' Billie was beginning to think that the chief was demob happy. *He* might already have his mind on exotic shores, but she wanted to focus on the job in hand. After a beat during which she crammed in more silent expletives than she had ever thought possible, she reluctantly conceded that he was fairly high profile from TV briefings, so maybe he was just being extra careful not to draw any unwanted attention to Hipsmouth tonight, by coming over to meet her.

'Can you spare Andy?' Now Billie had spent a few days supervising Derek Blythe's nephew, she could see that he had all the signs of being an even better detective than his uncle, having inherited Derek's obsession with fair play, but being naturally more politically correct due to his younger years. 'Send him out to the car park with his keys, I'll swap him for the van's. He can keep an eye out from that angle.'

'Will do. My guess is that after they've finished their nosebags, they will start dealing again round by the convenience-store trash.'

Billie ended the call, watched Boo bang on the door and bravely enter the Trap House, before heading quickly for the parked van. She was determined to get the meeting with the chief over and done with and speed back, ready to act should any trouble kick off.

28

PIGS MIGHT FLY

F*unny how a sunny day could turn so dark*, Billie thought as she parked the car in the near empty police headquarters and jumped out. She had positioned the pool vehicle close to the back door, in order to make a quick getaway. The chief's office was on the second floor, just along from the back staircase that led from this nondescript entrance, for staff use. Her mobile rang as she gathered speed. Ellis Darque's name flashed up.

'If you need an excuse to get away from the chief's oily clutches, tell him it's starting to kick off here. We could do with all hands back on deck.' Billie felt her tummy tighten with tension.

'What's up?' She stopped dead, wondering whether to disobey the chief and head straight back.

'Two of 'em have finished their tea and headed off. Dealing right now behind the store. But the elder, guarding the stash, has also snorted a fair bit and is going loco about his pizza not being up to scratch. Already pulled the gun on Boo once to put the frighteners on her.'

'I'm coming back now.' As she turned, distracted at the news, a figure darted out from behind, wrenching her backwards sharply, one arm tightly wrapped around her body like a vice. The other hand whipped into view holding a cloth, forcing it firmly across her nose and mouth. Billie struggled frantically for a moment, before her body relaxed. Something weird had just happened. But what, exactly? Her brain suddenly seemed a bit addled.

She felt herself being pushed forward from behind, as the door was opened.

'Now use your security fob to get through this next door,' the voice ordered. Billie looked around. Did she recognise that speaker? The voice sounded muffled. She realised that the person issuing instructions was wearing one of those balaclavas that only showed eyes and mouth. The vision made her smile for some reason. In fact, she felt sort of drunk, totally chilled out as she made her way up the back staircase and into the corridor.

'Check there's no one in the incident room,' the voice directed her. It seemed like a perfectly good idea, so Billie headed into the office, almost bumping into Daz, the security guard, doing his rounds.

'Everyone pulled an early shift tonight?' he asked, indicating the empty room.

'We're all out in Hipsmouth doing an undercover operation.' Billie smiled, holding her finger to her lips. 'Shh, don't tell anyone,' she added. 'It's top secret.' Daz reacted in surprise at the information.

'My sister lives down that way and my mother. In fact, most of my family. Should I warn them, if any trouble is going to kick off?' he asked.

'Maybe. If they're druggies or going to the convenience store that backs onto the scrubland.' Billie smiled sweetly. Daz frowned slightly, then continued on his route, taking out his mobile phone.

Billie looked around. Where could her new friend have gone

to? She suddenly noticed the person emerging through the door from the staircase, still wearing a balaclava.

'Move, quick,' came a whispered order. Billie acted on the suggestion, jogging towards the incident room, her captor close on her heels. 'Keep the light off. Now tell me everything you know about the inquiries into the murders of this lot.'

Billie felt happy to help, as she viewed the scene-of-crime photos still visible on the walls, via the light of a street lamp spilling into the room. She ran through the leads to date as her custodian strode back and forth across the room. Then she turned on a PC to double-check dates and times and people's names.

'There's no need to keep that face-thing on,' Billie finally said cheerfully. 'You don't have to play games, I know exactly who you are.' The figure stopped for a moment, then quickly crossed to the water dispenser in the corner of the room, grabbing a paper cup and filling it with water. Hastily, they reached into a jacket pocket and brought out a tiny clear bag containing white powder. The gloved hand sprinkled the contents of the packet into the drink. Billie looked on benignly as the darkly dressed figure mixed the concoction with a pen left on Boo's workplace.

'Sip this,' Billie's detainer ordered, holding the drink to Billie's lips. Her throat felt dry, so it seemed like a good idea to drink up. The person was close now.

'Are you in a sexual relationship with Max Strong?' the person asked. Billie sniggered. It sounded funny coming from them, bearing in mind they probably already knew the answer.

'He's waiting for me at the hotel,' Billie answered cheerily. 'Tonight might finally be the night.' She ran her tongue over her lips. They felt dry now too. She reached for the drink and took another sip.

'Which hotel?' the person persisted. Billie wanted to tell, she sincerely wanted to. Somehow it felt impossible to refuse. 'Beats me,' she finally answered truthfully. 'He might have texted the details.' She reached for her mobile.

'Sounds like you're up for some action tonight.' The body moved closer, running one finger down the dip in Billie's cleavage. Billie chuckled. She didn't think that the person before her should have been doing that. The room seemed to tilt on its axis for a moment. Billie reached out to grab her keeper's arm, but they were holding her tightly now, pressing up against her, undoing the buttons of her shirt and her jeans, their breathing heavy.

'Now turn around and bend over the desk.' The words were huskily demanding. Billie did as she was bid, a key effect of poisoning by Devil's Breath being that all free will is eliminated, the victim totally responsive to even the most horrific and shocking of suggestions.

Billie sang the words 'Tonight's gonna be a drug night' whilst clicking her fingers to the beat of a tune, as the car driven by her new amour, turned in to Hipsmouth High Street. Her guardian was wearing a hoodie pulled up and a face mask now. Billie suddenly yawned.

'Let's go to bed,' she suggested. 'To sleep this time,' she added, looking down at her unbuttoned shirt. Had she taken her clothes off recently? Looked like it, but she couldn't really remember. Somehow that seemed okay. The two of them were friends after all. Billie blinked. Her vision felt a little blurred. She could see little fish appearing to swim through the car. She glanced into the passenger mirror. There was a nice red rose behind her ear. When had she put that there?

'Are we going to the beach?' she asked. 'There's something

fishy around here.' She sniggered at the joke. Her friend must have seen the brightly coloured sea creatures on the dashboard too. They reminded Billie of those fishes in the tank at the mortuary.

'Where's the Trap House?' the driver asked. 'Point it out.' Billie noticed that her new lover didn't seem to be in such a fun mood anymore. She could see the convenience store now and Jo still hunkered down in the sleeping bag in the doorway.

'Aww, look. I told her she didn't have to stay on watch anymore,' Billie announced.

'Who's on watch?' The driver was speaking sharply now. Billie didn't like that, even though she wanted to tell them.

'The Cuckoo's in the nest right over there,' Billie pointed to the flat with Boo inside.

'And they've got live feeds and audio in there, right?' Billie's new friend demanded confirmation. Billie nodded enthusiastically, guessing that she must have told them that earlier, though she couldn't remember if she had or not. In fact, she was having trouble suddenly understanding who the driver of this car was. Did she know them? Her chauffeur pulled the car over by the kerb, before taking out a mobile and ringing a number.

'Game's up. Got trouble heading your way. Gather the stuff, pronto. Stay cool, open the door, use the shooter, then get the hell out. Fail to shut her up or lose the gear and you're dead.' The car door was pushed open.

'Get out and go inside the Trap House. They're waiting,' Billie was directed. She climbed out of the car. It sounded like a good plan. She walked down the street, crossed the road and turned to wave before giving a hard knock at the door. Billie didn't notice if the driver waved back. They appeared to have disappeared into thin air. Did she just dream all of that? She knocked again.

'Police!' she called loudly, when the door opened. A tall, muscular young man, who reeked of danger and smelled of the psychotic-inducing version of cannabis known as skunk, loomed in the opening. *If looks could kill*, Billie thought as she stepped inside. 'I was told to come,' she announced, on registering her less than effusive welcome. Even Boo, sitting in the middle of the room, looked absolutely horrified to see her.

'Hey.' She waved at Boo. 'How's it going with the bad boy here?' *Weird*, Billie thought, that Boo wasn't answering and also that the wallpaper pattern seemed to be moving. She couldn't quite remember how she had gotten here.

'Bitch Feds!' the youth shouted, grabbing a holdall from the table, scooping up stray wraps and throwing them into the bag as he angrily crossed to Boo. 'Don't mind if I stick you with this flicky, bitch!' – he grabbed a craft knife from his pocket and pushed it under Boo's chin, before spinning around – 'but the Beast says to take *you* out,' he screamed into Billie's face, pulling out a gun. Even in her mind-altered state she recognised it as a Colt 45.

Her reaction was to move her head to the side at the same instant that Boo seemed to fly through the air, flipping her wheelchair over and smashing the youth hard on the back of his head with her removable wheelchair footrest, swung like a shot-putter going for Olympic gold. The gun went off with an almighty bang as he dropped to the floor, the bullet ricocheting off the wall. Billie felt the weight of Boo covering her as she lay stunned on the shagpile carpet. The back door could be heard bursting open as Ellis and the team hurtled into the lounge.

'He's unconscious,' Billie heard Ellis inform the team as they crowded around the dealer. 'Stem the blood flow and call the paramedics in.' He crouched down beside Boo. 'You okay?' He put his arm around Boo's shoulders, as she sat back on the floor, shaken but nodding in confirmation.

'It's the boss I'm worried about.' Boo sounded a bit breathless. Billie could see them both staring at her with concern. She giggled.

'Did you see all those pigs come flying out of the wallpaper?' she asked, blinking hard. Was this some sort of crazy bad dream she'd just walked into?

29

WILDE BEAST

Billie felt deathly as she opened her eyes for a second and then closed them again. Her head was thumping, her mouth as dry as a sandstorm and every inch of her body ached. She tried lifting her eyelids once more, feeling something uncomfortable digging into her left hand. She moved to brush it away.

'Don't take the drip out. It's there for your own good.' The voice spoke in hushed tones. Billie tried opening her eyes again. White walls took shape in her vision and then white sheets. She was lying under them.

'What's going on?' she mumbled, trying to tug at her left hand once more, before Boo's face loomed into view.

'It's okay, Billie. You're safe, in hospital. Everything is fine.' Billie blinked hard as Boo's words cut through the wads of cotton that seemed to have taken the place of brain cells. Her memory was coming back – some of it anyway. She pushed the covers back, tried to pull herself upright.

'Here.' Boo reached over and adjusted Billie's pillows as she dragged herself into a sitting position. 'Drink this.' Billie sipped from the glass of water being offered from the top of the bedside locker, as instructed.

'Why am I here?' Billie remembered being with Boo in the pizza takeaway, swapping car keys with DC Andy Hines, driving back to base, taking a call from Ellis then, what? Her mind was utterly blank.

'You've been assaulted, Billie,' Boo explained. 'Last night someone drugged you and made you do things...'

'Like what?' Billie's mind was starting to clear now, enough to realise that Boo was trying to break some news to her – gently.

'Well, we don't know exactly what happened after you went back to base last night,' Boo started.

'The chief sent a message saying I had to go straight back.' Billie remembered that much. She hadn't entirely lost her mind. Boo clutched Billie's hand.

'Well, that's the thing. It wasn't actually the chief. He was out at the theatre with David's mum, he said.' Any news about David's mum was bad news, as far as Billie was concerned, but she had a feeling that it was about to get much worse. 'The call seemed to have come from inside headquarters, but the surveillance team were concentrating on the Trap House and just passed the message on to you.'

'So what? Did I pass out on the floor or something... and, what happened at the Trap House?' Billie felt her tummy tense.

'Daz on security met you on the way in. He said you were chattering away, looking totally normal – maybe too talkative, if anything. You were alone.'

'What did I say? Jesus, I can't seem to remember a thing.' Billie rubbed her head.

Boo lifted a folder, which had been tucked down the side of her wheelchair cushion, opened it and took out a photograph. She paused for a moment before turning it towards Billie. The photo showed Billie staring at the camera with a glazed look, her pupils dilated. Her dishevelled hair was decorated by a single dead rose, tucked behind her ear.

She swallowed hard as she took in the whole view. Her shirt was wide open, leaving little to the imagination. Around her neck a large card was hanging off a string necklace. The words on it read *Wilde Beast*.

'Where was this?' Billie felt sick.

'The Trap House,' Boo answered, already having guessed Billie's reaction. She pushed the sick bowl that had been left on the bedside locker under her chin just before Billie retched into it. Her mind ached, her body ached. One part of her anatomy in particular. She didn't have to be Einstein to guess why.

'I'm so sorry, Billie.' Boo stretched across and hugged Billie as the truth sank in.

'You've taken DNA samples?' Billie started, her detective head already pushing personal feelings of horror to one side. She was almost grateful that she had no memory of what had occurred. Boo nodded.

'Blood tests show that you had burandanga in your bloodstream. Ellis mentioned that you had discussed the drug with him and Max Strong.'

'Have you heard from Max?' Had he texted her his hotel address? Had she shared it, putting him in danger? Billie panicked. 'I need my mobile...' She opened the drawer of the locker.

'Got it here with me,' Boo replied, taking the mobile out of her folder. 'This photo seems to have been captured during the incident.' She pulled out another photo, this time a half headshot of someone wearing a balaclava, almost all of their face totally covered.

'Do you remember this person?' Boo coaxed gently. 'Or anyone bringing you back to the Trap House–'

'I can't believe that I did that. I could have gotten you kill–' Billie cut over her. Boo patted Billie's hand.

'Calm down. We'll go through events later. When you are feeling stronger. Good news is that we've got the senior dealer, who was apprehended in the house, in custody, along with his cocaine and heroin booty. He's not talking yet, got a bit of a headache himself.' She gave a small smile. 'But when we break the news of his likely sentence, his tongue will hopefully loosen.' Billie ran her fingers through her hair. Her default stress reflex. She scrolled through her mobile. There was no message from Max. Had her captor read one and wiped it? Was Max in trouble? How could her stalker be linked to both county lines drugs and also Max's recent activities? Her head thumped with the effort of attempting to unravel that terrifying question.

'We need to ring around all of the hotels in the Lake District,' she started, pulling the covers back from the bed.

'Not so fast.' Boo pushed Billie gently back against the pillows. 'Max Strong can take care of himself, I'm sure. Your mobile has been checked thoroughly. From the report, there were no text messages left, sent nor deleted last night.'

Billie tried to think. Maybe Max had rung to tell her of a change of plan, and she had simply forgotten that too? One memory did suddenly spring into her mind.

'I remember seeing Maya.' Billie recalled the conversation that she'd had with the young nanny, playing through her mind now. She looked at Boo. 'You said that she reminded you of someone you once knew,' Billie queried. 'Was it the environmentalist that Ellis had an affair with?'

Boo paused as though finding it difficult to summon the words to reply, but by the look on her face, Billie already knew the answer.

'She's his daughter?' Boo had a question in her voice, but Billie knew that she wasn't really asking. Billie nodded.

'Maya's the double of Angie, her mum.' Boo rubbed her hand over her eyes as if trying to wipe away her memories.

'You knew then that she was pregnant with Ellis's child?' Billie suddenly had the feeling that Boo was feeling even more sick than she was. Her friend nodded.

'I've got no excuses,' Boo finally said. 'Jealousy is a terrible thing. When he was whisked off the job, she thought he'd done a runner abroad, because a warrant was out for him. That was the cover story. Angie couldn't believe that he hadn't made any contact. I let her cry on my shoulder through many long nights and the whole UCO team moved out before she gave birth. I wasn't aware of the final outcome, until you introduced us the other day.'

'What else could you have done? It was meant to be an undercover operation,' Billie reasoned.

'That wasn't Maya's fault though, was it? I should have told the truth, refused to live the lie. Angie was a nice girl, just passionate about saving the planet.' Boo patted her legs. 'But bad deeds come back to haunt you. I didn't spill the beans to her, and I didn't tell Ellis that he was about to become a dad. Let's face it. I deserved to have a wall fall down on me. As far as I know, he still has no idea.' The conversation was suddenly interrupted by a knock. Ellis popped his head around the door.

'Speak of the devil,' Billie teased, to lighten the mood.

'The devil? That's this one here.' He thumbed towards Boo, grinning. 'Don't get on the wrong side of her when she's got a footrest in her hand. Billy Big Buns is still under guard on the next floor, suffering from concussion. Dent in his head the size of a dinner plate.' He chuckled. 'I spotted Ash coming in.' He turned to Boo. 'He said to get a move on, it's his turn to come and visit now. The nanny and kids are on their way in to see you as well. We need a booking system if you are going to be lazing around here for days, boss,' he joked.

'No way am I doing that. I'm checking out.' Billie glanced across to Boo and raised her eyebrows. Maya was on her way in. The time had come to put things straight. Boo was looking pensive but nodded in agreement. 'Ellis, Boo's going to take you down to the canteen. There's someone heading in that she'd like you to meet.'

'Not setting me up on a blind date, are you?' Ellis teased Boo. 'I'll see you down there. Just got to have another word with the watch outside your old housemate's room. Reassure him you're not heading his way again with that killer bit of gear clenched in your mitt.' He left, upbeat as always, no idea that his whole view of the world was about to be transformed in just a few minutes.

Billie hoped the life-changing news heading Ellis's way wouldn't cast dark shadows over his sunny disposition, but she had suffered parental deceit of her own. This was a secret screaming out to be told. 'Come here.' She gave Boo a tight hug. 'You can do it, sweetheart,' she whispered, 'and thanks. You'll always be an angel to me.' Boo gave a small smile before trundling out like a woman heading for the gallows.

Billie lay back on the pillows for a moment trying to absorb the various truths shared, fearing how many facts from the night before Boo may still be keeping from her, in an act of protective kindness, until she got her head back into gear. The wad of dressing between her legs and her aching insides meant that more horrors were about to unfold when DNA results came back. A harassed-looking nurse suddenly entered the room.

'How are you feeling, dear?' She plumped up Billie's pillows. 'We really don't recommend so many visitors at one time.'

'I'm perfectly fine,' Billie lied.

'All right then, I'll let her in.' The nurse responded as though she had given in on a battle that had been raging somewhere.

'Who?' Billie took another sip of her water. Her head was clearing a little more now.

'The woman giving me grief at the nurses' station. I'll be glad to get her off my back to be honest,' she added, in her lovely Irish lilt. 'Says she's the new press officer with you lot and the chief of police, no less, has told her to have a word with you. Now I don't want to get on the wrong side of him, do I?' The nurse checked the clipboard on the bottom of the bed and walked out.

Billie inwardly groaned. The last thing she needed right now, was a bright-eyed, bushy-tailed PR person desperate to make an impression in their brand-new job. Not when she still didn't know herself what had happened last night. But before she'd had a chance to direct the nurse to bar the latest visitor, the door was flung open, and Perry Gooch loomed into view.

'One step nearer and I'm hitting the emergency button,' Billie threatened. 'I thought you had been sent packing?'

'Lance Harris personally gave me the push if that makes you feel better. Not that I'm losing any sleep over that trash merchant,' Perry Gooch replied. 'I've won awards for my journalism. National broadsheets not local tittle-tattle papers, so no need to stress, dear. I'm well overqualified to broadcast police force tales of derring-do.'

Billie couldn't believe that the chief would have given a job to the journalist who had trashed his force. But then again, maybe he'd done a deal with his soon-to-be employer Lance Harris and Perry Gooch's dismissal was in truth, all for show.

'Don't let me keep you. If you're that clever. Head off for one of those important jobs instead.'

'Nice idea, but I'm a single mum with two teenage daughters to get through education in one piece and looking at the county lines gangs currently getting their feet under the table, that might be something of a tall order. I'm a jobbing journo – a pen for hire. I simply sell the tales I'm paid to tell. That doesn't mean I don't like to get my teeth into some solid stories when I get the chance, but my girls come first. I need a regular income.' Perry Gooch opened a folder that had been tucked under her arm.

'The chief has asked me to write a press release about the young officer and he tells me you thought very highly of her. My girls did too. She got them started in the local junior girls' roller derby team. Keeps them off the streets.'

'Jo Green?' Billie blinked hard. 'What about her?' she asked, a feeling of foreboding crawling through her body. There was a beat of silence, unusual for the journalist. It didn't quell Billie's stress response.

'She was murdered last night.' Perry Gooch, to her credit, spoke with regret, attempting to soften the blow, having detected in that split second that Billie had been left in the dark.

'How?' Billie's voice broke into a whisper.

'Her throat was slit in the doorway of the convenience store,' Perry Gooch answered.

The reaction in Billie was physical, like a hard blow to the stomach. If anyone had given her a prediction that she would be breaking her heart about a female that she had once detested, in the arms of a woman she had so recently wanted to destroy, Billie would have accused them of being totally insane. But the news that the eccentric young detective, once known as The Grass had been wiped off the face of the earth, made Billie burst into devastated wails.

Whilst Perry Gooch held her close, she sobbed rivers of snot and tears, stopping only to retch once more into the sick bowl. It seemed, for some time, as though she might never be able to stem the flow. Was it her fault? The suspicion that now stabbed through her mind and body was almost too shocking to even contemplate. Had she pointed out Jo's undercover location to the murderer? Had she been the one responsible for the young detective's death?

30

A KILLER DISCOVERY

'Thanks. It's good of you to drive me back to base.' Billie's face was still tear-stained, her eyes red and swollen from hearing the news of Jo Green's fate, as she looked out of Perry Gooch's car window. People passed by as though they didn't have a care in the world. Billie had almost forgotten what that felt like.

'It's the least that I could do,' Perry replied. 'You may think I'm a hard bitch, DSI Wilde' – Perry waved her hand out of the car window, holding up her middle finger to a speeding car overtaking dangerously towards them, as if to prove her point – 'but even I wouldn't just spring that sort of news on you. I thought that you had already been informed of Jo Green's murder.'

Billie felt a wave of shock threaten to surge up and envelop her once again, at the mention of the name. She ran her fingers through her hair, desperately trying to get control of her emotions. Clearly the team had planned to break the news to her gently, once she had first gotten acquainted with the fact that she had been drugged and raped the night before. Maybe the chief didn't wrap her in as much cotton wool as she had imagined, being his goddaughter. That thought offered some small relief. Perry Gooch ripped a pile of paper handkerchiefs from a box wedged next to the gear lever.

'Thanks.' Billie blew her nose, begging herself to get a grip. She decided to change the subject, to take her mind off the harrowing news. 'So, now you can tell me who fed you embargoed information on Christy Callaghan's murder and gave you an early heads-up on the address of Rupert Grey. I know we've got someone spilling sensitive information.' Billie thought of the Trap House in Amsterly, not that she was in any position to complain about tipping off criminals, after her behaviour the night before. She inwardly cringed, aware that it could only get worse when she eventually discovered the full facts.

'I'd have to kill you if I gave you names of my informants.' Perry chuckled. 'But let's just say that money talks and Lance Harris pays the local moles well, especially if they are telling tales about the fuzz. I will say that it's usually those new to the job, desperate to big up that they are on a major investigation who spill the beans most easily, or old-timers ready to throw in the towel, so want to top up their pension pots. Or sometimes security and even affiliated services. You would be surprised to find out how many of your working colleagues can't wait to hotfoot it to the nearest phone to share confidential intel, after you've just briefed them, if the price is right.' It was sobering information.

'That doesn't exactly narrow it down.' Billie gave a thin smile. 'I thought you were on our side now?' Perry shook her head genially.

'I don't usually take sides, that's a fact. Unless it's my kids we're talking about. I'm always on the side of my girls, DSI Wilde. When I was a proper journo with no one else to think of, all I wanted was to tell the world the truth. But now that I'm a fully paid-up card-carrying adult with responsibilities, I've learned that telling the truth doesn't always pay the rent and school fees are on the up.'

'Is that why you took the job at the *Herald* group?' Billie asked.

'Got it in one. I had to move my girls from our local school where they were getting bullied, to a fee-paying place. I'm glad to say they are both top of their class, so it all worked out for the best. Shame their old mum had to be put up with being browbeaten at work instead.' She smiled ruefully. 'But you make your choices and take the money,' she added. 'Believe me, there's no bigger bully than Lance Harris when he's whipping up his workforce to generate stories that people will rush to buy.'

'Truthful or not,' Billie added, though she felt less stung now by the lies Perry had written about her earlier, Jo Green's death having added some perspective to the slight. Perry Gooch nodded in agreement.

'Name of the game.' She stopped at a zebra crossing to allow some young boys on bikes to cross. Billie suddenly experienced a vivid image of Chip Little doing a wheelie on his gold bike, giving her a cheeky wink. Her emotions welled up again. She caught a single tear as it darted down her cheek, wiping her face. She still hadn't any recollection of what exactly had happened the night before, but somewhere in her subconscious the shock of the events appeared to be continuing to have an effect.

'The irony of it is, I've been sitting on the biggest story for the past few months, right on my doorstep. Thought of selling it to one of my old editors on a national paper, but it would have been a case of cutting off the hand that feeds me.' Perry glanced at Billie. 'Lance Harris isn't feeding me anymore though. Can I trust you, DSI Wilde?' Perry asked.

'Call me Billie,' came the reply. 'Is it illegal?' Billie asked. 'Your story?'

'It's about drugs, coming into this area. It's the kids I'm thinking about. My girls are the same ages as Sophie Grey and Chip Little. Someone's got to put a stop to this.' Billie sat up straight in her seat, suddenly alert.

'You're right about that. If you know anything–'

'I've seen lots of things, including the fact that some people in the police must also be in the know, or the whole drugs movement couldn't run so smoothly across the country. I don't want my girls to be orphans, that's the bottom line. I don't want a bullet through my head.'

'This conversation is confidential, I swear.' Billie didn't hold out any hope of the captured drugs dealer at the Trap House giving up anything that would shine much light on the enquiry. She had already learned that the cogs in the county lines wheel only knew enough to turn their own tiny bit of the structure. The investigation desperately needed someone who could show how the whole machine ran and who, ultimately, was the engine driver.

Perry's car pulled away from the crowded roads of the city now. Perhaps the view of fields all around and the sensation of space enabled her to feel it was finally safe to talk.

'I'm putting my girls' lives in your hands. If anything were to happen to them...' she warned sternly.

'You've got my word,' Billie insisted. 'Believe me, no one wants to put a stop to this more than I do. Once and for all.' Perry Gooch wiped her hand over her mouth in thought for a moment before speaking up.

'I believe that Lance Harris is using the *Herald* group of newspapers to distribute drugs around the country. It's big. We are talking regular and huge supplies delivered to various collection points, covering the whole of the UK. From the local county line hub location, the drugs are further cut or packaged into wraps and sent out with kids like Sophie Grey, to far-flung towns.

'The hub dealer, that is the person responsible for the Lucifer line in this area – my informants tell me he's known as the Beast – will be holding the line's encrypted phone. That's the number everyone phones, just like ordering a takeaway. The Beast then texts one of the dealers at the Trap House, who are using a burner phone that can be dumped if you lot get wind of the number. The Trap House dossers, if it's a major purchase, or one of the little kids on bikes locally, if the order is just a wrap or two, deliver into the hands of the users.'

Billie had already got the gist of how the drug distribution and sales ran in the towns, what she needed was information to enable her to catch those higher up.

'So are you telling me that Lance Harris is the Beast, the guy running the Lucifer line?' Billie questioned.

'No, he's bigger than just one county line. My guess is that he has international backers. After all, his own main home isn't even in the UK. He produces so-called local papers for areas right around the country and delivers to those regions every single day. This is how it works, listen up.' Perry pulled the car into a lay-by, looking all around, as though checking that she wasn't being followed. She appeared a lot more nervous now than the cocky journalist Billie had thought she had sussed so well.

'The drugs arrive in the country inside of giant aluminium reels of paper, we're talking two tons in weight and there are several deliveries per day, all shipped from countries where the drug cartels have set up newsprint businesses. The reels are sealed, so not opened until they arrive at the printing press. The *Herald* group owns some of the largest paper presses in the country. Most of the process is highly automated, so not many staff around to see any dirty dealings going on. The drugs are speedily removed from the reels and packed inside of sealed cellophane packets surrounded with those free advertising flyers and TV listing mags that you find in the middle of papers these days.'

'Newspaper dandruff.' Billie nodded. That's what her dad used to call it when the loose flyers would fall out all over the floor as he opened the papers.

'Expensive fallout this stuff, hence the packaging. It's common in all sorts of newspapers and magazines now, so the inserts don't draw undue attention. On different days, different papers are carrying the packages. Lorries are waiting to take them across the country every night. Everyone understands the need for speed with newspaper production, so there is rarely any intervention in the process. The trucks are owned by the *Herald* group and so are the newsagents they deliver to.

'When the papers arrive at specific newsagents, carefully hired staff remove the dandruff, as you call it, and separate the drugs from the flyers. All very smooth. Then arrangements are made for the kids to take deliveries out to other, often smaller county towns, from there. For extra insurance, these children rarely meet the head of each county line, simply taking instructions on constantly changing mobiles that are dumped every few days. One child delivers to another.

'Various-aged kids take on greater or lesser responsibility. The older teenagers carry weapons and police any trouble. Once the drugs are sold, the mule returns the money to the newsagents which launders the takings back to the county line owner. Another kid then takes their place, carrying drugs on their bodies or in school backpacks. If they're caught, kids are hard to prosecute and easy to replace. This area hadn't been touched until now, due to the local gang leaders having a very loyal clientele. But now the market's wide open.'

'Thanks to the murders of Christy Callaghan,' Billie

breathed out, 'and Jesus O'Brian on next door's patch.' Perry Gooch nodded.

'I'm guessing that's why Lance Harris is giving it the royal visit, bringing one international businessperson after another into the offices, pressing the flesh. He's going flat out to impress–'

'Looking for investors. Just like any big business,' said Billie, finishing her sentence. It all made sense and now he had the chief all starry-eyed for the international jet-setting lifestyle.

'I had to do a story for the woman's mag in the Friday paper, about the life cycle of a fashion garment or some such nonsense, from the frock being produced, to photographed on a model, printed in the magazine and so on, fluffy story for the gals. Anyway, I had to take some pics of the printing press. Turned up on location late one night after having had a flat tyre en route and stumbled across a drugs delivery in progress. Thank God no one spotted me.'

'How come none of the staff have spilled the beans?' Billie wanted to be sure of the truth of the story.

'My guess is that there are several coppers getting backhanders on forces up and down the country to keep the job running like clockwork.' Perry Gooch looked worried. 'Please tell me you are not one of those. Your reaction to Green's death is telling me that my hunch that you're one of the good guys is right?' Perry swallowed hard.

'You're safe, I swear,' Billie assured her. She suddenly wasn't as sure about the chief. Was he on the payroll of Lance Harris already? 'But I can see the problem of swooping on big printing presses without anyone giving Lance Harris and his backers a heads-up in advance, if what you're telling me is true. I don't suppose you've got wind of who the Beast is, the person running the Lucifer line hub here?' Billie asked. She was well aware that the answer to that question would offer her the golden ticket.

The word was that Cilla still wasn't spilling if she knew the truth.

'If we can sweep on that individual and grab a large quantity of drugs all wrapped in the freebie cellophane covers, produced at the *Herald* group's presses, there's no way that Lance Harris can wriggle out of being copped,' Billie thought out aloud. 'And for once I'll be happy for you to get straight on to every editor of the broadsheets and TV stations. It won't matter then how many friends Lance Harris might have in high places.'

'No idea as to the identity of the Beast.' Perry shrugged. 'Possibility it's someone out of the area, who's moved in specifically to carry out the job. The old days of local crooks like Christy Callaghan are over, I'm afraid.'

Billie damned herself once again for not having gotten the information that Josh had been so keen to give her. Hindsight was a wonderful thing.

'I've got a few extra photos I can give you from the day of Sophie Grey's death, now that I'm not employed by the *Herald*,' Perry suddenly offered. 'Used to work us like dogs across all of the publications at once, so I was doing some PR pics for a new business that day, offering big bucks for an advertising slot in the paper. The place was just up the road from the station, and I think I may have caught Sophie Grey and some kids following behind her, in the background of a couple of the shots.' Billie's ears pricked up.

'It would be brilliant if any of the others can be identified. They might be able to lead us to the Beast. The photos might well help us nail Sophie's actual killer too,' Billie reflected, not that she took any joy from nabbing the children responsible, but at least more murders of kids could be prevented in the future.

'I can pull in at my place and get them. It's just around the corner?' Perry offered.

'Cool.' Billie ran her fingers through her hair again, amazed at the leads this new and unexpected friendship was producing.

Perry parked her car outside of a new-build house on a modern estate. Billie followed her, still in some pain, up the short pathway, on either side of which neatly planted flowers fringed handkerchief-sized lawns. The street portrayed a sense of calm except for one thing. As Perry plucked out her house keys, Billie watched her open not one, but three separate locks.

'You're security conscious,' Billie said, suddenly also aware of a video surveillance camera positioned on the wall. 'This doesn't look like the sort of place that has regular break-ins,' she added, as Perry disengaged a beeping burglar alarm when they stepped into the tiny hallway.

'The neighbours don't. I just got lucky, with my own personal stalker,' Perry replied, as Billie noticed a panic button right next to her home telephone.

'You're kidding me?' Billie couldn't believe that not only her, but Jo and now Perry Gooch, who certainly wasn't a woman to be easily intimidated by anyone's standards, had all been stalked.

'I wish I was,' Perry answered. 'He or she comes and goes, but I haven't been able to shake them off in years. They've managed to get in here a few times. Smeared horseshit up the walls, sent video footage of my underwear drawer. Reacted to my writing a story about stalking for the paper by putting photos of my daughters on porn star bodies and sharing the results online, including the school website. Hence their change of school.'

Perry sighed, checking around the rooms even as she spoke to Billie, as though it had become so much of an ingrained habit that such inspections were a normal part of her life. Billie remembered Jo's recollections of similar abuse.

'It all seemed to start after I reported a woman's march. Claim the streets again at night sort of thing, after some old fart of a judge had suggested that in order to remain safe, women shouldn't go out after dark.'

Perry had walked halfway up the stairs and was making a sweep of the bedrooms from her viewpoint as she spoke in a matter-of-fact manner. 'The police officers got heavy-handed, knocking a couple of the women to the ground and I took pictures. It made the front page. Stuff started happening after that.' Perry walked back downstairs again.

'Have you set eyes on the perp?' Billie felt her breath catch. She knew that her own stalker had to be involved in the Lucifer line. The message around her neck when she had arrived at the Trap House last night had proved it, even though the note left with Chip Little's body had already left little room for doubt.

'Not that I'm aware of.' Perry sounded matter of fact about the situation. 'Believe me, I've racked my brains, but I'm probably a bit like you, weirdos are the meat and drink of my job. Could have been an irate copper policing that march, or someone who's worked in the house. On the other hand, maybe a random screwball simply reckoned that I was a good fit with their warped fantasies and decided to make me their new victim. Once, in the dead of night, I even got it into my mind that it was the shrink who runs the local group for stalked women that I interviewed, for the report. Now that would be a good cover.' Perry Gooch chuckled. Billie realised that she must be talking about Max. She shivered at the crazy joke.

'But then again, it might be a female,' Perry added. 'It's not entirely unknown after all.' Billie's mind strayed to Josta and Lola's stories on that subject. Billie didn't feel like sharing. The bruising she felt inside – surely that couldn't be the work of another woman?

'Have you reported it?' Billie pressed instead. Perry laughed at the question.

'Do you really think the police are going to trip over themselves to help out a journo who regularly flags up their shortcomings?' Perry shook her head at the absurdity of the thought.

'I'd just be sent packing. Called a hysterical woman, asked if I'd upset an old boyfriend perhaps? Maybe slept around with someone else just to annoy him or been drunk and given some poor innocent bloke the come-on, that sort of stuff. Same as when you go to a male doctor with a complaint and you're told you're probably just premenstrual or menopausal, or plain hormonal. Women are dying from abusers and undiagnosed illnesses all over the place, because it's acceptable to view grown women as generally unstable, their accounts not totally believable. No, DSI Wilde. I just manned up and learned how to live with it.'

Billie felt shocked at Perry's observation of her situation. Had Billie been trying to 'man up' too, making light of her own stalking episodes? What about Jo, who had also suffered in silence, worried that her serious abuse would be viewed as simply the nagging cries of a weak woman? Here she was, the morning after she had been sexually abused, pretending to 'man up' herself, rather than show the normal emotions of a woman who had clearly been subject to appalling treatment.

Billie vowed to step forward in future and use her own position of relative power to make sure that other women could share their harrowing experiences and be reassured that they would be taken seriously by law enforcers. She knew very well from her own experiences that women were no weaker than men. Perhaps different in their approach, yet sometimes even more dangerous. So why treat them any differently when they voiced concerns?

'Here are the photos...' Perry had moved into a small office area and started rifling through folders. She lifted one up, handing it to Billie as she led the way back in the direction of the front door. Billie stepped outside, opening the folder of photographs as Perry went through her locking-up procedure.

'You look more like a jail warden than a homeowner.' Billie couldn't believe her eyes.

'Tell me about it.' Perry sighed. 'But you do what you've got to do to survive. I don't want my daughters having to suffer any further upheaval.'

As Billie lifted the first photo out and viewed it, she could see Sophie Grey walking down the street, with three other people following behind. She lifted up a second photo, focused and then swore out loud, dropping the file onto the ground. The remaining photos toppled out across the crazy paved pathway.

'You all right?' Perry turned to check. Billie was speechless for a moment as she gazed at the scattered pictures. She definitely recognised the person dressed in hoodie and jeans, captured momentarily staring straight into the camera lens. Billie blinked hard, but it made no difference. 'It can't be...' she stammered, as Perry looked on, frowning. 'I know this person.' Billie gawped at the former journalist, utterly shocked as the name of one of Sophie Grey's probable killers formed on the tip of her tongue.

31

HER FINAL JOURNEY

Billie tried hard to focus on the conversation, though beads of clammy sweat had started to break out on her forehead. During the time she had received counselling following her last investigation, she had learned to deal with the sporadic distressing recollections, she had suffered, like scattered images on broken glass, painful moments from her childhood abuse. Now they were coming back, hopscotching through her mind, it seemed, in response to the events of the night before.

'Our Trap House playmate in the cells is still claiming "see no evil, speak no evil", but we've got his attempted murder of you on the cameras that were fitted inside the flat, and Boo also captured a good bit of footage on her wheelchair set-up.'

Billie nodded. Ash had already given her a personal viewing of the video recording of her surprise visit to the Trap House, quietly in her own office, to save the total embarrassment of her drugged and half-clothed, gate-crashing episode being the afternoon matinee on the incident room big screen.

The images had started then, with the noise of flapping wings and the sorrowful flash of a single magpie flying by. That's before she had given him bad news in return. Then he'd ran off like a scalded cat. Billie had tried to regain her equilibrium whilst waiting for Ellis to finish the interview with the drug dealer arrested the night before.

'You okay?' Ellis furrowed his brow as he looked at Billie. 'Aren't you still meant to be on rest and recuperation detail?'

'More to the point, are *you* all right?' Billie replied, forcing the scattered pictures out of her mind. Ellis breathed out heavily, understanding immediately what she was referring to.

'Yeah. I am actually. Can't say it wasn't a bit of a shock, but she seems like a good kid... looks the double of her mother...' he trailed off.

'Don't be too hard on Boo.' Billie touched his arm. He smiled slowly.

'No. In fact, in a selfish way, it makes me feel a tiny bit better about that whole period. Believe me, over the years I've beat myself up time and again about how unprofessionally I acted back then and how Boo suffered because of it. She wouldn't even see or speak to me after.'

'Not because of the wall collapsing, but for having reported you and then not feeling able to share the fact that Angie was having your child,' Billie reasoned.

'Yeah, well I dropped her right in it. I should have been there backing her up and the fact that I wasn't, wrecked her life. I didn't blame her for not wanting anything more to do with me. Thing was, I only started messing around with Angie to make Boo jealous. We were an ace working team... but in truth, I wanted more.'

'And Boo didn't?' Billie asked.

'No, well maybe. She was flirting around the idea. But she was still at the tail end of her marriage and Boo isn't the sort to play away from home.'

'So don't think too badly of yourself,' Billie answered.

'I do. I was an idiot. Not that Angie wasn't a nice girl, I'm not saying that, but it was just a couple of nights of madness. With Boo I was hoping for a lifetime partnership.'

'You're sure Maya *is* your daughter then?'

'You've seen the way we both react to the dog, with sneezing fits. My whole family's the same.' He smiled for a moment. Billie recalled that Boo clearly hadn't been in any doubt when Angie had confided in her. 'What makes you ask?' Ellis questioned.

Billie turned over some photos lying face down on her desk. They were the ones Perry had given to her.

'These are photos of Sophie Grey walking towards the station and to her death. The young people following behind are the same kids caught on CCTV as she fell onto the track.' She braced herself for Ellis's reaction.

'You are joking...' The blood drained from his face. The one young person who Perry had caught looking straight at the camera was physically striking and totally unmistakable.

'I wish I was, but you know I'm right,' Billie answered softly. Ellis nodded.

'Yep. It's definitely Maya.' Ellis had no option but to agree. The truth was literally staring him in the face.

The tide was turning. Powerful surges of water were running away choppily from the sandy beach. A dangerous time for anyone who might get caught in the rip current. Waves of tears ran down Maya's face as she gulped in air, unable to answer the questions being directed towards her, or perhaps unwilling, Billie considered, lest she be dragged into yet stormier waters.

The photos of Sophie on her way to meet her death train lay on the sand, framed by wisps of seaweed and fragile shells. Only a few feet away, Ash's children Indie and Happi were making sandcastles whilst the baby slept in her cradle, guarded by Kat the dog. It made a change from the overheated and airless room that Billie generally used to interrogate murder suspects. She was momentarily distracted by a squawking gull as it swooped overhead, ready to pounce on a pretty fish, perhaps.

'I didn't kill her,' Maya finally managed to stammer in between sobs, 'and I was telling the truth about being trained in childcare, honestly.' She turned to Ash. They had clearly already had *that* little discussion, Ash having hurtled home on seeing the photos shared by Billie. Nevertheless, by his shell-shocked face, he was still having trouble accepting the fact that he had left his precious girls in the hands of a possible murderess. Ellis was absolutely still. Maya dared a peek at him from under her lashes and then started sobbing again, her tears as salty as the spray from the waves crashing against the shore.

'I just wanted to find my dad. My mum said, when she was dying, that you might be with a northern force...' Maya whispered, daring a glance at Ellis again. He looked shamefaced. 'She found out that you were a policeman when I was about ten,' she added.

'Someone else who worked undercover with you, had eventually retired and had joined her environmental group. They told her everything. Said that they felt bad about that operation, but they'd had to follow orders. Everyone had stopped seeing environmentalists as being crazy people by then. She'd got an award. People liked my mum. She was kind and trusting,' Maya added. Ellis nodded sadly in agreement.

'I'm sorry. That must have been hard.' Ellis reached out and touched Maya's hand.

'I remember she was shocked, but she said that it had all turned out all right in the end. If it wasn't for you then there would have been no me. She said that everything happens for a reason. Mum wasn't the sort who bore a grudge, you see. Anyway, you had married someone else by then, the retired police friend said. Last we heard you had another daughter. Is that right?' Ellis rubbed his face and finally nodded. 'I do. Connie. She's two years old. Her mum and me aren't together anymore,' he added quietly.

'So I've got a little sister?' Maya perked up. Billie used the opportunity to get information.

'Let's get back to Sophie Grey first, Maya. Why were you there that day? Are you a member of the Lucifer line gang?' Billie asked.

'No!' Maya sounded shocked.

'So why were you following her then? Are you in another gang?' Ash demanded. Right now, he wasn't in such a forgiving mood.

'No!' Maya insisted. 'You've got to believe me. I wasn't anything to do with it!' Ellis flicked his head back and caught Maya's hand.

'Come on, tell your old dad about it then.' He pulled Maya towards him. Billie made a space for her as Ellis put his arm around the young girl's shoulders, rooting through his pocket to find a handkerchief. 'Blow your nose on that. We can share.' He bumped his head gently against Maya's, in a show of affection. She smiled between tears as she fought to regain control of her emotions.

'Um, when Mum died, I wanted to go to uni up here.' She glanced at Ellis. 'It was the only place that I sort of thought I might have some family.' Ellis closed his eyes tightly, pained at the information.

'Mum had a friend who came to her funeral. They had met at a retreat for women with cancer. They did yoga and meditation and stuff. She lives in this area and she offered to let me stay at her house for a while, until I found a room in a student house and a part-time job to see me through the course. I didn't have anywhere else. Mum just rented our place, so when she suddenly went downhill quickly then... I was given notice to leave...' Ellis sighed and rubbed his face, totally stressed as more painful details emerged. Billie took over.

'So I dropped you off at the house of your mother's friend, the other night?' Billie pulled her notebook and pencil out of her pocket ready to take details.

'No, I'd already left by then. I was sleeping rough. It didn't feel right to stay, not after what happened to Josh.' Billie's ears pricked up immediately.

'Josh Hallows?' Billie asked. Maya nodded.

'You know him?' Billie pressed.

'Yes. It was his mum who invited me to stay at their place.'

'You do know that Josh was about to tell me who killed Sophie Grey and a man called Christy Callaghan when he was murdered?' Billie spoke carefully. 'Maya, were you involved in both of those killings?' Maya blinked in shock.

'No! Ask the station if they have CCTV. You'll see what happened when Sophie went under the train! You'll see what I was wearing, match it to these photos. I was trying to talk them *out* of following Sophie, but they said they had to. I stood back. I couldn't believe my eyes when they did it.'

'Who did it, Maya?' Ellis kept his arm around her shoulder. 'Can you tell us the names of the two people who were in the tussle with Sophie Grey when she fell to her death?' Maya closed her eyes tightly as though she didn't want to relive the event, even in her mind's eye.

'Josh Hallows and Chip Little.' The names came out in a whisper. Billie felt a jolt of shock, as though a bolt of electricity had shot through her body.

'Josh and Chip?' She couldn't believe it. She certainly didn't want to imagine it could really be true. 'But Josh was going to tell me who did the murders–' Billie started.

'I know. He wanted to confess. He wanted out of the whole

gang thing. I begged him to stop.' Maya wiped the flowing tears away once again. 'But he said that he couldn't. It would affect other people.'

'But he won an award for his anti-bullying campaign.' Billie ran through the night of the award in her head. The smart young man stepping up onto the stage to shake her hand and take the award.

'Yes. His anti-bullying site was online. It was a good way to find kids who were feeling vulnerable, people who were being bullied at school, then befriend them, make them feel one of the gang... protected. That's how Sophie Grey contacted him. She was being beaten up at her new school. She just couldn't fit in. That's the sort of kids who are best for doing the drug deliveries, you see. Josh gave them the impression that they were important. He made them feel wanted. Sometimes the Beast himself even spoke to them on the phone.

'Of course, before they knew it, they were facing much worse abuse, but by then there was no way out. Josh said that when he first tried, the Beast took a photo of Josh's mum and put her head on a porn star's body and shared it online.' Billie thought of Perry Gooch's girls and her own treatment at the hands of her stalker. There could be no doubt now that her rapist was the same person.

'Did Josh find Chip Little via his bullying site too?' Billie got another vision of the cheeky imp that she was struggling to accept was involved in the attack on Sophie Grey.

'Chip Little? No, he was different. Nobody ever bullied him. He didn't have any feelings to hurt. He'd stab his own mother in the back for money. Josh said that Chip knew the Beast's girlfriend, that's how he got involved.' Her voice broke. 'He threatened to stab me one day, when I was begging Josh to stop. Said that I should shut up and join them. It would be the only way I'd ever be able to afford a house of my own.' Ellis found his voice at last.

'Maya, do you know who the Beast is?' The young girl shook her head slowly.

'Only Josh and Chip knew that. Josh was his right-hand man by the time I came to stay. But he was scared. He told me that him and Chip had to help the Beast do away with the nightclub owner, Christy Callaghan.' Maya shivered, wiping her nose again. 'He was shocked by that, but the Beast told him to keep quiet, or the same thing would happen to him...'

Maya trailed off as Billie's thoughts went back to Josh taking his last breath in her arms. He had decided not to stay silent, despite being aware of the danger to his life. But the Beast obviously didn't make idle threats. He had clearly got word of Chip Little's chat at police headquarters, too, somehow.

'Josh said the rumour was that someone in the police knew the Beast and was giving him a heads-up on all of the enquiries into drugs crimes in the area. But Josh had done his research, knew that you were straight, so he planned to tell you. He thought it was his only chance to break free...'

Billie sighed. Much good that had done him. Her mind was racing. If the Beast worked the county line in the area on behalf of Lance Harris, then the chief was as thick as thieves with the newspaper owner. Surely her own godfather couldn't be involved? The idea horrified Billie, but it was true that Perry Gooch had been given info on Christy Callaghan's death before it had been made public and also had the address of Sophie Grey's father. Had Lance Harris given Perry's editor that info, passed from a friend in a very high place?

'Sophie was only meant to be robbed by the boys, to make sure that she stayed in debt to the Lucifer line,' Maya continued. 'Josh said they did that every time a new kid went out on a delivery. Or sometimes they were stripped and made to do things, boys as well as girls, and the threat made to put the footage up online, to humiliate them. Just to make sure they didn't try to get out, or tell anyone what they were involved in.'

Billie, Ellis and Ash exchanged glances. Billie had no doubt that the two men were having murderous thoughts similar to her own, if only they could get their hands on this monster known as the Beast.

'But Sophie stumbled and went under the train.' Maya started crying again, giving Billie time to gather her thoughts. She was absolutely stunned.

'Do you know who killed Josh, Maya?' Billie felt that the truth was only a heartbeat away. Maya shook her head.

'I guess it must have been the Beast. But I wouldn't be surprised if Chip Little was involved somewhere. He knew that Josh was trying to find a way out and he would have earned extra money for giving the Beast a tip-off like that.' Billie had a sudden recollection of Chip Little winking cheekily at her, as he did a wheelie on the bike she had bought him, whilst Josh Hallows' father hung from a tree branch nearby. The recollection made her blood run cold. Had he delivered the Molotov cocktail onto the Hallows family doorstep?

'You could ask Josh's mum.' Maya appeared to Billie to sincerely want to help, though the senior detective was beginning to think that she had lost any ability to judge people at all with these latest revelations.

'She knew that Josh was involved with a drugs gang?' Billie's voice rose in disbelief.

'Yes. She was the one who told me. Asked me to help him stop. She even followed him one day to try and find the Beast himself, give him a piece of her mind...'

'Well done, sweetheart. You're doing great.' Ellis gave Maya a little hug. She offered a watery smile in response.

'That's all I know,' Maya pleaded.

'And did she find out who it was?' Billie's heart was in her mouth. Maya shook her head.

'No. Josh realised she was following him, and he beat her up.'

'What?' Billie and Ash questioned loudly together, causing Kat to give a bark.

'He felt terrible afterwards, what with her being nearly dead anyway...' Maya trailed off. Billie felt sick. She sprang up.

'Ellis, take her down to headquarters and do a formal report,' Billie directed. She had recorded the discussion on her mobile in any case.

'I'm not being arrested, am I?' Maya panicked. Ellis helped her upright and gave her another hug.

'No. You've been a great help to the enquiry, Maya.' Ellis spoke in soothing tones, obviously trying to make up for lost time in the fathering department.

'You're welcome to stay when you bring her back,' Billie called over her shoulder as she marched across the sand, to sit on nearby rocks, out of earshot of Ash's children. 'Grab a spare room,' Billie shouted, as she watched Ellis leading Maya from the beach. She realised that she was in danger of turning into the old woman who lived in a shoe. But right now, as she scrolled through her list of contacts, she wasn't feeling at all like that sweet old nursery rhyme lady. She was in a mood to put the boot in.

'Mrs Hallows? It's DSI Wilde,' Billie announced, as her mobile screen suddenly flashed into video mode. The drained and extremely ill-looking face of Lydia Hallows, now a childless widow, stared hollow-eyed at Billie. It looked as though she didn't have long left before she followed the men of the house on her final journey. The pitiful sight took the edge off Billie's anger that Lydia Hallows hadn't spilled the beans when she had first become aware of her son's drug-filled pastime. It could have saved many lives, including his.

'Yes. I've been expecting you.' Her voice was nearly a whisper.

'I've been talking to Maya,' Billie started.

'Then you know it all,' Mrs Hallows replied. 'She's a dear girl. She tried very hard to make Josh see sense. I had hoped that she would stay with us for longer.' Josh's mum shivered and pulled the shawl that she was wearing more tightly around her shoulders.

'I know that you attempted to persuade Josh, too, Mrs Hallows, and I want you to know that he listened. On the night of his award, he spoke with me. I believe that he wanted me to know about his dangerous entanglement with a drugs gang.' Billie decided not to give Lydia Hallows all of the grizzly details of her son's involvement in murder as well as drugs. At least she deserved some credit, Billie reflected, for having tried to intervene, even whilst struggling with her own battle between life and death.

'Maya tells me that he yearned to start afresh.' *Or to just get the hell away from the murdering Beast*, Billie guessed. She had no idea whether Josh's mum had any idea that she featured in online video footage looking like a porn queen and that it had been spread all over the internet. Billie didn't intend to share that news either. There was only so much that one woman could take and soon she would be past caring anyway.

'I blame myself. If I had handed him in earlier to the police, none of this would have happened. Josh and his father would still be alive now. I knew what he had been doing. I deserve what I've got coming, DSI Wilde.'

'I believe that you tried to follow Josh one day, Mrs Hallows, to find the person at the heart of the drug dealing in this area. Can you tell me where Josh went that day?'

A dark shadow passed over the face of Lydia Hallows, as she dredged harrowing memories up to the surface. She rubbed the side of her face. Billie guessed it was in the spot where Josh's fist had made contact.

'I only followed him as far as Barrow Wood. That's the stop where he got off the bus, I'm afraid, before he spotted me. I would never have made a good detective. I have no idea if he was simply meeting friends or getting up to underhand dealings on that occasion. We had a rather heated exchange, which put an end to my undercover operations once and for all.'

'Maya tells me that Josh was very sorry about the incident.' Billie tried to offer a smudge of soothing balm, to calm the painful memories.

'I'm the one who's sorry, DSI Wilde. Make no mistake. I had my sharpest carving knife in my bag. If I had got my hands on that Beast, I would have stuck it straight through him and relished every second. I had been thinking about it day and night. It's ironic that I'm the only person in my family that hasn't been involved in criminal activities. I certainly premeditated killing that devil. The fact that I failed in the task will be the biggest regret of what's left of my sorry life.' The woman looked utterly exhausted by the conversation. Billie wondered if she would last out the week.

She ended the call, trying hard to eradicate the dark feelings enveloping her soul. Like Lydia Hallows she had missed her chance – to get Josh Hallows to speak, to find the truth about Chip Little and to suss out Cilla at the first opportunity. Was she losing her edge? What's more she still hadn't heard from Max. Was he suffering somewhere right now, because she'd allowed herself to get drugged up and given away his location to a crazy killer? There was one shard of light at the end of her dark tunnel of gloom. She scrolled through her contacts before finding the number she wanted.

'Dexie, it's Billie.' She tried her best to sound upbeat as Derek Blythe's messaging service kicked in. 'I need to come down to that lovely allotment of yours over in Barrow Wood to return your jacket and pick your brains. Will you be there in an hour or so? Please say yes. I've never needed your help so much.'

She hoped that Derek would quickly reply to confirm that he would be on-site. Who better than Dexie to assist her in pinpointing a drug dealer in his area? He may have been determined to turn his back on the force, but Billie was ready to use absolutely all of her powers of persuasion on him. He had years of experience and was bound to have his ear on the ground on his own patch. If Josh had been heading for a meeting with the Beast nearby, this might be the chance to pick up a crucial piece of information in order to finally tear apart the Lucifer line.

Billie ran her fingers through her hair as she watched the tide turning. Nothing stood still. The chief had decided to move across the world. Could he have already moved his allegiance from law enforcement to using his knowledge to assist big league drugs barons? Billie shivered at the thought that he had wanted to take her with him.

Her mobile buzzed as a text message came through. *You just can't leave me alone. See you in an hour x.* Billie smiled. That was Dexie, always the joker. It would be good to have some lightness on this day of dark revelations.

As she stood up, still sore, she saw the figure moving along the empty shoreline. She blinked then rubbed her eyes. It wasn't some sort of mirage caused by the sea spray and low sun bouncing off the waves, it was a flesh-and-blood man. Even better, it was Max and he was walking towards her.

Billie's aching body gathered speed as she wiped away

thoughts that her mind was playing tricks. As she drew closer, he smiled that slow smile of his as they made eye contact.

'You had me bloody worried sick!' Billie slapped Max's arm as they approached one another.

'Isn't that normally my line?' He laughed, catching her in his arms and pulling her close, burying his face in her hair. 'You can't imagine what thoughts have been running through my head.' He sighed.

Billie felt tears run down her cheeks. She had held back her feelings of grief and pain due to the events of the night before, the horrific slaying of Jo and her terror that Max might have met the same fate, but now a tidal wave of emotion threatened to overwhelm her.

As she pulled back to wipe her face with the cuff of her sleeve, Max took the opportunity to cup her face in his hands, before bending forward to kiss her, softly and deeply, his lips tasting of salt and warmth.

'I heard about what happened last night.' Max frowned as they eventually broke free. 'Josta's on her way back to work. Nothing will stop her. Not me, that's for sure. She wants to be there...'

'For Jo.' Billie nodded. 'She was fond of her. So was I, in the end...' She trailed off, still trying hard to accept the demise of the young detective, who should have been at home safe and sound. Instead, she had given her life for the job.

'I heard that you fell victim to the Devil's Breath.' He spoke softly, as he stroked her hair. 'You do realise that you had no free will whilst under its influence?' he reminded Billie. She couldn't help dwelling on the fact that he might be following her own train of thought, that maybe she had pointed out Jo's hiding place.

'But what I don't understand, is what the Devil's Breath has to do with county lines and my stalker? One person seems to be connected to them all.' Billie desperately wished that she could make sense of it.

'I believe the actions of one person are the root cause.' Max clicked on his phone and showed Billie a photo. It was a pretty, slightly built young woman smiling at the camera.

'This was taken around fifteen years ago, when we were at university together in Bogotá. Then, she was bright and sweet, passionate about environmental issues. We would get involved in marches and protests together thinking that we could change the world...' Max rolled his eyes at his naivety. Billie stared at the photo. If he had been the one taking the snap, then she could tell by the look of adoration radiating from the girl's eyes that they had been up to more than just protests together. Billie frowned. The girl looked vaguely familiar.

'She used to tell me that her family were poor simple farmers. Indeed, perhaps they really had been a few generations back, but even by then she was playing a game, perhaps deluding herself, pretending to be a normal student. In truth, her family run one of the most dangerous drug cartels in Columbia.' Billie's brain cells finally began to connect.

'One of the family hasn't recently been eradicated during a hostage situation by any chance?' Billie raised her eyebrows, willing Max to come clean at last.

'Her oldest brother,' he finally answered. 'Hostage taking is quite a profitable sideline within that particular cartel. The sweet young lady you see in the photos is almost unrecognisable today. Regular plastic surgery has changed the shape of her face and her body. It's known as narco-aesthetics in South America. The perfect female form as far as drug barons are concerned is voluptuous and highly sexualised. Barbie doll beautiful. Not that she needs to play the part of a trophy wife today.

'I knew her as Maria Garcia. It turned out to be a false name. Today she is recognised as La Reina del Cielo – the Queen of the

Sky, because as the highest-ranking female drug cartel leader in South America, she is always on the move, flying around the world, disguised as different people, setting up drug-trafficking deals. Often her cover is in full view. She thrives on the danger. So far, no one can catch her.'

'Was it you who took out her brother?' Billie guessed the answer. Max didn't reply. He was instead scrolling through his phone.

'Let's say it's believed that she was in Europe when she got news of his demise and is set on revenge. This is how she looked when a rare photo was taken a year ago.' He turned the mobile to face Billie.

'Luciana Martinez,' Billie gasped. 'The person who asked me to work for her! She made a speech about the environment...' – Billie ran her fingers through her hair – '...the chief has agreed to join her security team.' Billie wondered if he already had.

Max's face clouded over. 'She loves playing games. It amuses her to change identity and outwit those who are trying to stop her. We're facing a very formidable enemy, Billie. Make no mistake. She's clever and ruthless. I have no doubt she has brought the Devil's Breath with her for personal reasons, whilst she oversees a new network of drugs distribution in the UK.'

'She told me she was leaving.'

'When?' Max asked.

'The day after I came to yours for dinner–' Billie started.

'The same day that Jamie Squires was murdered, using Devil's Breath,' Max finished.

'She knows newspaper owner Lance Harris. I've had information he's been involved in drug distribution around the UK. I think that the Beast, who runs the new Lucifer line is my stalker as well as Jo Green's, so a local person...' She trailed off for a moment. Perry was also known to the chief. Her mind shot back to the night before. She felt sick. *Could it have been my godfather... the stalker... my rapist?*

'Are you okay?' Max asked. She did feel shaky. Maybe he had just watched the blood drain from her face. Her mobile buzzed again.

Here already and waiting, the message read.

'I've got to go. I'm meeting Derek Blythe. He might be able to give me the vital piece of information that will lead us to the Beast. If we can just catch a delivery in progress, then we can prove how the drugs are distributed around the country.'

'I'm driving.' Max had a look on his face that brooked no argument. A sudden bark from behind alerted them to the presence of Kat the dog, bounding along the beach to join them, forgotten for the past few minutes, amongst the various dramas involving the others.

'Looks like we're taking an extra passenger.' Billie grabbed Kat's collar as she gave slobbering licks to Max on arrival. 'We need all the help we can get and this one's a bonafide drugs detective.'

32

LEAVING ON A DEATH TRAIN

'I see they've sent the A-team then?' Wilf, king of leeks, had started marching over to the car even before Max had brought it to a halt beside Derek Blythe's allotment. Billie climbed out, reaching in the back for Derek's loaned jacket to return it, but Kat was fast asleep dribbling happily over the fleece. Remembering that Derek had said he was allergic to the dog, she decided to leave the piece of clothing in situ, then take it home to wash it before dropping it off later. She left the back door open, so that Kat wouldn't overheat, though there was already a chill in the early evening air.

'Hi. Wilf, isn't it? We met last time I visited.'

'Yes, and I told you about those kids on bikes causing trouble. I'm taking it that's why you've turned up? I've been ringing the local cop shop day and night asking for someone to sort them out. My leeks are in danger and I'm hoping for first prize next week at the summer show.' Wilf was full of high dudgeon.

'Hasn't Derek seen them off?' Billie looked around. There was no sign of him yet. Wilf scowled.

'I'd stay clear of him if I were you. He's been getting more and more miserable, ever since he lost out on that promotion. Some slip of a lass got upgraded and he'd got nowt. That's why he left, but I expect you know all that, having been his boss.' Billie frowned.

'He never said,' she answered. Though it was true, Derek had never liked Jo Green.

'Said he was surprised. Always thought you had a real soft spot for him.' Wilf winked. 'Come and see my leeks, officer.' He waved Max towards his allotment, mistaking him for a detective. 'I've got a marrow that would make your eyes water,' the pensioner added, 'and an onion the size of a four-year-old. I'm going for a world record with that one, if those kids don't destroy the lot.'

Max made eye contact with Billie. She smiled as he started to follow Wilf.

'Actually, Wilf, this is Dr Max Strong. He deals with mental health issues,' Billie announced.

'Is that right?' Wilf looked Max up and down. 'Well, maybe you can work out what gets into the heads of the types of parents that let their kids roam wild all night around here.'

Billie looked at the playground next to the allotment. She guessed that the children were simply looking for somewhere to hang out, there being little other provision made for youngsters to entertain themselves these days, as youth clubs and playing fields made way for cardboard housing estates.

She followed Wilf along the pathway to his vast greenhouse where he was shepherding Max, who, to his credit, was engaging Wilf in animated conversation about his vegetables. She guessed that Max had immediately sussed that the elderly man was, in truth, after companionship rather than police protection.

'Go in there an' you'll see a swede twice the size of your head.' Wilf urged Max forward. Max dutifully moved inside, whilst Billie scanned around for Derek. 'I've booked a tractor to get that pumpkin out. Wreck the suspension of your average car that would.' Wilf pointed towards another vast vegetable. Max turned and caught Billie's eye again.

'That's an impressive cucumber you have there, Wilf, must be a metre long.' Max shook his head in disbelief. Wilf, standing at the doorway, looked as pleased as punch, totally oblivious to the fact that his vegetables had never been in more danger, only inches away from a man who appeared to have a Columbian hit squad searching for him right at that moment.

'Any sign of Derek today?' Billie asked the elderly gardener as Max wandered amongst the mind-blowing vegetables inside the greenhouse. She checked her watch, desperate to get some intel to shop the Beast. If anyone could enlighten them with the jackpot local info it would be Dexie. Billie felt a buzz as though she was finally onto something, if only Derek would show. Instead, she was being eaten alive by midges and discussing the proportions of obscenely sized vegetables.

'Saw him earlier, love, but these days I keep my distance. He's usually in his second allotment, behind that long shed there. The building that looks like Fort Knox. Went over the other day to mention the lads causing a commotion and he pointed a gun at me.'

'What, Derek?' Billie answered, startled. Wilf grimaced, folding his arms.

'Maybe some old police trophy. Thought you'd have to hand such things in when you retire, but I'm just a moaning old goat that knows nothing. That's what he called me. He's changed since he gave up the police.' Billie wondered if the old man had some sort of dementia. She couldn't imagine that Derek would have a gun.

'Mind you, I'd be bad tempered too, if I had to get up at five o'clock in the morning to open the newsagents.' Billie's ears pricked up.

'What newsagents?' she asked.

'The big one up on the high street. Used to belong to his girlfriend's mother. Family had it for generations. Flo was a lovely woman. Ran it herself when Reggie died. Then a couple of months ago, she just keeled over in bed. I couldn't believe it. I saw her at the club the night before and she was as right as rain. Up on the dance floor all night. Fit as a flea. But her daughter, Cilla, said it was just one of those unaccountable funny turns. She just seems to have stopped breathing.'

'What did you say her daughter's name is?' Billie caught her breath.

'Cilla Saunders. Derek's fancy woman. Been seeing each other for a year or so now. She used to be a dancer at some smart club, owned by that Christy Callaghan, but it looks like they're managing the newsagents now. See her son in there sometimes, as well, when he's not working on the ships.'

Billie's mind was racing. Max was way at the far end of Wilf's long greenhouse now, dutifully surveying the tubers. She desperately wanted to run her thoughts by him, ensure that she wasn't going mad. But she didn't want to alert Wilf to the urgent concerns that she had. God knows she'd had madcap suspicions about so many people lately – including both of Max's mothers, for heaven's sake. Were the thoughts now forming in her mind just another of her flights of fantasy?

'I doubt he'll be entering his roses into the show this year. Normally wins a rosette, but he hasn't given them much attention lately. They're running wil–' Wilf started.

'Roses? Where are they?' Billie's voice was firm. She decided that she wanted answers. Wilf blinked; a bit taken aback by her change of tone. He stepped back out of his greenhouse and led her down his garden path, to the far boundary of what seemed to be Derek's allotment.

'There.' Wilf pointed, as they rounded the far end of a shed.

A sea of wild red roses reached from the back of Derek's shed across a stretch of land, to another long, low metal building. Beyond, a tangle of brambles and high weeds stretched away to abandoned pigeon sheds and smallholdings. They didn't quite cover the sight of an old black Mercedes car. The front bumper and light were smashed in, paintwork matching the car Jo Green had been driving when they had been rammed over the cliff, clearly visible. Billie's heart started beating fast. It was a perfect hiding place.

'Just look at that.' Wilf nodded to a piece of golden metal, surrounded by long grass, catching in the light, beyond the perimeter fencing.

'Dumped bike by the looks of it. Bet it's been nicked,' Wilf added. 'He wants to get this cleaned up. Weeds are mushrooming over my side and he hasn't spread his horse manure this year. That's why these flies are everywhere. It's a stinking eyesore.' It was more than that, Billie realised. It was Chip Little's bike. The one she had bought him just before he had been murdered, half dumped in horseshit – a favourite weapon of the local stalker.

A sudden bark caught their attention, as Kat the dog raced along the pathway, not even stopping for a pat before she jumped a broken fence and, nose down, forged through the undergrowth and brambles in the direction of Derek's second hidden building.

'That your dog, love?' Wilf called after Billie as she started to follow the bloodhound. It had its nose down and was totally focused on following the scent that it had presumably picked up from Derek's jacket in the car.

'Best get a hold of it before Derek grabs his gun. He's made it plain he doesn't like cold callers.'

Billie took off in chase, the brambles scratching her arms

and legs. She wasn't a cold caller; she was absolutely boiling with fury.

'Kat,' Billie half whispered, as the large dog pushed through the half open solid metal door of the long low building ahead. Billie was surprised. By the look of the steel bars and shutters on all of the windows, this didn't appear to be the sort of structure to be kept casually open. But then Billie remembered the text from Derek an hour earlier. *Here already and waiting.* She wasn't an unexpected guest. He was lying in wait for her.

'Derek?' Billie called, as she followed Kat through a second door and into a corridor with openings off it. Kat ran ahead and snuffled inside the first one. Billie caught up, grabbing the dog's collar as she looked inside, blinking in recognition. She had just entered a drugs factory.

The crack-cocaine smell of flowery scent and burning plastic put Billie in the mind of a local nail salon she had raided once for money laundering. An electric cooker and several microwave ovens, somehow rigged to the local supply, skirting the edge of the allotments, almost made the room look like a downmarket takeaway joint.

As Billie stepped inside, she saw waxy lumps, in a huge bowl on a long Formica-topped table. If she hadn't known better, Billie might have thought that Derek was halfway through a recipe for home-made fudge, perhaps a competition entry at the coming country show which was the focus of Wilf's giant vegetable-growing mania. Instead, she realised that she was staring at fat pieces of newly cooked crack cocaine. This bowl alone, Billie estimated, from everything that Ellis had taught her, would have a street value of around £500,000. Looking at the sight of other containers scattered around, along with piles of cellophane fillets from newspapers, containing pure white cocaine powder in its raw form, it was clear to Billie that she was looking at the sort of fortune that would put a gold mine to shame.

At one side of the room, spilling out of a holdall, were bags of what Billie was pretty sure was heroin. From the luggage tags still tied on the bag, it had come in via the ferry from Amsterdam to the Port of Tyne. Perhaps Cilla's son had more than middle-of-the-road music and stormy seas on his mind during his daily trips back and forth across the North Sea? A sudden noise alerted Billie to another room leading off from the far corner.

'Stay,' she whispered to Kat, who wagged her tail, pleased to have tracked the smell of crack from Derek's jacket on the back seat of the car, to the location of the drug's creation.

Billie crept across the room and peered around the door, momentarily stunned at the view inside.

The walls were covered with photos of women, clearly taken without their knowledge. Sometimes Derek had positioned himself in shot, appearing to be taking a selfie, whilst the targets went about their business, totally oblivious in the background. Amongst them were photos of Jo Green and Perry Gooch and her daughters. Compilation photos, mostly of a pornographic nature, featured those same faces. There were also various natural and compiled photo mock-ups of other females, covering every wall surface. Billie spotted Lydia Hallows' head on one particularly offensively displayed body.

Blown-up copies of messages much like those that Billie had received, were also stuck on the walls, along with a photo of a Molotov cocktail, in the hand of a smiling Chip Little, here in the allotment, before he had set off to deliver it on the doorstep of the Hallows home. One large photo showed Derek and his nephew, Andy, in the incident room grinning to the camera. It suddenly made sense of Perry Gooch's words on the people who were most likely to feed the press information. Those new to the force who wanted to big themselves up and those heading for retirement.

Turning around, Billie was suddenly horrified to find herself facing an entire wall devoted exclusively to her. One photo, which immediately caught her eye, was a shot taken from above. She was cradling Josh Hallows, as his life had ebbed away. The photographer, clearly in a hurry, had caught his own arm in shot, wearing the fleece jacket loaned to Billie straight after the incident – by Derek. Billie's emotions flared as she recalled handing him the red rose – that she now realised he had planted in her car moments earlier – in totally ignorant thanks.

There were many more photos, taken when she was at work and also off duty. Billie felt queasy as she spotted another horrific scenario, realising that it must have been captured in the incident room the night before. She had her shirt fully open, facing the camera with a dazed expression. A second picture which also appeared to have been snapped at the same time, made bile rise to the back of her throat. She was bent over a desk, the undressed view leaving little to the imagination. Behind her, Derek Blythe had lifted his dark balaclava and was triumphantly facing the camera.

'Hi, Billie.' Derek's voice made Billie spin around, ready for attack.

'You bastard! You're the Beast!' she screamed, starting to propel Derek backwards. As he staggered, she realised that he wasn't putting up a fight. She suddenly spotted another figure standing in the doorway. The person was holding a golden-plated, engraved and jewel-bedecked gun. In a gallery it might have been considered to be a thing of exquisite beauty, but here, it was simply a deadly weapon. It was pointed straight at Billie.

'This might look like a beautiful toy.' The woman that Billie knew as Dr Luciana Martinez stared directly at her as she moved forward. 'But believe me. It has killed many people. I won't hesitate to use it.' Billie glanced sideways at Derek. He had the slightly glazed smile that Billie had recognised in Jas Sanghera as having been drug induced.

'Take the cable ties and fasten her wrists.' Luciana handed the nylon plant ties to Derek, whilst she kept the gun trained on Billie. He did as he was bid, Billie's skin crawling at his touch.

'I can see your anger, Billie.' Luciana nodded to the photos of her from the night before. 'The man is an amateur. The Borrachero is for expert use only. Lance Harris will pay for bringing him into our organisation.' Derek still had the same dopey smile on his face.

'I used the Devil's Breath,' he offered.

'Looks like you've fed him some yourself.' Billie ignored Derek and spoke to Luciana directly. 'Just like you or your lackeys dosed up Lola Strong and Jas Sanghera.' Luciana smiled.

'So clever, DSI Wilde. It's a shame I couldn't convince you to join my team.' She sighed.

'Like you've persuaded the chief?' Billie asked. 'Or maybe he's already working for you?' Billie winced as Derek pulled the ties tightly, drawing her wrists painfully together behind her back. Luciana shook her head. 'Alas not. He was just a passing plaything, *mi amor*. One stupid law enforcement officer is quite enough.'

Billie glanced at Derek who had come back to stand alongside Luciana. He was rubbing his crotch.

'You were good last night, Billie, better than I ever dreamed.'

The movement was so quick and the silencer on the gun so effective that for a split second, Billie's brain failed to process that Luciana had shot him. His smile suddenly dropped, his eyes registered shock, before he toppled forward towards Billie, almost in slow motion. She jumped back, pinned against the wall as a volcano of blood suddenly erupted from Derek Blythe's mouth towards her, before he slammed face down, onto the cold hard floor, dead.

'Billie?' Luciana slowly smiled as she heard Max's voice calling.

'Ah, yes. This was worth waiting a few more days for. Let's move.' She flicked her head, stepping over the body of Derek Blythe without another glance, the gun now pushed behind Billie's right ear as Luciana spun her around and moved her forward, back through the room full of drugs and onwards around the main greenhouse, the one that actually contained fruit and vegetables.

Max could now be seen by the car, looking around, whilst fussing Kat the dog who had given up guarding drugs and headed for the man who she had licked almost to death on the journey to the allotment.

'Max, run!' Billie screamed as she was pushed out from behind Derek's greenhouse by Luciana, who had one arm around her shoulder, as though they were amigos, the other hand covered by Billie's curls, holding the golden gun, pinned firmly to the nape of her skull. Max's head flicked up in their direction, his face darkening immediately on recognition of Billie's companion.

'Ahh, just beautiful,' Luciana whispered in Billie's ear. 'See how he is concerned for you? Just as you would risk your life to give him warning. This is even better than I planned.' She propelled Billie forward. 'I'm not going to shoot him, unless you refuse to do exactly as I tell you.' Luciana's voice was quiet but completely focused. Billie could feel the strength running through the body that presented as a perfect female prototype of narco beauty. Her mind was racing. Whatever Luciana was planning couldn't have a happy ending whatever sweet nothings she was whispering in her ear.

Just behind Max, children enjoying an outdoor birthday party were skipping around the play park, jumping on slides and swings and roundabouts which had been created to look like farmyard animals, holding balloons on strings, totally unaware of the drama going on just inches away from them. Billie hoped to keep it that way.

'Move.' Luciana flicked her head to the side as she and Billie emerged through the wooden gate to the allotments and moved sideways across the grass.

'Let her go.' Max moved in a parallel line to Billie and Luciana, stopping as they came across a tiny stream. 'This is nothing to do with Billie,' he reasoned.

'But it is everything to do with us, Max!' Billie felt the surge of anger which made Luciana's hand shake, the extra pressure of the gun rammed against her skull. The look on Max's face. Glancing down, she watched the tiny river trickle by. Billie wondered if this was to be her final resting place. Would any stoned shrimp be feasting on her blown-out brains, there on the edge of the children's playground, she wondered? 'Keep walking!' Luciana pressed the gun even harder, so that Billie had no option but to move down the slippery slope and through the ice-cool water. She felt a shiver of fear run up her spine. There could be only one place that this scenario was going to end.

'Why shouldn't I kill your clever little lover?' Luciana goaded Max.

'We're colleagues, not lovers.' Billie tried to sound calm. The way things were going, that momentary connection on the beach was likely to be the final kiss of death on their relationship, so there was some truth in her plea. Luciana laughed. There was no warmth in it.

'You are deluding yourself, DSI Wilde. I saw that look of love he has for you in the newspaper photograph. I can see it now. It was once directed at me after all...'

'I didn't know who you really were then,' Max answered quietly. 'You're still living a lie now, pretending to protect your people and the environment, looking after the local community...'

'Our people are poor farmers!' Luciana answered. 'The land we had has been taken by corporations that don't give a damn about families,' she hissed. 'Like the one your father ran. Your army is working for them. Killing our people. My brother!' Luciana's voice broke for a moment. Billie held her breath, expecting the gun to go off at any second, as she was half dragged over the river and up onto a grassy bank.

Below, ran the main East Coast railway line, where superfast trains crossed the UK from north to south. Across the track, Billie spotted an identical poster to the one that had loomed above Sophie Grey's shattered body, reading 'Crime Doesn't Pay'. In other circumstances, she might have laughed at the irony, but she felt that one wrong move at that moment might cause a vastly expensive bejewelled gun to wipe the smile right off her face.

'Maybe your family *were* poor farmers, way back in the past, but not anymore. *You* are the multinational corporation now. The true poverty-stricken farmers are forced to flee their homes when your drug cartel moves in, when you plant landmines to protect your illegal processing plants and decimate the rainforest with your pollutants,' Max replied.

A little girl dressed in a princess outfit, with freckles across her nose like Sophie Grey's, ran towards them, following the ever-inquisitive Kat the dog. The girl, dressed in a pretty princess costume and holding a pink balloon, stopped for a moment on the riverbank, dark afro hair waving in the breeze, her large brown eyes staring at the adults, perhaps imagining that a game was underway.

'Go and play back over there, little one.' Max managed a soft smile, hoping that the child would take the hint and run back to join the party.

'No, no,' Luciana interjected, smiling at the girl. A wolf in sheep's clothing, showing her perfect whiter than white teeth. 'We're playing a game. Bring the dog. Sit on the bank here and watch. It's going to be quite a show.' She chuckled, as the girl did as she was bid. Billie couldn't help wishing for a split second that Kat was one of the police dogs trained to attack. The bloodhound sadly had more chance of licking the drugs queen into submission.

'I intend to make you pay for the death of my brother, my one-time lover,' Luciana announced, making it clear that Max's argument had fallen on deaf ears.

'Don't harm him, please,' Billie begged.

'It is not me, but *you* who will break his heart, DSI Wilde. Just as he has broken mine by taking my brother. A train will be coming any minute now. You are going to throw yourself under it and he will watch.'

'No,' Max cried softly, moving forward.

'Stay where you are,' Luciana snapped. 'One more move and I will take out the little princess here and the dog.'

Billie could already hear the train track below, crackling with electricity as the fast train approached from the direction of Scotland. Luciana had clearly heard it too. She pushed Billie onto the crest of the bank. Billie dared to peep at the steep slope, wondering if she could roll down the hill and somehow miss landing on the tracks.

'If you don't come to rest in front of the train, the child and dog will die, along with some of her little friends in the farmyard over there.' Luciana seemed to have read her mind. Billie glanced to the children chasing balloons in the playground. 'I can assure you that I never miss my targets. As for Max, well, he will be losing his kneecaps whilst I wave adios anyway, but he'll live with that pain and the more agonising knowledge that he let his lover walk to her death. Not for the first time I believe, Max?' she goaded.

It was at that moment that the little princess's balloon burst with a loud pop. Luciana, startled, spun around to face the sound. Max swiftly made his move, yanking Billie forcefully to one side, whilst in one totally precise movement, thrusting Luciana at speed over the top of the embankment. She bounced once, at the base of the hill before landing on the track, looking upwards for a split second, her dark eyes wide with shock, before the train, with absolutely no time to stop, hit her at full pelt.

What was for certain was that the last tune that she heard on this earth was not the hauntingly beautiful 'Pavane for a Dead Princess', which had accompanied Sophie Grey on her final journey. Instead, it was the voices of children in a playground farmyard, singing 'Ee-i, adio the farmer's in his den'. It probably never crossed Luciana's mind that the devastation about to be caused to her body was only a fragment of the pain inflicted on families right across the world, from the rainforests of Columbia to the far-flung country towns of England, because of the carnage created by the Devil's Line.

33

A GAME OF SMOKE AND MIRRORS

The date she was born, was also the date that she died. It turned out that it had been Jo Green's birthday when her throat was slashed, in a cold and dark convenience store doorway. She could have been celebrating, but instead, the young detective had given her life for the force. Her teammates at the local roller derby club had organised a surprise party for their number one player that night. But *she* had been the one to quietly spring the anniversary shocker, carrying on a family tradition of grizzly bombshells.

Today a crowd had gathered to commemorate her unique life at the local crematorium. It had been standing room only and then some. Billie blinked back tears at the thought, regretful that she had not reached out earlier, got to know Jo better, in the brief time that they had shared together on this earth.

'Surprise to me, about her helping kids, through the roller derby club,' the chief said, as Billie joined him in the Garden of Remembrance, watching people mill around reading the messages attached to the many floral tributes to the young officer. 'If she'd only mentioned, I could have pulled some strings with our community fund grant. Funny how you only discover this sort of stuff about people at their funerals, when it's too late to do anything about it.'

'Funny I only found out about Derek Blythe a minute before he croaked. Jo Green saved my life on the last investigation,' Billie answered, 'where was I when she needed me to watch her back? Where was I when those kids needed protection? Sophie Grey, Josh Hallows, Chip Little and Milly Lloyd, she was just a kid too.' Billie sighed and shook her head in disbelief. The chief nudged her with his elbow as he stood straight in his dapper uniform.

'Don't start a self-pity party on me, Billie. You can't save the world. Next thing you'll be blaming yourself for Christy Callaghan's downfall.'

'Ricky Hallows would still be here, if I had opened my eyes and realised that the Beast was sitting right in the middle of my team, starting up the Lucifer line under my bloody nose.'

'It was me who sent him off on all those drugs prevention courses, so lay the blame on me if you want. I was also the one who gave his nephew the job. I should have spotted what was going on a mile off. It's a good job that I'm soon to hang up my cap, Billie. I'm clearly not as sharp as I was. Just a shame I'm not going to be spending my dotage in some exotic location. You killed off that little fantasy too, if you feel like adding to your list of crimes against humanity.' The chief teased gently.

'You've still got David's doting mum,' Billie nudged him back, rolling her eyes. The chief grinned.

'You're never going to be her greatest fan, are you?'

'Nope, but then I used to look up to Derek as some sort of mentor, rather than a crazed drug dealing stalker and rapist who resented my every move. That shows what a fantastic judge of character I am.'

Billie felt a sudden pang of grief for the loss of the person she had believed Derek to have been. It had been hard to come to terms with the truth. She recalled the picture of him on the front page of the local paper, playing the local hero, when in reality, he had stepped out of harm's way when the Molotov cocktail had burst through the window, having encouraged Ricky Hallows to carry out the evil deed.

'Hi. I've made a decision,' Billie hadn't noticed Maya approaching. 'After hearing all about Jo, I've decided to change courses at uni. I'm going to take a BSc in Professional Policing,' she announced, a wide grin on her face.

'Congratulations, young lady. You see, Billie, somebody still has confidence in us,' the chief answered as Ellis joined them, putting his arm around Maya's shoulders.

'Just when I'm thinking of giving up,' Ellis announced. Billie and the chief turned to him in astonishment.

'But you're an amazing copper,' Billie said. She meant it. She'd learned so much from him.

'The best,' the chief agreed.

'But it's all drugs these days. It's a mug's game. We're fighting a losing battle. Don't get me wrong, you've done a great job here in wiping out the Lucifer line, but eventually someone else will come in and fill the space.'

'That thought is depressing,' Billie answered.

'Drugs have become part of the world economy.' Ellis shrugged. 'Permeated the system until they've become indistinct from it. Banks, big business, politicians' far-reaching decisions; the entire world economy is infused with drug activities. People all over the planet want the product, and it's never going to run out. It also makes vastly more money than anything else.'

'So what's the answer?' Billie ran her fingers through her hair. She couldn't face the thought of investigating yet more murders in which children were both the victims and the perpetrators.

'Legalise drugs,' the chief answered. His words shocked

Billie. 'I'm not the only one in the force who's reluctantly come to that conclusion. Right now it's like Prohibition in America, when alcohol was banned. It didn't stop the production of alcohol. Just meant that criminal gangs controlled it, causing more crime and more deaths and lowered tax revenues. People will always want to experiment with mind-altering substances. We need to regulate the market.'

'He's right,' Ellis said. 'At least if drugs were legalised, the products would be controlled and made safer. Half the time it's the crap they bulk the pure stuff out with that kills people; rat poison, anaesthetics, and detergents, for example. We need to take the power out of the hands of the criminal gangs. Because the way that the business is run now, crime definitely *does* pay, for the likes of Luciana Martinez and the big cartels. They are rich beyond belief.'

'But it's the krill who suffer,' Billie answered thoughtfully, thinking about the stoned shrimps in the rivers of the UK.

'Yeah, those scraping away at the bottom of the barrel, like Chip Little,' Ellis pointed out. '*They* are the people getting nicked every day, to make law enforcement look like it's winning a war, that we have in reality, totally lost. All those little people, doing time inside and suffering a life sentence outside, for little reward. The worst thing is all of those childhoods destructed. Innocent kids, who are easily controlled and totally expendable. They end up dead in a gutter or with a record that stops them going any further in life and it's happening the world over.'

It was a sobering thought. Legalising drugs went against everything that Billie had ever considered to be desirable, but surely things couldn't go on like this? What future would the children have? She wished that she had a crystal ball.

She glanced over to Max who had just laid a wreath and was now walking towards her. The sight lifted her spirits. Their relationship had moved forward at last, consummated on the night that he had saved her from hurtling onto the rail tracks. They were still at the stage where they could hardly keep their hands off one another.

'Ready to go?' He held out his hand and she caught it, desperate to have some respite from talk of death, drugs, and destruction. She already had some ideas playing on her mind on how they might make the stresses of the day fade away.

'Hi, you're Max, aren't you?' A young woman caught Max's arm. He turned to face her as she looked from Max to Billie.

'I'm Zoe. We met at the wedding.' She smiled. Max's face was a blank for a moment. 'Natalie's cousin,' she clarified. Billie felt Max's fingers slip out from hers.

'Oh, yes. Of course,' Max appeared to politely fib. The young woman's eyes filled with tears.

'Poor Nat and her being three months gone as well, when it all blew up.' Zoe dabbed her eyes with a crumpled handkerchief in her hand.

'Sorry?' Billie looked from Zoe to Max. His face was white.

'No–' he shook his head. Zoe frowned as Max walked away in the direction of a memorial plaque, looking shocked.

'Max,' Billie called after him. He continued walking. Billie turned back to Zoe. 'It seems to be news to him. Are you sure that his wife was pregnant?'

'Course I am. She sent me a copy of the twelve-week scan. I think she had it done on the quiet, so she wouldn't be sent home. She wanted to stay on duty out there with him for as long as possible. The two of them were so loved up,' Zoe replied.

Billie watched as the chief approached Max. He waved him away. It was clear that he needed a moment alone. Her mobile suddenly rang.

'DSI Billie Wilde,' Billie announced in answer to her work tune.

'I'm not interrupting the service, am I?' Boo whispered. She had stayed back at base to hold the fort.

'No. All done and dusted.' Billie stepped away from Zoe, who shrugged and wandered away to join the other mourners.

'Call just come in of a suspicious death,' Boo said.

'Where?' Billie asked.

'Body found in a grave,' Boo replied. Billie waited for a beat, expecting Boo to continue talking. She didn't.

'Yeah, so what's the punchline?' Billie finally asked, looking distractedly towards Max. He was standing at the perimeter of the Crematorium, clearly not laughing. The chief was ambling back over to join her.

'It's not a joke,' Boo answered. 'A call has just come in from a member of the public. The victim has serious head injuries and is partially buried on top of another corpse in an actual grave.'

'Oh Christ. Right. Sorry.' Billie was suddenly on red alert.

'Ash is already heading there,' Boo added. 'I just thought you would kill me if I didn't let you know. Day off or not.' Billie glanced across to Max, feeling momentarily torn. She had planned to celebrate a life and spend precious time with her new love. But he didn't look like he was in the mood for company anymore.

'I've got to run. Big job just come in,' Billie called over to the chief.

'That's my girl. I'll give Max a lift back. No worries,' the chief answered, much to Billie's relief.

'I'm on my way.' She spoke to Boo, heading fast towards her car.

'Okay. The victim is dressed in female clothing but appears to be male…'

Boo started reading out the initial details of the discovery, as Billie jumped into her car, backing out of the parking space so quickly that it was a miracle that she didn't create any fatalities.

She caught sight of Max in the rear-view mirror, at a distance, as she made her getaway. Hopefully, he would forgive her for going on the run, unable to resist the call to sniff out the truth and find where the bodies were buried – just like a bloodhound obsessed with a bone. She would always be Wilde by name and forever wild, by nature.

THE END

ACKNOWLEDGEMENTS

Thank you so much for reading *The Devil's Line*.

Creating a book is a team effort and whilst I'm let loose to make up stories, a whole host of other people are standing by to bring my imaginings to life in the shape of a fully-fledged novel, making sure that it reaches the people who want to read it.

The team at Bloodhound Books, with Betsy and Fred Reavley at the helm, create absolute magic. They are always encouraging and full of enthusiasm, at hand every step of the way, to ensure that my words are shaped into the best entertainment package possible.

My editor, Ian Skewis, is an absolute star, full of gentle wisdom and fantastic suggestions. Proofreader Shirley Khan has the eyes of a hawk, scouring for any spelling mistakes that may be hiding betwixt the pages. Production Manager Tara Lyons keeps everything on track and patiently deals with endless questions and Maria Slocombe does a spectacular job of spreading the word when books go out into the big wide world.

The Devil's Line is my second book and the thing that has come as something of a surprise has been the support offered by my fellow Bloodhound authors. Many of them are best-selling writers, busy working on their own latest novels, but always happy to be on hand with advice and encouragement. Too many lovely people to mention them all here, but Keri Beevis is very much to the fore. A huge thanks to her for her endless kindness.

Last, but very much not least, my family, with my wonderful husband Bob Whittaker at the helm. He guards my writing space, feeds me endless tea and snacks, and lets me ramble on about storylines and characters for hours without ever having resorted to locking me away inside a darkened room. Love you forever x

If you would like to contact me, I would love to hear from readers:

Facebook: Marrisse Whittaker Author
Twitter: @MarrisseWhitt
Instagram: MarrisseWhittakerAuthor

A NOTE FROM THE PUBLISHER

Thank you for reading this book. If you enjoyed it please do consider leaving a review on Amazon to help others find it too.

We hate typos. All of our books have been rigorously edited and proofread, but sometimes mistakes do slip through. If you have spotted a typo, please do let us know and we can get it amended within hours.

info@bloodhoundbooks.com

Lightning Source UK Ltd.
Milton Keynes UK
UKHW010824291021
393032UK00003B/106